BOUND FOR THE TOP

by

SARAH DEAN

Published by **CHIMERA**
ISBN 9781780807126

CHAPTER ONE

Jane's First Assignment

Ben Handford, the producer of *Extraordinary Lives*, strode into the conference room of the shabby Camden offices for his regular Monday production meeting. His team of twelve researchers and producers were waiting for him, clutching cartons of coffee, their youthful faces ashen from the excesses of the weekend and the prospect of another week of punishing schedules. Jane Carter tried to adopt their air of urban cynicism as she found a seat at the far end of the table. She had only been on the programme for six weeks. It was part of her three-month trial as a junior researcher and the first step on the long road to becoming a television presenter.

'Okay you useless bunch of shits - whose lives are we destroying this week?' Ben growled down at them, the Adam's apple bobbing in his throat. He'd earned his reputation during his heyday as a probing television current affairs producer. His demise came when a primetime interview with a junior cabinet minister brought him before a government select committee. The outcome was his sacking and the minister's promotion.

'I've got a lap dancer who's had a sex change,' drawled one of the young men, brushing back his mop of floppy hair.

'Fucking muscles bulging over a g-string? Not my idea of a wet dream.

'Exposure!' Ben yelled the word in their faces. 'That's what this programme wants. Exposure!' He had lost none of his zeal or wit, whatever the subject matter.

'What about that woman in North London who makes Victorian corsets as a sideline? Did anyone look into her story?'

Jane tensed at the far end of the table. She thought everybody had overlooked the story about Georgina Brentwood, the forty-year-old Islington schoolteacher. But not Ben Handford. He spent his Sundays alone, scouring every newspaper for snippets of scandal as obsessively as he had once done for political gossip. That's how she'd got the job. He'd read a piece she'd written for her local paper and liked her Yorkshire honesty. At the end of each Monday meeting he would dump his bundle of cuttings onto the conference table and there would be an unseemly scrabble for the best stories. Two weeks ago there was an article about a schoolteacher being fined for running her business from home. It turned out that the house was unwittingly owned by an un-named member of Her Majesty's government. The paper had printed some rather salacious pictures and suggestive editorial. The article on a middle-aged woman making a few extra pennies was discarded by the rest of the team in favour of a footballer's prowess in bed and the sordid secrets of assorted celebrities.

Jane needed to find a story of her own if she was going to make an impression, but most of the articles Ben cut out concerned worlds of which she had no knowledge. In fact, Jane had little knowledge of any world outside the small Yorkshire village where she'd been raised. Her father, a wild straw-haired Southerner, from whom she inherited her blonde hair and sense of adventure, left home before Jane was born. Her mother, burdened with her newborn child, was forced to move in with her spinster sister, Judith. Aunt Judith, a village schoolmistress, exercised her authority over the children in her charge while Jane's mother kept house and spent her spare moments embroidering evening dresses for expensive shops in York.

It hadn't been much fun for Jane, a feisty and curious child. When she finished helping her mother she would escape to the neighbouring farm and muck out the stables, in exchange for rides on the cart ponies. At night she watched the tiny black and white television in her attic bedroom, squinting at the fuzzy screen and dreaming of another life. Her mother ignored her ambitions and her aunt scoffed, but neither made much effort to discourage her from leaving the village. By the time she was sixteen her unruly curls and beguiling smile had begun to create too much attention amongst the local men and friction between the two unmarried sisters.

'I said did anyone look into the fucking story about the schoolteacher?' Ben repeated his question. Jane felt the heat rising through her.

'I did.' Twelve pairs of eyes turned and bored into her. 'Her name is Ms Brentwood. I went to see her last week. I didn't say anything. I'm not really sure if she...' Jane faltered, her embarrassment consuming her, '...if she has an *Extraordinary Life*.'

'I'll decide that,' Ben turned on her. 'What the fuck are you doing, going off meeting some woman without telling anyone? What cover did you use?'

Jane stared down at the table, summoning up the courage to continue.

'I told her I wanted to have a corset fitted.' She tried to ignore her colleagues' sniggers. 'She makes authentic Victorian corsets and I told her I wanted it to wear under a particular evening dress.'

Jane stopped, clasping her hands in front of her as she remembered how she had stood, dressed in nothing but her white panties in the suburban dining room while Georgina Brentwood measured her. She rarely wore a bra because she didn't need to; her breasts were firm and rounded and she disliked the restriction.

'So who does she sell them to? Presumably not dumb kids who can't think up a decent cover.' Ben fired his questions, his body stiffening as he sensed the taste of a story.

It was a warm April evening when Georgina Brentwood had brusquely guided Jane into the dining room of her Islington terraced house. She introduced herself as Ms Brentwood and addressed Jane as Miss Carter. She was tall and elegant and wore her black hair pulled back in a bun. She was dressed in a fifties style dark tailored suit with a peplum ruffle drawing attention to her trim waist. Jane wasn't going to tell Ben and all these smart young people in their designer clothes all the details; what it had been like, feeling Ms Brentwood's hands firmly raising her limbs, commanding her to sit, stand and bend forward so that she could be measured in every position. Or her embarrassment when the tape was finally passed around her breasts and her nipples hardened and swelled. The heavy blinds shut out the warmth of the evening sun. She shivered as Ms Brentwood noted down every detail of her body, making professional comments as she worked.

'Waist, twenty-four. That can be reduced by at least six inches. Hips thirty-two. They can be accentuated.' She was completely absorbed in her task and her remarks were as much to herself as to her young client.

When finished she handed Jane a thin silk robe to cover herself. Jane thought she detected the faintest trace of a Scottish accent as Ms Brentwood briefly indulged in small talk, enquiring how long Jane had been in London. That's when the older

3

woman suggested that Jane attend an evening where her full collection was displayed. It would help her select a choice of style. However, the preliminary work on the garment would be ready within the week.

Now as Jane stood in front of her colleagues, she struggled to find words that could answer Ben's questions.

'I have to go back tonight for the first fitting,' Jane blurted out, 'and she's asked me to go to some sort of fashion show afterwards. It's at something called the Ruskin Club, I think...'

Ben Handford lowered his voice and an almost seductive smile softened the sharpness of his features. 'So little Jane's found herself a story, has she? Go and see Matt later and get him to fix you up with a camera. Come and see me and I'll give you a press pass. You might be on to something with this Ruskin Club. Seems your cover wasn't so bad, after all. It beats the old, *I've got something you'll want routine*. Well done.' Jane blushed shyly.

Ben brought the meeting to an abrupt close, dumping down his usual Sunday bundle. She noticed that several of the girls were regarding her with suspicion but that some of the men seemed to have noticed her for the first time. One of them stayed behind to help her clear up.

'So *little Jane*, you like dressing up in corsets, do you?' He patted her bottom, pressed into tight jeans, as she bent to retrieve some papers.

'I just told her that. It was the best I could think of,' she protested, dodging his unexpected attention.

'Come on. Don't be coy. You're pretty gorgeous, you know. I bet you look great all bound up like that. How about coming out for a drink with us after work on Friday?'

Jane had longed to be asked to join them in the noisy bar opposite the office where the drinkers spilled onto the pavement, laughing together, releasing the stress of their weeks. Instead she made her way alone to the station and travelled back to her dismal rented room in South London, but now, although her colleague's suggestive remarks made her feel a little awkward, she was flattered by his invitation.

Jane's excitement was still bubbling as she sat on the underground among the other commuters heading north, to keep her seven o'clock appointment with Ms Brentwood. She kept glancing down at her lap, checking on the fashionable canvas backpack Matt had given her. Matt's specialty was finding ways of hiding a camera. His ingenuity had led to hiding cameras in footballs, wing mirrors and beer bottles, so the backpack had not presented a problem.

Ms Brentwood opened the door. This time, although her manner was formal, she didn't lead Jane into the dining room as she did on her previous visit. Instead they crossed the hall, and Jane had to hide her surprise when they entered a sumptuously furnished drawing room, already shielded from the fading daylight by heavy velvet drapes. Despite the warm evening a wood fire burned in the grate.

'I thought we would have a sherry before your fitting, Miss Carter.' Ms Brentwood had already lifted a cut glass decanter from a silver tray.

Jane nodded as she took in her surroundings. Every item in the room served to create a perfect Victorian drawing room. Deep brocade sofas sat either side of the marble fireplace, above which hung a vibrant oil painting in a heavy, gilded frame. Gas lamps provided the only lighting, leaving shadowy corners where the light didn't fall. A musky smell pervaded the air, and Jane's confidence started to crumble in the oppressive atmosphere of the peculiar room, taken from another age.

Her unease increased when she took in Ms Brentwood's outfit. The tailored suit had been replaced by a long black taffeta dress that swept the floor with its hem. The older woman stood with her back to her as she poured from the decanter, and Jane could see the shape of the bustle that protruded over her buttocks. When she turned and crossed the room, holding the two glasses of dark liquid, Jane saw the high neckline and the row of buttons that ran down between her full, sculpted breasts. The tight bodice plunged down into a V-shape that ended low on her hips, and the skirt was full but not frivolously so. It was the kind of dress worn by a Victorian governess, and for a terrible moment Jane was reminded of Aunt Judith. She had dressed in similar, austere clothing. Jane had too often been the subject of her classroom ridicule, believing that her own niece must receive equal, if not more discipline than her contemporaries. Seeing Ms Brentwood dressed in the same style took her back to memories she would rather forget.

Except that the effect of the costume on Ms Brentwood was quite different. She was a very handsome woman with her hair swept back from her face showing off her high cheekbones. She had a broad forehead and penetrating brown eyes that Jane found impossible to meet. Although Jane hardly drank alcohol, she was grateful to be handed the delicate crystal glass. She twisted it between her fingers in an attempt to disguise her confusion.

'Have you brought your dress with you, Miss Carter? The one you want to wear over the corset?' Ms Brentwood's eyes looked expectantly at the canvas bag by Jane's side.

'No, I mean, I didn't think I would need to...' Jane's voice trailed away and she felt the colour rising as she fibbed.

'I see. I thought I made it clear that I needed to see the dress for this fitting.' Jane didn't answer and stared into her glass, her heart pounding as she remembered how her aunt punished her fibs.

'There is no dress, is there, Miss Carter?' She waited again for a response.

'Yes, yes, it's at the cleaners.' Jane was terrified that Ms Brentwood had seen though her cover and that at any moment she might demand to see the contents of the bag. She gulped at her drink and felt the stuffiness of the room closing around her.

'I see,' Ms Brentwood repeated. 'In that case we will go upstairs for the fitting and I must lend you a dress to wear to the Ruskin Club.'

'Look, I'm not sure I can come tonight. I have to get home. I said I would meet someone.'

'Nonsense. I don't know why you did come to see me, Miss Carter, but you clearly have an interest in proper undergarments. I am glad to find that voluntarily in a modern lass and it is to be encouraged. Now follow me.' The woman's Scottish burr was clear when she raised her voice in irritation.

She should have protested but the sherry and Ms Brentwood's imperious tone made Jane follow her out into the hall and up the polished staircase. She told herself to calm down. The woman was bizarre but if she wanted to make it in a ruthless business, it was no use faltering at the first obstacle.

The bedroom was in the same Victorian style as the drawing room, and also dimly lit by gaslight. A large four-poster bed dominated the room, its canopy festooned with elaborate curtains. The linen was snowy white and the pile of lace pillows looked momentarily inviting as Jane tried to compose herself. Ms Brentwood opened the big mahogany wardrobe.

'I have your corset here. Undress now, Miss Carter. Behind the screen if you would.'

Jane was more than grateful for the privacy of the hand-painted screen depicting Pre-Raphaelite maidens bathing by pools of water. She kicked off her trainers and peeled off her jeans and jumper. After a few deep breaths, she stepped back into the room as before, in just her panties.

Ms Brentwood was completing the lacing that joined together the two panels of the corset, and Jane's hands lifted instinctively to cover her breasts as the older woman looked up from her work and gazed frankly at her almost naked body.

'Everything off today, Miss Carter. That underwear is not suitable. I will provide some once I have fitted the corset.'

'B-but surely I can k-keep them on while...' Jane stuttered wildly.

'Miss Carter!' Ms Brentwood's voice took on an edge that Jane recognised only too well from her childhood. 'We have a car collecting us at eight and I don't intend to be late. Please undress and stand by the foot of the bed.'

Jane felt her legs start to weaken and clutched her arms even tighter across her front, but if she were to get the story she needed she would have to comply. She wished Ms Brentwood would stop staring at her, but she didn't so eventually she was forced to lower her arms and slip her panties over the curve of her hips to reveal the soft triangle of fair hair between her thighs.

'Good lass.' Ms Brentwood's voice dropped to little more than a whisper as she beckoned the naked girl to approach the bed.

In all her confusion, Jane had given little thought to the garment itself, and was shocked to see how stiff and unrelenting the two panels looked. They were made of cream satin and there were no adornments. The one continuous lace was loosely crisscrossed through metal eyelets at the back, and the surplus hung in two long loops at either side of the waist. It was quite unlike the fashionable elasticised corsets that filled the market stalls around Camden.

'Raise your arms above your head and I'll fasten the front.'

Starting from the top, Ms Brentwood's deft fingers quickly closed the stainless steel clasps that joined the two panels together at the front. Jane stiffened as Ms Brentwood's hands brushed against her breasts... her stomach... and lower still as she fastened the final clasp. Ms Brentwood stood back to admire her work. The corset, even before it was tightened, traced the shape of Jane's body perfectly. It reached from the middle of her breasts to low on her tummy, and both the top and bottom edges were completely straight.

'Now place your hands at shoulder height on the bedpost please, Miss Carter.' Jane gripped the thick wooden post and tried to breathe normally as Ms Brentwood used her expertise to tighten the laces, gradually pulling them equally, top and bottom, towards her waist.

Jane was surprised to feel a surge of pride in Ms Brentwood's words, and even more when she began to enjoy the unaccustomed hugging sensation. Perhaps this wasn't going to be such an ordeal after all. Her mind drifted to the office - to Ben and the questions she would have to face in the morning. How would she make a story about what was happening to her in a weird Victorian house, and its occupant, lost in another era? But there was still the Ruskin Club; perhaps that would give her what she needed.

'However,' Ms Brentwood continued, 'there is a great deal of room for improvement. Your breasts, for instance, have been left unrestricted for too long, which will damage the delicate skin. That is why I have selected a mid-bust style that will provide them with proper support for the time being.'

For the time being? She didn't think Jane was going to put herself through this indignity again, did she? Not even for her career. But just as the moment of defiance rose in her, Jane felt a strong pull on the upper lace and the corset tightened around her ribs. She looked down with alarm and saw the top of the corset cut into her breasts, just above her nipples, crushing them and forcing the soft flesh into two swollen globes above the satin edging. She breathed in sharply just in time to feel the lower lace shortening so that her buttocks were squeezed together, held by the unrelenting metal rods sown into the seams. As Ms Brentwood snatched a sharp tug at her waist, Jane could remain silent no longer.

'Oh, really, I think that's enough,' she said as calmly as she could. 'It feels very tight now.'

'My dear girl, we have hardly begun,' was Ms Brentwood's response. 'Now stand still. You may grip the post higher.'

Panic was starting to rise but Jane lifted her hands to about head height. She felt the satin edge bite harder into her breasts, and it was becoming difficult to take a full breath as Ms Brentwood tugged vigorously at the lower lace. Finally Jane could stand no more and dropped her hands from the post, clutching herself around her considerably reduced waist.

'No honestly, Ms Brentwood, I can't...'

'Put your hands back up at once and compose yourself!' the woman snapped. 'Keep still, lass!' Jane could hear the anger in Ms Brentwood's voice, but it only increased her desire to be free and she fought against the grip even harder.

She was still struggling when she felt the first sharp sting of Ms Brentwood's palm landing squarely on her buttocks. She screamed in shock. The next two blows came quickly and just as hard, and her screams turned to sobs as the pain seeped into her.

'I had hoped we weren't going to have trouble tonight, Miss Carter.' Ms Brentwood allowed Jane, limp and quivering, to stand. She held the woman's shoulders firmly while she found her balance. 'Now be a good girl for me.' Ms Brentwood used the same coaxing tone that she had earlier.

She took Jane's hands and gently replaced them in their former position on the bedpost, but ignored the tears running freely down her young client's cheeks and continued with her task. Jane was too stunned to know what to do but try to tolerate the vicelike grip as her body was drawn in ever tighter. The burning spreading through her bottom distracted her, but not enough. She sobbed and begged openly, her fingers clenched around the post to maintain her balance as the laces continued to close around her.

'I hope you appreciate, Miss Carter, that this would have been a great deal easier if you'd started your training at an early age. You have a great deal of neglect to put right. Do you understand?' Ms Brentwood was once again the imperious corsetiere.

Jane continued to sob, her misery overwhelming.

'I said, do you understand?' Before Jane had a chance to reply another blow smacked down, biting against the already reddened skin.

'Yes,' Jane whimpered.

'Yes, Ms Brentwood. Your manners, Miss Carter, need some improving too, I fear. Before you dress, Miss Carter, I need to see how the corset fits when you walk. So if you would cross over to the window now.'

Jane would have to humour the woman for a bit longer, but she wasn't at all sure she would be able to make it the twelve or so paces to the window. But she felt Ms Brentwood's warning hand encircle her waist and her hesitation was short-lived. She didn't want to risk another spanking, so she broke free and set off across the room, snatching short breaths as best she could. When she reached the window she leaned on the sill in relief, although she knew she was giving her tormentor a perfect view of her naked and reddened backside.

'Back to the bed now, please.' Jane made her way back, using her arms to balance herself as the blood spun around her head.

'Good. Now put your hands behind your neck and display yourself properly.' Jane was shocked by her words but gingerly raised her arms. As she clasped her fingers together she looked down to see her nipples emerging from the top of the low-cut corset, and flinched as Ms Brentwood slipped her hands inside and used the opportunity to run her fingers over the hard little buds.

'I think there are some adjustments needed here, Miss Carter. Now keep your hands clasped behind your head and continue.'

Jane weaved her way several times up and down the room. Gradually her head cleared and her balance began to return.

'That's it. Head up, elbows out wide. Much better.'

The restriction of the corset forced her to take much smaller steps than she was used to as she teetered across the room. Slowly the stiff fabric warmed and moulded itself to her lithe young body. Jane found herself walking, turning, walking, and turning, almost in a trance, Ms Brentwood's words coming at her from a distance.

'Very good, my dear, you learn fast,' Ms Brentwood purred through the flickering light.

As Jane turned for the fourth time she caught sight of herself in the full-length mirror, and saw how her body had changed shape. Each time she turned she let her eyes linger a little longer, taking in her breasts forced high by the tight lacing. Her nipples peeped over the creamy satin and her waist was tiny. The corset held her back completely straight and her bottom jutted out just below where the laces ended. She saw the marks that the four slaps had left across her buttocks. The skin was tight and flushed but the sharpness of the pain had subsided. She liked the way her body was sculpted into such a perfect shape and her confidence grew, bolstered by Ms Brentwood's words of encouragement. She almost forgot the reason she was there at all, as she paraded in nothing more than the satin corset and black stockings.

'You may stop now, Miss Carter. I'll make the alterations later but it fits well enough for the time being. Come here to the mirror and I will complete your outfit.'

The woman's words cut across Jane's composure, but she was relieved when Ms Brentwood invited her to step into the pair of long, pure white cotton drawers, trimmed with fine lace just above the knee. The cool fabric felt soothing on her hot buttocks, but as the drawstrings were fastened round her waist she realised that the garment was not joined at the gusset. The two legs hung from the tapes independently, leaving an opening running down her stomach, between her legs and up into the small of her back.

'I don't believe in this modern fad of not allowing air to circulate, Miss Carter,' Ms Brentwood said when she saw Jane's reaction. 'It is unhygienic.'

The midnight-blue velvet dress Ms Brentwood had selected was a perfect fit, and Jane looked at her reflection in the mirror as the woman fastened the hooks at the back. The neck was cut low with a ribbon run in to tighten the shoulders, so that with each breath her breasts swelled and strained against the fabric. The bodice was a tight fit and the full-length skirt flowed over her rounded hips, accentuating her trimmed waist.

'There, now what was all that fuss about?' Ms Brentwood smiled with undisguised admiration. Jane did indeed look very beautiful. She could hardly believe the transformation as she gazed at the stranger in the mirror.

Jane stuffed her clothes into the valise. Lying on the floor was the canvas backpack containing Matt's camera, a jarring reminder of her real purpose for being in the strange house. Yet she had to admit that she loved the softness of the velvet and how graceful the exquisite dress made her feel. Perhaps she'd been foolish to make a fuss, and whatever Ms Brentwood's motives were for treating her as she had, the results were very pleasing. If she breathed lightly and didn't exert herself the corset was quite tolerable. She heard Ms Brentwood returning and hastily tucked the canvas bag into a corner of the valise.

'The car is here, Miss Carter.'

CHAPTER TWO

The Ruskin Club

Jane sat next to Ms Brentwood in the back of the chauffeured limousine formulating her plan. When the time came all she had to do was open the clasp on the valise and activate the camera by pressing the button on the side of the backpack. She looked out at the evening crowds, milling in and out of the bars and restaurants. The girls in their short skirts made her even more aware of her own incongruous clothing.

'I will have to blindfold you in a moment. Our members insist on absolute discretion in the case of new visitors.'

Members? Blindfolds? Jane's mind was racing. What was this Ruskin Club and who were these members who insisted on such secrecy? It seemed increasingly likely that Ben's instincts - and hers - had been right. She must get something on camera although what, she had no idea. She would go along with Ms Brentwood for as long as it took. Then, somehow, she would slip out into the night and escape back to her rented room, and for once it seemed an appealing prospect.

They drove on in silence for ten minutes or so, when Ms Brentwood reached into her purse and produced a black silk scarf.

Jane felt anything but comfortable behind the blindfold. Depriving her of one sense had awakened others and now the heat from the spanking burned into her again and her ribs ached. Her courage had all but evaporated when after what seemed like an eternity the car came to a halt and Ms Brentwood slipped off the blindfold.

Jane blinked into the night as the driver opened the door. He was a tall, dark-haired young man, immaculate in his grey uniform. Jane was too embarrassed to meet his eye. He looked only a few years older than her and must have wondered why she had allowed her companion to blindfold her during the journey. If he did he disguised it well, holding the door in the decorous manner of a professional servant to let them step out into the deserted street.

Jane followed Ms Brentwood up the steps of what seemed to be an abandoned theatre. Peeling billboards hung forlornly from the red brick building and the glass in the leaded windows was black with grime. As they entered the deserted foyer Jane heard the low hum of voices through the dim, dusty light. Her heart was beating fast and the poise she'd acquired earlier abandoned her.

An extraordinary sight greeted her as Ms Brentwood pushed open the creaking door to the auditorium. The orchestra pit was ablaze with hundreds of church candles throwing their light up onto the stage, and the audience was seated on some of the more serviceable velvet seats, arranged in the front rows. Every man rose to his feet as Jane and Ms Brentwood paused, framed in the doorway.

'Ms Brentwood, good evening.' A tall figure, dressed in a long black opera cloak, the hood raised to conceal his features, bowed in their direction. 'And you've brought us a guest this evening. We are honoured.'

'Good evening, Sir John. May I present Miss Carter to the membership?'

Jane shrank as every eye turned on her, but Ms Brentwood's firm hand in the small of her back urged her forward. Two seats had been reserved at the end of the front row, either side of the hooded man. She had the briefest of moments to take in the fifty or so men and women who made up the audience. They ranged from girls of her own age to portly gentlemen, all dressed in clothing from a similar period to her own. As she took her seat at the end of the row, next to Sir John, she tried to calm herself.

But her hopes were short-lived as the tattered curtains were heaved back from behind by two invisible figures. A young woman was seated to one side of the stage; a cello balanced between her parted legs. She was exquisitely lovely. Long, glossy curls as black as Jane's were blonde, tumbled down to her slim, pale shoulders. Her face was almost too delicate for the pools of blue that gazed out into some distant place far beyond her audience. She was dressed in an oyster-pink corset much shorter than Jane's. It started just below her breasts and ended on her hips. It had been laced over a fine cotton chemise that gathered round her breasts, doing little to hide their fullness and the dark buds that jutted through the thin material. Her lower body was covered by cotton drawers that ended, as Jane's did, just above her knees. Her shapely black-stockinged legs emerged beneath them, the calves raised by the heels of her shoes.

Jane recognised the evocative opening notes to Elgar's Cello Concerto at once.

Aunt Judith had played it often on the ancient old gramophone during long evenings spent striking her red pen systematically through the endeavours of her pupils. As the young musician swayed gently, the white cotton material that covered her lower body moved enough for Jane to see that the instrument was all that was covering her modesty.

The line of women was led into the shadows at the back of the stage, and a balding, round-faced man dressed in a black evening suit with a high starched collar stepped forward to address the audience.

'Good evening my, lords, ladies and gentlemen, I am your chairman for the evening,' he began in a loud, pompous voice. 'Tonight I have ten of Ms Brentwood's most finely crafted creations for your visual entertainment. And for the highest bidders, the opportunity to take one of those creations home for your personal enjoyment.'

Jane felt Sir John's bony thigh stiffen with anticipation as the chairman beckoned the first model forward into the light of the candles. She looked in her thirties, a tall, willowy woman with her face draped by the sweep of her brown hair. She was dressed in nothing but a scarlet satin corset and black stockings, the equally lustrous dark patch of hair plainly visible between her toned thighs. Jane shifted in her seat at the sight of the bold, semi-naked creature.

'Display!' the chairman instructed, and Jane's disquiet increased as the woman raised her hands and clasped them behind her neck, just as Jane had been made to earlier. The movement caused her large breasts to rise out of the small cups that supported them, revealing nipples standing erect and proud.

'Here we have a creation, developed from suggestions by Ms Brentwood's most discerning customers. The colour signifies the burning passion that such a creation inspires. The strongest rods have been used in the making,' the chairman announced. 'Turn.'

The woman obeyed without a flicker of change in her expression and stood with her legs slightly apart, her elbows wide. The cellist continued her accompaniment, the notes echoing around the sparsely populated auditorium. Below the laces the smooth, creamy expanse of the woman's bottom contrasted with the vividness of the fabric.

On a further cue from the chairman she began to walk up and down the stage, slowly, elegantly, her head high, apparently oblivious to the murmurings in the assembled audience.

'What am I bid for this superb creation? One hundred guineas from the gentleman to my right... one hundred and fifty guineas from the lady in green...'

Jane could barely believe her eyes as they darted from the stage to the faces in the dim light behind her.

'Sold to you, sir. Two hundred and twenty guineas.'

Jane turned in time to see a young man raise a silver-topped cane in acknowledgement of his purchase. The audience applauded as the woman finally lowered her arms and stepped forward into a low curtsey. One foot was placed in front of the other, her knees pointing outwards so that Jane, and most of the audience, had a clear view of the ripe flesh her position exposed. She heard Sir John exhale a long, low breath.

The chairman beckoned forward the next in line. She was a short plump girl, no more than twenty, with a sullen expression.

'Our celebrated corsetiere has had to use excessively strong flax in this creation. With some additional work this will make a most serviceable possession.'

The corset was made of heavy white cotton. A well-constructed underwire supported the breasts, but the mounds of flesh spilled over the top, the fat brown nipples large and disc-like. Her waist was pulled impossibly tight and her hips and stomach bulged out beneath it, the triangle of bushy red hair sprouting from between fleshy thighs. The girl was asked to turn, exposing the laces crossed and straining across her broad back and the large, dimpled cheeks bulging out below.

'As you can see, ladies and gentleman, this creation requires a strong hand.'

The girl moved despondently up and down the stage, her eyes fixed firmly to the floor.

'Come on, get her shoulders back!' a male voice shouted from the back of the hall.

'Get her arms up!' another jeered.

'Tie 'em back if you have to!'

Suddenly the hall was in uproar as men and women harangued the unfortunate girl, and she responded by insolently raising her arms and throwing out her vast bosom. Jane looked on in dismay as she moved awkwardly up and down the stage. To her left she saw Sir John's manicured fingers emerge from beneath his cloak and grip his thigh. Beyond him Ms Brentwood stared at the stage, light drops of moisture visible on her upper lip. The voices got louder and louder and all the time the cellist played on, seemingly lost in the beauty of her music, oblivious to the mayhem around her.

Jane wondered what she'd gotten herself into, although there was no doubt in her mind now that there was a story to be had - a much bigger story than even Ben Handford could have suspected. It was now or never.

She used the cover of the audience's excitement to reach down and open the clasp on the leather bag placed at her feet. She fumbled to position the lens where it would have a clear view of the stage, and by the time she felt along the strap and found the hidden switch the audience had settled down again and the auction was once more underway.

Jane sat back, her heart pumping faster and faster against the restriction of the laces, amazed at her own courage. She longed to take in a full breath to stop the spinning in her head, but the corset made that impossible.

'Sold to the lady with the feather boa,' announced the balding chairman. 'A very astute choice, madam.'

The plump girl lowered herself into an ungainly curtsey, exposing the fat, moist lips between her hefty thighs.

The auction continued but Jane was distracted by the low but persistent whirring of the camera at her feet, only partly disguised by the music. The women stepped forward in turn; a stout matronly type, her ample but womanly curves encased in black silk; a petite Oriental girl wearing a tiny corset that cinched her waist and left her pert breasts and narrow hips exposed; a tall, arrogant, ebony-skinned beauty whose muscular physique fought proudly beneath a corset of the whitest lace.

Each woman followed the rehearsed routine; standing, turning, raising her arms and parading as the crowd roared their approval or displeasure. They wore black stockings held up by garters, and high heels.

Who were they? Had they been coerced, or were they compliant participants? Jane regretted her own inexperience as she searched their faces for answers.

An awed suspense pervaded the audience as the last was called forward, and the aristocratic, flaxen-haired beauty took even Jane aback, and her fascination increased when she saw the corset she was wearing was made from course grey horsehair.

'I start the bidding at two hundred guineas for this creation, guaranteed to temper the vanity to which well bred ladies are prone,' the chairman called, wiping perspiration from his face with a large white hanky, and Jane had to admit that she, too, was fascinated by the ice-cold vision of loveliness. Her haughty expression left no doubt about her breeding.

'Three hundred... three hundred and fifty...'

The rough fabric had chaffed her ivory skin, leaving livid blotches where it cut across her magnificent breasts. But still she crossed the stage, with a confidence that Jane would have envied under any circumstances.

'Four hundred and thirty... four hundred and eighty guineas.'

Men and women jostled to have their bids acknowledged. Every stride must have caused the corset to dig at and irritate her tender flesh, but it didn't stop her moving as if covered in the finest silks.

'Five hundred and fifty guineas... *sold* to Sir John!'

Her curtsy was lower and longer than any of her forerunners, but even though the hair between her legs had been removed, she revealed none of her intimate secrets.

Five hundred and fifty guineas for a corset?

Jane was snatched back to reality when the cellist let her bow sweep across the strings in one final flourish. Her arms fell limply into her lap and she closed her deep blue eyes in contemplation. She was helped to her feet by a burly stagehand. Sir John stood and the audience took this as their cue to depart. Jane fumbled frantically in the bag for the button to turn off the camera but it was too late. Her host was extending his arm to her, so she snapped the clasp closed and clambered to her feet.

'You will join us for a glass of port in the committee room, Miss Carter,' he said in a deep voice, barely muffled by the hood that disguised his identity so effectively. 'Paul will look after your bag.' The dark-haired driver appeared in his liveried uniform and waited, expectantly, for her to hand over the bag.

'It's all right, I can manage...' Jane gripped the leather handle tightly.

'I'll take care of it, miss.' Paul reached out respectfully and took hold of it, but she appealed to him silently, her eyes wide with panic, and he relaxed his grip.

'Miss Carter, give Paul the bag at once and don't argue with Sir John,' Ms Brentwood intervened, and Jane had no option but to comply.

As she was led away towards the side of the stage on the arm of the mysterious hooded stranger, her only hope was that she'd been right about the sympathy in the deep brown eyes that had met hers for a brief moment. Would he hear the camera? And if he did, would he expose her? Should she turn and flee right now? It must be well past ten o'clock and her last train was at eleven-thirty, except she had no idea where she was. She must have been mad to think she could handle such an assignment.

The committee room was no more than an area screened off behind the stage. Two velvet couches had been dragged into position and strewn with brightly embroidered shawls to hide their years of wear. A few wooden chairs were the only other seating. Three men were already there when Sir John brought the two women into the small enclosure.

'Ladies, may I present the committee of the Ruskin Club.'

In turn the men were introduced, and Jane followed Ms Brentwood's lead, extending her right hand to be kissed.

'Major Hunt.' The first to be presented was a stocky, balding man with a ruddy face and broad shoulders. His muscular neck strained at his wing collar, and Jane noticed his calloused knuckles as his hand gripped hers.

'Lord Waterhouse.' A tall, foppish, younger man dressed in a deep green frock coat with a broad velvet collar, bent low to plant his kiss. A sharp goatee beard jutted from below his clean-shaven upper lip and pricked her skin, and she pulled away as his wet tongue darted out and licked her hand like a venomous snake.

'And Doctor Morris.' An austere gentleman wearing a full-length black opera cloak, similar to Sir John's, was the last to be introduced. But he lowered his hood to reveal sallow cheeks and grey eyes when he bent formally to press dry lips to the back of her hand.

Jane was guided to a sofa and perched nervously on the edge. Ms Brentwood chose one of the upright chairs.

'Ah, some refreshments,' Sir John announced as the fat girl who'd been the butt of the audience's jibes appeared, carrying a tray of glasses filled with a ruby liquid. She was still bound tightly into the cotton garment and had been given nothing to cover herself further.

'I must compliment you, Ms Brentwood, on your collection,' said the major, his voice as gruff and robust as his physique.

They sipped their drinks, and in turn each of the men came to sit beside Jane, enquiring politely about her reaction and attempting to relieve her disquiet. Ms Brentwood kept a constant watch, but Jane said little, her embarrassment compounded by the presence of the plump girl who hovered nearby, her hands folded loosely behind her back, exposing the thatch of hair between her slightly parted thighs. Eventually Jane's relief was almost overwhelming when Ms

Brentwood rose to her feet and concluded the conversations, veiled with undertones that Jane did not fully understand.

'It is late, gentlemen,' the woman decreed, but before any more could be said Paul appeared from behind a screen. Jane wondered how long he'd been there, and then she saw the leather bag still in his hand.

'Your car is waiting, madam,' he said formally, as in sheer relief at the sight of her bag Jane rushed forward to grab it from him. However, in her haste she forgot to gather the long folds of her velvet skirt, which wrapped around her legs and she staggered forward, tumbling helplessly to the floor.

Paul reacted swiftly, bending to help her back up to her feet. The men gathered around her. Even Ms Brentwood seemed concerned as she rearranged the skirt of the dress. Jane assured them she was all right, when to her horror she looked behind them and saw the leather valise, the clasp knocked open when Paul dropped it. The canvas backpack had spilled out and was clearly visible. She struggled to break free from the circle of people surrounding her, but it was too late.

A piercing bleep, like an air raid siren to poor Jane, signalled that the battery had run flat. She froze, paralysed with fear.

'Bring the bag here, Paul,' Sir John said curtly from within his hood, and it took him but moments to pull out the miniature camera Matt had concealed. Then he examined the contents of her purse, producing the laminated press pass. She'd been so proud when Ben handed it to her earlier in the day, but now it was about to condemn her.

'So, Miss Carter, not quite the innocent Yorkshire lass, it seems.' He rounded on her as he spoke. 'Do you have any other items of equipment concealed on your person?'

Jane looked desperately around for a means of escape, but she was trapped, all eyes staring at her accusingly, waiting for a reply that did not come.

'Very well, Miss Carter, it seems we must find out for ourselves. Come here, Bessie.' He beckoned to the plump girl, who was watching the whole episode.

'Help Miss Carter undress.'

The girl obeyed Sir John's instructions at once and moved behind Jane, and the feel of her hands groping at her waist shocked Jane back to life.

'No stop, please! It's not necessary. There is nothing else. Ms Brentwood knows...' Jane's voice was taut with fear as she turned to the woman, her eyes imploring her to stop the indignity. But the woman stared back, grim-faced, her lips tight with fury.

'Hold her still, Major Hunt.' Ms Brentwood's tone was as cold as her eyes. She returned to her seat and the major needed no encouragement. He moved between Jane and Sir John and his brutish hands gripped her slender shoulders like a vice.

'No, please, you mustn't,' Jane babbled, squirming and wriggling, but to no avail. 'Please.' The man was powerful and an eighteen-year-old girl was no match for him.

'You've brought this upon yourself, Miss Carter, with your deceit.' Sir John spoke as he and the other two men took their former seats in a semi-circle around her. Only Paul remained standing, guarding the entrance to the stage. 'The sooner you submit to a search, the sooner we'll know where we stand,' Sir John added.

Jane felt the tears well up as she closed her eyes in resignation. How could she have let things go this far? And who were these people? She could feel the major's hot breath on her face and feel his barrel chest occasionally rubbing against her breasts as he held her ever more firmly. Behind her, the girl continued to fumble clumsily at the fastenings.

Them Jane almost slumped to her knees when the major relaxed his grip just enough to slide the tight velvet bodice off her shoulders, and before she could object the heavy material fell to a pool at her feet. She was left standing in just the drawers and the creamy satin corset.

He moved nimbly for a big man, lifting her so that Bessie could scramble beneath and gather up the folds of blue velvet. Then he spun Jane round, placed her back on the floor and pinned her arms behind her back.

Cringing with fear she opened her eyes and saw the lascivious stares crawling over her semi-exposed body. Lord Waterhouse, the youngest of the men, drooled openly, his slack mouth revealing a reptilian tongue. The doctor absorbed every curve, his grim face set in a frown of concentration. But Sir John never lowered his hood and she could only guess at his response to her degradation.

Well they could stare all they liked, she decided, lifting her chin defiantly. Anyone could see there was nothing concealed in the tightly laced satin and the white cotton drawers. If she could just endure their stares a moment longer, perhaps she might be allowed to dress in her own clothes and leave.

At that moment Sir John broke the silence. 'Fetch Miss Carter a chair, Paul.'

Jane welcomed his words; hopefully they indicated a softening of their stance and would bring her ordeal nearer to a close. Paul brought a wooden chair and put it down in front of Jane.

'Ms Brentwood, would you be so kind as to conduct a more intimate search?' said Sir John, and Jane felt her legs weaken as Ms Brentwood rose. Surely they couldn't mean...?

'Bend over, Miss Carter,' Ms Brentwood's voice cut through the tense atmosphere like a knife, 'and brace yourself on the back of the chair.' The shocked girl tried to speak, but she could already feel Ms Brentwood's cool palm sliding into the slit at the back of the drawers, squeezing her still tender flesh.

'You are a lying, conniving girl who set out from the start to deceive me,' the woman accused vehemently. 'But you are intelligent enough to understand that unless you submit to a search, it will be concluded by force.'

'Y-yes,' Jane whispered miserably, but Ms Brentwood's nails dug into her buttocks, causing her to exhale sharply. 'Yes, Ms Brentwood,' she said hastily, fighting back the tears.

'Now do as you're told and bend over.'

Jane obeyed, and Ms Brentwood opened the back of the cotton draws and reached round to spread the front, sliding the material around the drawstring until the stage's cold drafts crept around and between Jane's naked thighs.

'Spread your legs, Miss Carter.' Ms Brentwood was unbuttoning and rolling back the tight cuffs on her own costume.

Jane shuffled her feet apart as she steadied herself over the seat of the chair.

'I see you've had to chastise Miss Carter already,' Sir John noted.

'Yes,' Ms Brentwood confirmed, 'but it seems it was not warning enough. She is a defiant and wilful girl, although I suspect from her relative tolerance that it's not the first time she's been punished.'

Jane's shame on that terrible night, a few months before she left home, came flooding back to her. What had begun as an innocent evening walk with a boy from the farm had ended in a furtive screw in a cowshed. It was the first time for both of them and afterwards they fell asleep in each other's arms, and when Jane eventually got home, close to midnight, her aunt was waiting for her.

Aunt Judith had never made any pretence of her strong belief in physical discipline, and a few times Jane had actually suffered the weight of her heavy hand through her school knickers. But that all stopped, naturally, as Jane grew older... until that night when she returned home late.

Aunt Judith called her into the kitchen and told her to place her hands flat on the scrubbed tabletop and bend forward. Jane reluctantly obeyed, and felt her fingers raising the hem of her skirt in disbelief, her humiliation complete when her aunt pulled down her damp knickers; all the incriminating evidence the woman needed.

Aunt Judith delivered six harsh blows to Jane's naked bottom with a wooden spatula. Each swat stung worse than the last, but Jane kept bravely silent as the wood whipped through the air and smacked into her bare flesh.

Afterwards she crept upstairs and crawled stiffly into bed, and in her misery slipped her hands under her nightdress, tentatively touching the raised weals the kitchen implement had left. Then she let her fingers drift to the bud between her thighs and used them to drive away the memory of the cruel spanking.

A few days later the letter arrived offering her a new job and life in London, and she thought she'd escaped the shame of that night forever...

Ms Brentwood moved to Jane's side, and to the girl's horror, placed her hands on both buttocks and spread them wide, exposing the shadowy valley that ran between them. It was unbearable to be so humiliated in front of strangers, and Jane sobbed as she felt a finger probe her vagina lips.

'She's very tight,' Ms Brentwood stated.

'Has she been fucked, do you think?' Lord Waterhouse sounded a little breathless with excitement.

'I would say yes, she has,' Ms Brentwood replied.

'Please stop,' Jane begged. 'I can't bear it. I'm hiding nothing else, I swear.' She pleaded through tears.

Ms Brentwood moved her finger, but only to locate her other, tiny, puckered entrance, and as soon as Jane realised her vile intention she shrieked a protest.

'Be quiet!' Ms Brentwood admonished, slapping Jane's buttocks. 'You've already proved yourself to be untrustworthy. I put nothing past you, and whoever it was who sent you here.'

Ms Brentwood's other hand was pressing down on the small of her back, pinning her against the chair-back, her muscles tensed in her dismay as Ms Brentwood's finger started to work at the tiny, intimate star. It was awful, and to know the whole shameful act was being observed, not just by the men but by the sulky girl as well, was almost too much to bear.

'No, please, you have to stop this,' she begged, and then flinched and gasped as Ms Brentwood's finger broke through the tight ring of muscle. She jerked her hips hopelessly from side to side, but the invading digit remained firmly lodged inside her.

'Be a good girl and relax, and it will soon be over,' Ms Brentwood whispered, the same coaxing tone she'd used in the bedroom, and sure enough, a few seconds later the offending hand withdrew.

'My search is complete, Sir John,' Ms Brentwood declared.

'Very well, Ms Brentwood,' he responded, 'if you would like to come with us we will discuss this unfortunate situation. In the meantime, Miss Carter, you will sit and wait.'

Jane sank onto the wooden chair, her head reeling with bewilderment as she straightened her scant clothing. Why was she allowing herself to be controlled by such bizarre people? She had to get away. She glanced round at Paul and the girl. Were they friend or foe?

'Please help me,' she ventured. 'I have to get away from here.'

'Shut up or you'll make it bad for all of us,' the girl hissed back, glancing nervously through a gap in the screens, at the group who were talking in low, conspiratorial voices.

A few minutes later the group returned. 'Miss Carter,' Sir John's voice was cold and clipped within the hood, as he addressed the terrified girl. 'You have invaded the Ruskin Club in an attempt to expose it for the salacious entertainment of modern society - a society who would do well to learn from our beliefs. You deceived Ms Brentwood into believing you are a girl of moral standing who would benefit from an introduction to our membership, and as a result she placed her trust in you by bringing you here tonight.'

Jane stared helplessly down at her lap, her face burning with shame as Sir John continued, his harsh words making her feel strangely guilty for her behaviour.

'You have been very foolish, Miss Carter, and have left us with few alternatives. We would prefer to place you with Ms Brentwood for a period of correction, but she is otherwise occupied for the next few days so you will go with Dr Morris, until other arrangements can be made.'

What was he talking about? She wasn't going anywhere with any of them and they couldn't make her. She was on her feet in one movement, a protestation poised to burst forth, but the doctor, like a predator judging the reactions of his prey perfectly, grabbed her around the waist, his arms closing upon her struggling body, that brave protest muffled by a hand that clamped over her mouth.

'Get the rope,' he demanded, clearly enjoying the sport. 'This little livewire's not going to cooperate.' He managed to get his cloak over her struggling form, and then rope was bound around her, pulling the cloak tight at her ankles, gathering it round her waist and across her breasts, pinning her arms to her sides. She fought with all her strength but she knew there was more than one pair of restraining hands as they worked to bind her, then as the rope was tied off she fell to the floor, the cloak encasing her up to her throat like a sack.

The doctor stared down at her coldly, his hawk-like eyes watching her as she gasped for breath. 'Gag and blindfold her,' he instructed. 'I don't want any trouble from this little one.'

Jane could no longer tell whose hands slipped the blindfold over her eyes, pushed the solid rubber ball into her mouth, and pulled the black hood back over her head.

CHAPTER THREE

The Proposition

Jane's eyes strained to hear the sound of the night traffic as she lay bundled on the floor of the moving car. She couldn't believe what was happening to her. It can't have been more than five hours since she'd set out so positively from the bustling Camden streets on the road to fulfilling her ambitions. What did these people intend to do with her? They couldn't keep her prisoner forever. Her friends and the office would try to find her, surely? She couldn't rely on any efforts from her family; she'd had little contact with her mother and aunt since she left Yorkshire.

After what Jane judged to be about twenty minutes the car drew into a gravelled driveway, and she felt herself being lifted into the night air.

'We have an unexpected guest, my dear.' The door was opened to his knock and the doctor spoke in clipped tones. 'I'll take her straight upstairs.'

Jane lay helplessly in his arms. Her jaw ached from the gag and the tears stung her eyes under the blindfold. He appeared to climb some stairs effortlessly, despite his burden, then a few moments later Jane sensed being manoeuvred through a doorway, carried a little further, and then bedsprings squeaked as she was dumped down.

His hands worked quickly to undo the uncomfortable knots, the heavy cloak was peeled away, he pulled off the blindfold, and the glare of a naked light bulb made her wince and flinch to protect her eyes.

'My wife will attend to you in a while.' His voice betrayed nothing as he gathered up the cloak from beside her and then left the room, closing and locking the door behind him.

Jane lay still until she was sure he was gone, before she removed the gag. She flexed her jaw and sat gingerly up. It was a poky attic room with sloping ceilings and a tiny dormer window. It contained almost no furniture, just the metal bedstead she'd been dumped on, covered with a thin mattress, a marble-topped washstand and a wooden chair.

Jane awoke from a miserable doze to hear the key turning in the lock, and was surprised to recognise the woman who entered and set a jug down on the washstand. It was the stout woman who'd paraded on the stage so freely earlier in the evening, her ample curves encased in black silk. Now she wore a long brocade dressing gown.

'Well, young lady,' she said, 'you have been a foolish girl. My husband is most displeased.' Her voice was rich and fruity as she busied herself pouring the water into the china washbowl. Jane looked at her short blonde curls and rosy cheeks and judged her to be around forty years old.

Mrs Morris beckoned Jane to her, the sound of cool water splashing in the bowl and the prospect of a refreshing wash lured her, and despite her aching body she climbed slowly off the bed and crossed to the expectant woman.

'That's it,' Mrs Morris encouraged, 'lean on here and I'll loosen those laces for you.'

Jane placed her hands on the cool marble, and the sense of relief and release was exquisite as the woman loosened the laces at her back. Then, although her ribs ached she was enjoying the first deep lungful of air, when she felt the cotton drawers drop to the floor. The doctor's wife then released the front clasps and the corset fell away, leaving her naked again, except for the black stockings encasing her shapely legs.

'Now we'll give you a good wash,' the woman said, lathering a bar of soap on a face flannel, Jane drained and beyond resistance as Mrs Morris started to scrub her vigorously. She closed her eyes and felt her skin tingling where it had been trapped by the tight lacing, and had to admit to herself that it felt really, really good, even when the flannel brushed against her still tender buttocks. And when she felt it soaping the backs of her legs she couldn't resist parting them slightly, so that her inner thighs could receive the same soothing treatment.

'Turn around now, young lady,' Mrs Morris directed, then applied more soap to the flannel.

Jane kept her eyes closed and allowed the woman to wash her face, neck and throat, and she didn't flinch or protest when the flannel drifted down over her breasts, caressing her nipples.

'Come and lie on the bed,' the doctor's wife coaxed, having completed a full body wash and gently dried the girl with a towel, her voice suddenly lower, more sultry. 'You must be very tired.'

Jane lay back on the thin, lumpy mattress and closed her eyes tight, wondering why she was accepting such treatment without even a murmur of complaint.

The friction of the towel increased and she didn't complain that it was centred on the sensitive bud of her clitoris. Her head lolled to one side and a hand stroked her hair away from her forehead. She opened her eyes, for just long enough to see the doctor looming, his usual grey pallor replaced with a red flush. But nothing could stop the waves of delight that were building inside her. She moved her hips, perhaps lewdly, against the towel, her body consumed by its quest for pleasure. Heat permeated her as the doctor's wife continued to tease her sensitive clitoris with the towel, and she couldn't suppress the sobs that whispered around the attic room as the orgasm burst inside her.

Jane felt her legs being closed and straightened and a cotton slip being passed over her head, but her shame prevented her from opening her eyes.

'Sleep well, young lady,' the doctor said. 'Tomorrow you will begin your new life; a life for which you are obviously ready. A life where you will see all your ambitions realised. You have nothing to fear.'

The exhausted girl's eyes fluttered open as the doctor's homely wife leaned over and planted a warm kiss on her lips. She heard them leave the room, but this time they did not turn the key in the lock. Her body felt leaden, and as her pleasure seeped away she could still feel the woman's kiss on her mouth and the stickiness between her thighs. Where was she and who were these people? What had the doctor meant about her ambitions?

Jane pulled the thin grey blanket over herself. She would think about her predicament when she'd slept a little. Just a little sleep, that's all she wanted.

Jane awoke surprisingly refreshed, and looked up at the low sloping ceiling. For a fleeting moment she thought she was at home in the tiny bedroom that had been her childhood refuge. But then she recalled the events of the previous evening, and her cheeks flushed at the memory of her ordeal at the theatre in front of the secretive Sir John and his 'committee'.

She sat up and tried to banish the thoughts from her head. She must focus on her reason for being there; Extraordinary Lives - Ben Handford. She conjured up his face and remembered the encouraging smile he'd given her as she left the office. Yesterday - it seemed a million light years away.

She must decide what to do before the doctor and his wife reappeared. She got off the bed and checked the door. It was open. She crept down the stairs to the landing below, her heart pounding. She could see down to the wooden front door, with brass bolts glinting in shafts of morning light, and knew that within seconds she could run down the stairs, pull back those bolts and dash to freedom.

So why did she hesitate and go back up to the attic room? Was it just her ambition to see the story through?

Jane was perched on the edge of the old bed when Mrs Morris entered.

'Oh, an early riser,' she announced cheerfully. 'Excellent. I've brought you some clothes. My husband expects you at breakfast, so we must hurry.'

Some of Jane's resolve left her as she saw her outfit, but she cooperated, allowing herself to be dressed once again. But this time the corset was lined with a coarser material that scratched her skin. It was no more than ten inches deep, cinching her waist and leaving her breasts entirely exposed. As the laces tightened she forced herself to relax and accept their restrictions, although Mrs Morris was not as severe in her lacing as Ms Brentwood had been.

'You're a natural student for body modification, my dear girl,' Mrs Morris observed, as she rolled black stockings up Jane's legs, and held them up with garters around her thighs. Jane looked with distaste at the long-sleeved, grey woollen dress that was dropped over her head. It hung shapelessly around her slim body, and for a moment she even longed for the soft, velvet gown she'd worn to the Ruskin Club.

'Sit down and I'll lace your boots.' Jane sat on the edge of the bed and allowed the woman to lace her feet tightly into brown leather, high-heeled ankle boots. 'Now, follow me.'

Dr Morris was waiting for them down in the entrance hall. 'Paul is here to collect you, my dear,' he said, holding out a cloak, similar to the one Jane had been wrapped in the previous night. Now they stood together Jane estimated there must be at least twenty years between them.

'And he's brought your delivery, I hope?' Mrs Morris responded.

'He has,' Dr Morris confirmed. 'It's been put in the kitchen.'

'Oh, please, may I just peek before I go?' Mrs Morris pleaded flirtatiously as he placed the cloak around her.

'Now, my dear, you know the rules,' he admonished mildly. 'Off you go and I'll see you in a few days.'

Jane listened to their conversation in alarm. The presence of Mrs Morris, another female, had afforded her some semblance of reassurance, however slight, but the doctor opened the front door and ushered his wife out. Jane caught a glimpse of Paul, standing in the driveway, and yearned to be leaving too.

'You will join me for breakfast,' the doctor said crisply, as he slid the brass bolts back into position.

Jane followed him into the dining room. Two places had been set at the mahogany table, and he indicated that she should sit at the one to the side, while he sat at the head.

'You may serve Miss Carter some porridge now, Matilda,' the doctor instructed, and Jane sat uncomfortably as she saw the defiant flash in the woman's piercing dark eyes. She carried the steaming dish towards Jane, moving across the floor with the grace of a stalking cat. She served a ladle of its contents into the bowl in front of Jane, and then did the same for the doctor.

'Sir John has telephoned this morning,' the man said to Jane, 'and we have a proposition for you.' He raised his spoon and began to eat, as Matilda backed away and stood quietly beside the closed door.

Jane looked at him curiously, and the doctor smiled confidently at her unformed question. 'You must not underestimate the powers of the Ruskin Club, Jane. We are prepared to resort to modern methods when we have to. Our membership has influence at the highest levels. Influence in many areas that could be of benefit to you, in fact. These are unusual circumstances, but Sir John is prepared to introduce you into our society... under certain conditions.'

Jane felt her stomach knot with apprehension, and tried to steady her voice before she spoke. '*Conditions?*' she echoed. 'What exactly do you mean by *conditions?*' She paused, recalling Ms Brentwood's admonishments of the previous night. 'Please, Dr Morris, what do you mean?'

'You will submit to a period of one month's training by the committee,' he elaborated. 'That is myself, Major Hunt and Lord Waterhouse. Ultimately Sir John will decide on your progress, and if he is satisfied you will be afforded all the favours that are open to our membership.' He dabbed his linen napkin to his lips. 'I can assure you, Jane, that if you live up to expectations you will not be disappointed.'

Jane fought hard to maintain her composure. 'And if I refuse?' she asked, in the boldest tone she could muster.

'I don't think you will. Firstly, because we have a valuable camera for which you are responsible, but also because you are too ambitious and too curious. You have demonstrated that already.' He challenged her deliberately as he spoke.

How could he be so presumptuous? Jane felt the heat rise to her cheeks, but she was determined to delve further into their activities. 'The training... what will that involve?' she asked cautiously.

The doctor rested his palms together, as if in prayer. 'Matilda can tell you that, can't you Matilda?' Jane looked up at the proud beauty watching her intently. Every sinew rippled with disdain as she ignored his question.

'"Silence is the most perfect expression of scorn",' the doctor quoted. 'You are familiar with the works of George Bernard Shaw, Jane?'

'Yes,' she answered, his question confusing her. She was in no mood for a literary discussion.

'Good. Suffice to say that your training at the Ruskin Club will complete your education. Now do I have your agreement?'

Jane's heart was pounding, the woollen dress increasingly irritated her skin, but she slowly nodded her confirmation nonetheless.

'Excellent! I shall inform Sir John. You will write the letters later. Of course there will be a further letter implicating you in the theft of the camera, which we shall hold in the event of you breaking your word.' The doctor made no attempt to disguise his delight as he poured himself a cup of tea from a silver pot.

'You seem to find your dress uncomfortable, my dear,' the doctor observed with ill-feigned concern. 'Matilda finds her clothes uncomfortable too, but for different reasons. Is that not so, Matilda?'

'You may dress me as a servant but I will never serve willingly.' The woman's voice indicated little sign of respect for the man, and he slammed his fist down onto the table, causing Jane to flinch with shock.

'But serve you will!' the doctor roared back at her, Jane trembling at his sudden rage, but the woman remained unmoved. 'Since it seems you're both unhappy with the clothes you've been provided with, I suggest you remove them.' His eyes darted furiously between the two.

Panic gripped Jane. Surely the powerful woman wasn't going to comply? But to Jane's horror she did, reaching behind her waist to untie her white apron. Then slowly she unbuttoned the high neck, never losing her composure.

23

'Take your dress off too, Jane.' The doctor looked at her slyly from the corner of his eye, but kept his attention focused on Matilda. Jane, too, was transfixed as the maid let the apron and dress fall to the floor, then stood, virtually naked, the stiff white corset contrasting beautifully with her ebony skin. At almost six foot tall she looked superb. Her full breasts stood firm and the dark brown nipples tilted upward. Threaded through them was a cluster of fine silver rings, and Jane's hands rose protectively to her own breasts as she imagined the pain the woman must have experienced during their insertion. Between her muscular thighs was a nest of tight black curls, trimmed enough to reveal the glint of more rings and the full, fleshy lips to which they were attached.

'I see your defiance has earned you additional penalties since you were last here, Matilda,' the doctor observed. 'Now, Jane,' he faced the spellbound girl, 'will you undress yourself or do you need Matilda to help you?'

Jane turned scarlet, but knew that resistance was futile, so taking a deep breath to calm her nerves, she fumbled clumsily with the buttons down her front.

Jane felt sick with trepidation as she trailed upstairs, following the doctor and maid. In the room they entered on the first landing an old-fashioned medical couch dominated its centre. A glass partition separated it from the adjoining space. Jane lingered in the doorway, shifting uneasily from one foot to the other.

'Up on the couch, please,' the doctor said, ushering her in and closing the door. Jane froze as he took off his jacket and started to roll up the sleeves of his crisp white shirt.

'No, please...' she mumbled, feeling the tears starting, too shocked to put up any resistance, the maid too strong and too practiced. Soon Jane was supine on the couch, broad leather straps attaching her ankles and wrists to the four corners, the tears meandering down her cheeks. She looked up helplessly at Matilda, but the woman was no ally. She'd shown none of her usual resistance in obeying the command to bind her to the couch.

'Take off her corset,' the doctor instructed, and Matilda worked enthusiastically, unlacing the stiff garment until Jane lay naked but for the stockings.

'I need to examine you so I can report on your condition at the start of your training.' Dr Morris flexed his fingers, before placing them over each of Jane's breasts and squeezing pensively. She shuddered with distaste and turned her head away. His cold hands travelled down over her flat stomach, occasionally pressing, occasionally prodding. Jane kept her eyes tightly shut, but her vulnerability and shame consumed her when his hand cupped her pubic mound, between her parted thighs. He let his fingers investigate between her moist sex lips, where they located and brushed over her clitoris, causing her to gasp, and then gasp again as his fingers and thumb lingered to pinch the tiny bud. Jane whimpered with shame as she felt it respond to his touch. She was overcome by bittersweet waves. She felt the rush of pleasure, and knew she was anointing his artful fingers with her juices as the orgasm rippled through her.

'I thought as much,' he pondered. 'Such abandon must be tempered, young lady.

Pass me a plug, Matilda.'

Jane let out a long low moan as the doctor eased the instrument into her vagina, forcing the lips apart, stretching the narrow entrance and holding it wide.

'You will learn to control and embrace your discomfort,' the doctor decreed. 'Prepare her and then bring her downstairs,' he said to the maid, then turned, picked up his jacket, and left the room.

Matilda moved to Jane's side and unbuckled the straps that secured her wrists. 'One day, honey,' the statuesque woman whispered, 'I'm going to suck you into another world.' Jane blushed at the vulgarity and her own secret, suspended cravings.

'Now keep still while I give you a little trim,' she said, and before Jane could react she produced a small pair of medical scissors and began to snip meticulously at the silky hairs that shielded her sex. Jane held her breath with trepidation and lay quite still, her feet on the couch and her knees bent, not daring to move a muscle. By the time Matilda was satisfied the ripe pinkness of her sex lips peeped through the light down.

'Now get up, and careful you hold the plug in.' Matilda helped her off the couch. Her legs felt as if they were wedged apart and she had to steady herself against it while she struggled to arrange her thoughts.

'I saw you at the auction of Ms Brentwood's corsets...' Jane said hesitantly, but Matilda let out a snort of derision.

'Corsets? You didn't think that was what they were selling? You're more naïve than you look if you did.' She reached into a drawer beside the couch. 'Now turn around.'

Jane looked down at the narrow leather belt being fastened around her waist, and when she realised its purpose she tried to pull away, but Matilda held her firmly and administered a smart slap to her bottom. The belt was part of a harness designed to run down over her stomach and back up between her buttocks. Matilda deftly arranged the straps where they split into two at the front, positioning them so that the newly exposed sex lips were lewdly displayed. Jane shuddered; the harness held the rubber plug inside her so that nothing could dislodge it.

'Oh, are they going to have some fun with you...' The coloured woman spoke in an awed whisper as she held Jane's hips and gazed at the vision before her.

'Wh-what did you mean about the auction?' Matilda seemed transfixed by the site in front of her, so Jane continued; emboldened by the effect she was clearly having on the maid. 'Was it the women being auctioned?'

Matilda looked up at her, her large dark eyes burning with desire. 'You got it, honey,' she confirmed, and Jane suppressed a fearful shudder as her suspicions were confirmed.

'So you were bought by... the doctor?' she asked, and Matilda nodded. 'Is he really a doctor?'

'Sure he is,' the woman sneered. 'He owns half the private clinics in Harley Street. That's where I met him. I was a nurse in one of them.' Matilda smiled ruefully.

'But who were the other women?' Jane pressed. 'And who is Sir John? Why do you let them treat you like this?'

'Shhh... let's just say we all have our reasons.' She stroked and kissed Jane's throat, her warm lips like velvet against her bare skin, stilling Jane's questions. 'You have your reasons, too,' Matilda purred, pulling back a little and looking intently at Jane, her eyes burning with unmistakable lust, 'and I for one will enjoy discovering them.'

The tense moment of intimacy ended suddenly, Matilda stepping back and her detachment returning. 'Follow me, and hurry,' she ordered. 'You'll learn not to keep them waiting.'

Jane clung to the mahogany handrail as she descended the stairs, catching her breath, the plug between her thighs tormenting her with every step. She could feel the leather straps biting into her sensitive flesh, but it was the shame of how she was displayed, more than the discomfort, that concerned her. And Matilda had re-laced the corset far tighter than the doctor's wife did that morning, oblivious to Jane's objections.

Matilda delivered Jane to the library, where the doctor was waiting, and left her standing awkwardly, staring at the floor.

'I think that is enough of your coyness, young lady,' the doctor said uncompromisingly. 'In future, on the command *display* you will adopt the position you saw last night. Do you understand?'

'Yes, doctor,' Jane said miserably.

'Very well, display,' he ordered, and she cringed with embarrassment as she raised her arms and clasped her hands behind her neck, her bare breasts jutting forward, completely exposed above the trim corset. The movement caused the harness to tighten and she felt the plug force itself even deeper. 'Now move your feet apart,' he said, and she complied as he approached, her head spinning as she tried to absorb and understand what was happening to her.

The warmth and atmosphere in the room was making her feel light-headed as the doctor guided her towards the desk and chair, and made her sit, causing her to flinch as the plug embedded itself even further.

'Be sensible,' he said, lowering his voice conspiratorially and placing a pen in her hand. 'When you've written the letters you may go to your room and rest for a while.'

CHAPTER FOUR

Matilda's Trials

Jane copied out the letters as instructed, and sat stiffly as the doctor read them through. Before he dismissed her he attached a tiny silver padlock to the buckle of the harness. 'In case you are tempted to loosen it,' he warned, tucking the key into his breast pocket.

In her room she found the white cotton slip laid over the chair. She took off her boots and stockings and put it on, relieved to cover herself at last. A plate of cold meats and a jug of water had been set out for her. She ate gratefully, then lay down on the bed, fingering the padlock, consumed with discomfort and confusion.

She was woken by a shriek and sat up on the bed, wondering what it was all about. The sound came again, so she eased herself off the bed, clothed only in the white slip, and crept barefoot to the door and out onto the narrow staircase. It was much later, for the house was in partial darkness. She must have been asleep for quite some time.

The anguished cries rose with increasing frequency from the landing below, and her heart pounded as she tiptoed down the stairs. The door to the room she'd earlier been examined in was ajar, and the light spilled out onto the darkened landing, so she crept to it and carefully peered inside.

Jane had to stifle the gasp that rose in her throat at the sight inside the room. Matilda hung facing her, completely naked, suspended by her wrists from the ceiling. Her head was slumped forward, her knees slightly bent and her tormented cries had been replaced by weary groans. Her body glistened from the rivulets of sweat that trickled down her dark flesh.

'So, Matilda, I ask you again; will you allow me to fuck you?' The doctor stepped into Jane's view. In his hand was a long bamboo cane, which he tapped against his thigh. Matilda barely raised her head, but shook it in defiant response.

'Very well, then we must continue.' The doctor simmered with contained anger, lifting the cane and flexing it. 'Six more strokes.' He reached up for a rope above the woman's wrists and Jane watched, incredulous, as a pulley system raised Matilda's limp body until her feet just touched the floor. The doctor ran the cane up the inside of her thighs until she parted her legs. Then he positioned himself a few feet behind and to the side of her and lifted the instrument to shoulder height. Matilda raised her head, her eyes tightly closed, and braced herself. The doctor swept the cane down viciously across her buttocks. Her firm breasts juddered and the silver rings shimmered as the blow resounded through her body.

The next stroke fell before she had time to recover from the first but she held her stance, the muscles in her thighs drawn taut with the effort. The soft curls between them revealed the rings that lined each lip. The doctor paused and stroked his target, and Jane saw the flash of resentment as Matilda's eyes briefly opened.

He aimed the third blow at her left buttock, and the fourth at her right. Jane crouched in the doorway, terrified by the growls now coming from deep inside the bound beauty.

'Two more, and you will ask for them when you are ready.' The doctor used his handkerchief to mop his brow and wipe the cane free of Matilda's sweat. The silence hung in the room for more than a minute as Jane watched, careful to keep herself concealed.

'I am ready... doctor,' Matilda said eventually, steeling her muscles and raising her head proudly.

Jane held her breath as the doctor aimed the two final blows with great accuracy. The starched sleeves of his shirt flashed behind the woman's dark torso as the cane whipped through the air. The *swit* of its descent and the smack of its contact reverberated in Jane's own body. She couldn't believe what she was witnessing, and her relief when all six blows had been delivered caused her to exhale - too loudly.

'I think we have an audience, Matilda,' the doctor mused, and Jane froze as he reached for the pulley and lowered his victim, although her wrists still supported the weight of her exhausted body.

'In you come, Jane.' The watching girl trembled with terror as she emerged from her hiding place. 'It seems your curiosity has gotten the better of you again, young lady,' the doctor said, fixing her with a beady stare. 'But now you are here you may as well watch the conclusion of Matilda's session.'

He indicated that she should sit on a wooden chair by the side of the pulley mechanism. So she crossed the room, skirting Matilda's sagging form and sat down, rigid with fear, and then the doctor moved swiftly, flicked a hidden catch on each arm of the chair, and before Jane had time to react her wrists were clamped by metal bands that snapped into position.

'Please, let me go,' she begged, struggling to stand but falling back hopelessly.

'It's too late for that,' he laughed contemptuously. 'Now Matilda,' he turned his attention back to the woman hanging from the rope pulley, her bottom crisscrossed with livid purple stripes, evidence of far more than the six strokes Jane had just witnessed. The doctor moved his hand between her thighs and Matilda moaned softly.

'For the final time, Matilda, will you allow yourself to be fucked here?' he asked quietly, leaning close to her ear.

Matilda barely paused, and Jane jumped at the vehemence in her voice. 'Never!' she spat, snatching her hips away from his exploring hand. 'Never, whatever you do to me!'

'In that case you have earned yourself another piercing,' he stated, toying with the rings between her legs. 'We shall decide where it is to be later, but you have left us with few options. In the meantime I'll employ another part of your anatomy.'

Sinews tensed as she drew herself up to her full height, but the doctor reached up and unclipped the pulley suddenly, and she sank wearily to the floor.

'Watch carefully, Jane, and learn,' he said, unbuttoning his trousers, exposing his erection, and then callously feeding it into Matilda's mouth. He started to sigh, rasping sounds that came from his slackened mouth, and Jane watched, sickened but spellbound as Matilda curled her fingers around the shaft impaling her mouth and pumped it, her breasts pressed against his legs as she concentrated on her task. The doctor's breathing increased in tempo and intensity. Matilda persisted skilfully with hand and mouth, until he withdrew from between her parted lips and directed jets of creamy sperm onto her dark flesh, splashing her face and watching it trickle down between her breasts, seeping down her tensed stomach, nestling in the black curls between her thighs.

The tension in the room was broken when the doorbell chimed. The doctor wiped the last drop of his seed against Matilda's face before fastening his trousers. 'You will answer that,' he said to Jane, releasing the catches on the arms of the chair, the metal bands springing back with a loud snap. 'I don't think Matilda is quite presentable.'

Jane scurried from the room. It wasn't too late to escape. She dashed down the stairs, hardly aware of the constraints of the harness under her thin slip. She heaved at the brass bolts and flung open the front door, the hum of traffic beckoning her as she started to descend the stone steps to the driveway.

'Get her inside!'

Jane's exhilaration at being free was a fleeting one as Ms Brentwood appeared from the shadows, and Paul instantly obeyed the order to easily manhandle her back into the house.

'Good evening, Ms Brentwood.' The doctor was at the top of the stairs, checking his gold watch. 'I'm afraid I was distracted by Miss Carter. It seems she is even more inquisitive than we thought.' Jane struggled feebly against Paul's hold as the doctor's eyes burned into her. 'And wilful too, I see. Bring her back up here. We may as well begin her trial immediately.'

Jane let out a shriek of panic as they went up to the examination room. Matilda had been strapped facedown on the couch, a cushion placed under her hips to raise her buttocks, highlighting the diagonal patterns of raised weals, turning red and purple against her dark skin.

'I assume you were no more successful than your fellow members, doctor?' Ms Brentwood said, approaching the spread-eagled woman. She stroked the inflamed flesh and Matilda stifled her reaction to the pain. 'Your resolve is remarkable, Matilda,' Ms Brentwood said, and Jane thought she detected a faint note of approval before she continued in a harsher tone. 'However, you know what you agreed to and your treatment will continue until you submit voluntarily.' She moved her fingers between Matilda's buttocks until she found the entrance to her sex, and Matilda moaned as she slipped two fingers inside her.

'You like that, don't you?' Ms Brentwood goaded, then stabbed with her fingers, the force lifting the naked woman's hips off the cushion. In spite of her dire situation, the Negress rolled her hips onto the other woman's fist. 'If you'd just let the doctor fuck you, your suffering would be over,' she whispered, before withdrawing her hand. 'I've already called Kurt. He'll be here shortly.'

Paul held Jane firmly and she whimpered as her buttocks brushed against the swell in his trousers. Was he really part of all the depravity?

'We'll use the pulley for the girl.' The doctor's stern voice cut across her thoughts. 'I think it will afford us the best view.' He was lowering the mechanism and Ms Brentwood beckoned Paul to move Jane forward, every fibre of Jane's body trembling with trepidation. She raised her arms while Ms Brentwood lifted the thin slip over her head, and stood cringing in nothing but the lewd harness. She wished they would at least dismiss Paul, but instead he was instructed to place a metal bar at her feet, and when they chained her ankles to each end her legs gave way, but she was prevented from falling by the rope drawing her wrists upward, her body stretched taut, straining against the enforced position.

The doctor produced the tiny key from his breast pocket and released the padlock. 'The plug will have done its work by now, Ms Brentwood,' he said, and Jane wasn't prepared for the sensations that flooded her as Ms Brentwood withdrew the crude implement from her.

'A few questions first,' Ms Brentwood said, feeling Jane's vulnerable sex. 'How many times have you been fucked?'

'Answer Ms Brentwood, Jane, we need to know,' the doctor urged.

'Just... just once,' Jane muttered miserably.

'I see.' She withdrew her finger and found the puckered entrance to Jane's rear passage. 'And here?'

Jane became more agitated and shook her head determinedly. 'No, never, Ms Brentwood,' she answered. The woman faced her, grasping her chin viciously and squeezing her cheeks until she was forced to open her mouth wide, and Ms Brentwood passed her fingers over the neat white teeth as if Jane were a young animal at market.

'And here?'

Jane gulped as her chin was released. 'No, Ms Brentwood.' She couldn't hold back the tears any longer as she recalled the site of Matilda on her knees in front of the doctor, his erection filling her mouth. The very thought of performing such an act on him filled her with apprehension and dread.

'I will begin the examination now,' Ms Brentwood stated. 'A blindfold please, Dr Morris. I need to be certain of purity for the source of her stimulation.' Jane had time to see Ms Brentwood open a drawer of what looked like medical instruments, before they slipped a leather blindfold over her eyes.

'In the event that your diagnosis is correct, doctor, we will prepare to administer the first treatment,' she heard Ms Brentwood say, then strained to hear the movements in the room - the muttered voices, the sound of furniture being moved close to her.

Several minutes passed, and behind the blindfold she fell in to her own world. So when with no warning she felt something hard touch her thigh, she allowed the new sensation to travel over her bare skin and rest on the swelling bud of her clitoris. When it began to vibrate her mind became centred on that one small place, as if no other part of her existed. She edged her hips forward as the vibrations increased, seeking out the source of her pleasure, rotating her hips, thrusting out her breasts, oblivious to anything but the need to release her desire.

When it came she felt it grip her whole body. If she hadn't been suspended by her wrists she might have slumped to the floor with the ferocity of it.

When the blindfold was removed the light made Jane squint, but after a few seconds she saw Ms Brentwood sitting on the wooden chair in front of her, holding out a kidney-shaped metal dish, and the doctor standing behind her checking his watch.

Jane started to struggle against the bonds as the doctor produced a short leather paddle and circled her suspended body. He slapped it threateningly against the palm of one hand while he held the stiff handle in the other. When she realised what he intended she begged and pleaded, but to no avail, and when she heard the rustle of his starched sleeve behind her she could do no more than close her eyes in dreaded anticipation.

The slap of the leather meeting her buttocks filled the room, and Jane wailed as the sharp pain suffused her body.

'Be quiet, girl!' Ms Brentwood barked as the doctor raised his arm again. Jane bit her lip and started to shake uncontrollably, despite her bonds. He struck again and the pain made her open her eyes wide, to see Ms Brentwood sitting in front of her, smiling enigmatically.

'She can take two more, doctor,' the woman decreed, her normally sallow cheeks flushed with suppressed excitement.

Jane looked at her pleadingly, but the heat in her buttocks had started to mingle with the dying embers of her orgasm. She felt the heaviness low in her stomach as the next blow fell. The strength of it thrust her hips forward towards Ms Brentwood.

But the severity of the final stroke forced the breath from her lungs and she hung limp from the pulley, moaning softly.

Ms Brentwood stood, and they released Jane's ankles and lowered her onto the wooden chair. The metal rings swiftly imprisoned her wrists and she could do nothing to wipe away the tears that glistened on her flushed cheeks.

'The treatment must be repeated three times a day for the next five days. Every orgasm, administered by the device I have provided, must be followed immediately by four hard strokes with the leather paddle.' Ms Brentwood was addressing the doctor, as if Jane didn't exist. 'As you know, I have recent experience of this unusual condition.'

'So I understand,' the doctor said, carefully returning the leather paddle to the drawer. 'Sir John commended you yesterday on your success in another case.'

'It is simple enough, doctor. Excessive orgasms indicate a lustful nature, which must be tempered and controlled. I suspect she has possessed this trait for some time.' Ms Brentwood's eyes fixed on Jane's nipples, still erect. 'It is best harnessed if the mind is conditioned to pay the price. Once that connection is made she will be capable of extraordinary service.'

Jane averted her eyes as Ms Brentwood continued to appraise her with cool detachment. 'She should be confined to her room during the period of treatment and deprived of all but her basic needs. I suggest that the plug is inserted for several hours a day.'

'That may also help to curb her headstrong nature,' the doctor concurred, cupping one of Jane's breasts and squeezing cruelly. 'Will you join me in the drawing room until Kurt arrives? I think we can safely leave these two alone for a while.'

'We have to escape,' Jane whispered desperately. 'Will Paul help us?'

Matilda raised her head and chuckled sardonically. 'He won't help us. He wants to be one of them. I guess you'd call it a kind of apprenticeship. And there's no sense trying to escape; they'll come after you and make your life a misery.'

Jane was taken aback by her negativity. 'But I don't understand, after what the doctor did to you. The way he made you suffer...'

'The more I let them make me suffer, the more I get what I want.' Matilda's voice was filled with pride as she raised her head and looked at Jane. 'That's why I hold out.'

The silence hung between them for several moments before Jane ventured further. 'But I don't understand what I was punished for.'

Again Matilda scoffed at her innocence. 'They'll always find something to punish you for.'

Jane was more confused than ever by Matilda's somewhat cryptic responses, but just then the doorbell chimed downstairs again. Matilda lowered her head and groaned.

'Who's that?' Jane asked urgently.

'You'll see soon enough.' Matilda closed her eyes, ending the brief conversation.

The doctor led the group back into the room, a large man carrying a black case having joined them.

'Help me turn her over, Paul, while Kurt prepares.' The doctor started to unbuckle the straps that fastened Matilda's wrists. The stranger set out his case on the small table, Jane noticing the tattoos that covered his sturdy forearms. He produced a rubber apron, slipped it over his head and tied it around his belly. Matilda had been turned onto her back and her wrists tied low down to a bar around the underside of the couch. She looked towards Jane and fixed her with a stare of determined resignation.

'I'll need her in stirrups,' the man said gruffly, eyeing Matilda's naked body.

'I think we should move Miss Carter a little closer so she can learn what comes of obstinacy,' Ms Brentwood said, lowering the apparatus that hung at the foot of the examination couch.

'So where do you want it?' Kurt asked bluntly, leaning forward to peer at Matilda's exposed sex. 'Doesn't look like there's much room.' Jane cringed as he roughly parted the lips, exposing the rich crimson flesh, and her alarm increased when she saw how thoroughly both the inner and outer labia were lined with metal rings, the naked peak of her clitoris clearly visible.

'She's left us no option,' Ms Brentwood placed her finger directly over Matilda's clitoris. 'And I want it done while it's erect.' A slow smile spread over her handsome face as she observed Matilda's reaction.

Kurt smiled too, lasciviously, the veins in his stout neck raised with anticipation. 'I'll do the honours then, shall I?' He moved Ms Brentwood's hand away and started to rub the exposed bud. 'How long's this bitch been here?' he asked.

'Three months,' the doctor stated precisely. 'She leaves in four weeks so we need space for at least four more piercings. Unless, of course, she submits,' he added.

'I won't get any more in her nipples, so they're going to have to go here.' The man continued the friction on her clitoris. 'Do you want me to do it without numbing her?'

'I told you, I want it erect,' Ms Brentwood snapped. 'Now get on with it.'

Matilda stared resolutely at the ceiling, her nostrils flaring as she inhaled and exhaled deeply, blocking out what was happening to her. She didn't see him reach for the metal piercing gun, already primed with a fine silver ring, but she stopped mid-breath when she felt the cold metal between her legs. The room fell silent while the man adjusted the head of the gun until the jaws closed against the erect peak. Jane saw Ms Brentwood nod her head, and then heard the click of the gun driving the bolt home.

Matilda spasmed, but hardly made a sound as she fought to re-establish the rhythmic breathing pattern she'd adopted to prepare for the ordeal.

Jane sat motionless, watching the beads of sweat forming between the firmness of Matilda's breasts, and to her utter amazement a slow smile creeping across her ruby lips. When she looked down at her own breasts she was horrified to see her nipples standing erect, the areola puckered and dark.

'Take Miss Carter to her room, Paul, and lock her in this time,' the doctor instructed, his keen eyes observing her body's reaction.

'Sure you don't want her done too?' Kurt offered eagerly, leering at Jane.

'Get her upstairs, Paul.' Jane sensed the note of disapproval from Ms Brentwood toward Kurt's lecherous tone.

Paul released her from the chair, urged her out of the humid room, and up the narrow staircase in silence. After Matilda's warning about him she didn't dare appeal for his help.

He pushed her into the bleak little attic room. 'Don't worry, you'll get used to it. If you do as they tell you, you won't come to any harm,' he said quickly before he left her, locking the door behind him, his hint of compassion merely heightening her despair.

Jane was perched on the edge of the bed, sorrowfully holding her head in her hands, when Ms Brentwood unlocked the door and entered.

'I've brought the garments you'll be required to wear for the next five days.' She laid two corsets on the bed beside Jane. 'One is for daywear, and the other you will wear at night. Matilda will dress you while you're here.'

Jane hung her head sullenly, averting her eyes from the two stiff garments that lay beside her, but Ms Brentwood grasped her chin and Jane grimaced with pain as her head was jerked up and back.

'You made quite a display of yourself earlier, young lady. Perhaps it's time you gave a little pleasure instead of receiving it.' She slowly raised her long skirt, keeping a firm grasp on Jane's chin as she exposed her sex, richly covered in lustrous brown hair curling around the full, ripe lips. Jane panted softly as the grip moved to her neck, tightened and pulled her closer, until she was breathing in the heavy scent of another woman's arousal.

'Have you done this before?' Ms Brentwood asked quietly, but Jane looked up into her deep dark eyes without answering, so the woman pulled her closer, pressing her flushed face between her thighs.

'Take it slowly...' she whispered, her words fading as Jane instinctively used her lips to coax and tease the hot, moist flesh.

As the sitting girl tasted the woman's juices she instinctively raised her arms and squeezed them around her thighs, cupping the smooth globes of Ms Brentwood's naked buttocks. The woman raised her dress higher and exposed the area of perfect white flesh above her black stockings. Jane's tongue found the woman's bud and she lapped at it, flicking her tongue around it, fascinated as she felt it grow and harden under her touch, and the warmth flowed through her own stomach. She slid her tongue lower, and felt how the bud sought it out again. She played the game several times until she was sure of her power. Then she closed her teeth lightly over the woman's engorged clitoris, and glowed proudly as she heard the first gasp, the brief shudder, and then the long exhale of breath that concluded their fleeting liaison.

Ms Brentwood moved back and lowered her dress. Her cheeks were ablaze and her eyes sparkled.

'Sleep well, my dear.' She stroked Jane's hair, toying for a moment with her damp fringe, before she left the room.

Jane sank back on the uncomfortable mattress, reeling in disbelief at what she'd just done, and when the doctor appeared moments later she lay passive and allowed him to chain her to the metal bedstead. He threw the thin blanket over her dismissively and locked the door as he left.

Jane tested the chains. They were long enough to let her alter position slightly but too short to allow her to soothe the torment between her thighs. She blushed at her own wantonness. Had she been coerced, or had she agreed willingly to lick another woman? Was it only twenty-four hours ago that she left her Camden office and set out on her first assignment? She wondered if anyone had noticed her absence. Probably not. Not yet, anyway.

CHAPTER FIVE

Ben Uncovers

Ben Handford read through Jane's letter several times. Something didn't make sense. He'd had high hopes for Jane Carter. She had a hunger and an ambition he recognised in himself at the same age. He remembered her naïve enthusiasm at her interview and how she had almost kissed him when he gave her the job, but now she was bolting back to Yorkshire at a moment's notice, with some stuff about her roommate returning the camera later. He was sure he'd overheard her saying she lived alone. He checked himself. He knew the signs when he was taking too much interest in a woman colleague. Not that she was a woman. No more than a kid just out of college, really.

'I'm going out. Probably won't be back today.' Ben stuffed the letter in his pocket and marched through the cramped outer office. He sensed the knowing looks exchanged behind his departing back: *one of Ben's benders*.

He headed down Tottenham Court Road towards Soho. He kept his head down, ignoring the groups of fashion groupies and tourists seated outside the pavement cafés. He remembered the area when it was a bohemian village populated by artists and tarts. As a struggling young journalist he had found a natural habitat in the pubs and after hours drinking clubs. That's where he'd met Sadie, between one of her bookings. He used to watch the girls scurrying up and down Dean Street, in and out of the seedy strip clubs, checking their watches. He bought them drinks, which they swilled down, never daring to be late to take off their clothes for the punters out for an afternoon's titilation. But Sadie was too smart to stick at that for long.

Ben turned up Greek Street in search of the familiar doorbell.

'She's up in the salon.' A brunette in a skimpy robe was on duty at the reception desk.

Sadie had owned the whole building for over ten years now and Ben climbed the carpeted stairs to the first floor room. It was furnished with plush red velvet sofas and gilded mirrors in the style of a high-class French bordello.

'Darlin'.' For all her success, Sadie hadn't lost her East End accent. 'Where you been? You never comes to see your true love any more.' Sadie enveloped him in an elaborate embrace, and Ben allowed himself a moment of delicious comfort. As he hugged her to him he was once again the gauche young man in love with the crazy, streetwise kid.

'You look great, Sadie.' Ben held her away from him and looked into her dancing eyes. He wanted to kiss her full lips and stroke the sleek blonde hair that framed her ageless face. 'There's something I want to talk to you about,' he said instead. 'I think you might be able to help...'

Ben couldn't help but be distracted by the tall, shapely girl who joined them at that moment. She was zipped into a tight black leather bask, stockings and thigh high, stiletto-heeled boots. Her red, manicured fingernails tapped impatiently on the ridges of a leather riding crop.

'In a while, my love,' Sadie said. 'This is Lola, from Brazil.' Lola did no more than nod in Ben's direction. 'I'm afraid we're expecting a client,' Sadie continued. 'But why don't you watch from the viewing booth? We'll only be half an hour and then you can ask me whatever you want.' She tossed her head coquettishly and urged him towards the door at the back of the room.

Ben tried to object. He wasn't sure he was in the mood for one of Sadie's sessions, but she insisted and soon he was sitting on a comfortable seat behind the one-way mirror, a glass of champagne in his hand and the rest of the bottle on ice in front of him. So he settled back and let the bubbles tickle his nose and throat.

The booth looked out onto a strangely furnished room. At first glance it could have been a gym. There was a leather vaulting horse, rows of parallel rails lined one wall, and around the others hung a variety of ingenious metal and leather instruments.

Minutes later Sadie led her clients through from the salon. The man was short and portly. His blue blazer was buttoned over his rotund stomach and he ran a hand distractedly through his thinning hair. His wife was an entirely ordinary, mousy-haired woman dressed in a rather shapeless tweed overcoat. They looked like respectable members of their local golf club.

'Did you have a good journey, sir?' Sadie enquired. She looked just as respectable as her clients, if a little more soigné. Her tight black dress hugged her trim figure and the red leather shoes showed off her shapely legs and ankles. Ben found her as desirable as ever.

Sadie offered the man a seat, but his wife remained standing. 'Now, sir, how has your wife's behaviour been since your last visit?'

'Not satisfactory, I'm afraid,' the man replied, somewhat pompously.

'Oh, I'm sorry to hear that.' Sadie played her part to perfection. 'Perhaps you'd better take off your coat and explain why your husband is so displeased with you,' she said to the woman, holding out her arm, the woman letting her coat slip off her shoulders and affording Ben a perfect view of her naked body as she handed the garment to Sadie. Underneath the coat she wore nothing but sheer black stockings held up with garters, and a pair of court shoes. Her figure was surprisingly curvy, with pert breasts and neatly rounded hips. Ben took a long swig of his chilled drink as he pictured the outwardly respectable couple leaving their immaculate home and making their journey into the city, hiding the shared knowledge of her nudity from their fellow travellers.

'Tell Mistress Sadie how you have disobeyed me, my dear.' The man licked his fleshy lips and looked sternly at his vulnerable wife.

Sadie made great play of hanging the shapeless tweed garment on a wooden hanger, before she spun round and demanded sharply, 'And how many times did you defy your husband's ruling?'

The woman spoke quietly but clearly. 'I wore an apron to cook supper on

Tuesday... and on Thursday there was dust on the hall table... I can be seen from the street when I'm polishing it...' Her voice trailed away apologetically as she looked nervously at her inquisitors. 'And on Friday I wore underwear when I visited the dentist.' She hung her head at the confession.

'So you would like her to be punished?' Sadie asked rhetorically of the man. 'I suggest two strokes each for the domestic failures and four for the more serious transgression.' Ben smiled to himself. He could see that Sadie enjoyed her work.

'Lola!' Sadie clapped her hands and the magnificent Brazilian beauty proudly entered the room, slapping the riding crop meaningfully against her thigh.

'Fasten her to the rails,' the man instructed hoarsely.

The ropes were already dangling from the wooden bars, and Lola skilfully tied them around the wrists and ankles of the woman so she was pinned, her arms held high, her legs parted, and her breasts pressed against the wall. She accepted the treatment without complaint.

Ben shifted in his seat and poured himself another drink. He had to admit, he was intrigued to see how the woman would endure her punishment.

'If you will excuse me, I'll leave you with Lola,' said Sadie. 'I have some other business to attend to.' She stroked her hand down the woman's back and let it linger over her bottom, before she left the room.

Moments later she slipped silently into the little booth and settled herself next to Ben, just in time to see Lola raising the crop for the first time.

'Start counting,' the man instructed his wife.

'One,' her voice quavered slightly. The crop swished through the air and landed squarely. The woman accepted the first blow stoically.

'Two.' Lola wielded the crop for the second time. The woman pressed her hips harder against the rails.

'Three.' The pitch of her voice rose each time she was expected to invite her punishment. After the next blow there was a longer pause, during which Lola stroked the crop threateningly over her reddening buttocks.

'Four,' the woman said quickly.

Ben leaned forward in his seat and felt the warmth of Sadie's thigh against his. He wasn't much of a voyeur, but the combination of the naked suburban housewife being so liberally chastised by an exotic, leather-clad Amazon, stirred him, the bulge in his trousers becoming obvious evidence of that fact. His appetite was not as jaded as he thought.

'I told you you'd enjoy it,' Sadie whispered conspiratorially, and brushed her fingers teasingly over his lap. 'He brings her here every Wednesday.'

'Seven.' The woman seemed to have gone into some sort of trance, but Lola had lost none of her vigour.

'Eight.' The woman's voice seemed to come from deep within her consciousness. Lola's golden skin glowed with the exertion as she swept the last stroke down with all her considerable strength. Ben winced and even Sadie looked momentarily concerned.

'Thank you, Mistress Lola,' the woman said eventually, and with a sincerity that took Ben by surprise.

Sadie stood up. 'Let me show you the horse,' she enthused. 'It's my new venture. I've just sold my latest deluxe model to some rich old major in Norfolk. Got my cousin makin' 'em for me in Wapping.'

Ben smiled as she left the booth. Sadie never missed a chance to make a few quid. For years she'd had half her family making the ingenious instruments of torture that decorated her walls, and sold them on as a nice little sideline.

She reappeared in the room as Lola was untying the woman from the wall bars. 'Five minutes on the horse I think, don't you, sir?' she said brightly to the husband, and he nodded his approval, sweat glistening on his bald patch.

Sadie moved to the vaulting horse. It was covered in brown leather, with two authentic looking support handles in the centre, set a few feet apart. Ben doubted that they had ever been used for their intended purpose, although he fleetingly imagined how diverting a nude gymnastics display might be.

Sadie opened a compartment set between the handles. Inside there appeared to be a mechanism from which she raised a large leather dildo. She glanced mischievously in Ben's direction as she applied a viscous lubricant to its supple surface, stroking it suggestively.

'Front or back, sir?' she enquired with mock innocence.

'Back,' the husband said, hesitating for not a moment, and his wife lost control for the first time since they'd arrived.

'No, please, not that,' she begged her husband as Lola guided her over to the contraption. 'Have me beaten again,' she offered. 'Anything!'

Lola effortlessly lifted the slighter woman over the handles, Sadie held her legs apart, and when she felt the tip of the dildo nudging between her buttocks her babbling became indecipherable.

'Compose yourself, my dear,' her husband said sternly. 'It is your inhibitions that cause you such distress and you must let Mistress Sadie help you overcome them.' He had moved to the foot of the horse, his wife immediately fell silent, and while Sadie held her hips she allowed Lola to lower her onto the glistening leather column.

As it started to fill her, her eyes opened wide and she threw her head back. Her breasts were full and swollen and her nipples stood out, pink and hard. How different she looked to the conventional Mrs Suburbia who'd arrived not so long before. Lola lowered her with care, her strong hands under the woman's armpits. Inch by inch the dildo disappeared until the woman was sitting between the two handles, her expression revealing experiences Ben could only imagine at.

Sadie flicked the switch and stood back, her eyes sparkling with devilish pride. The whole contraption began to move slowly backwards and forwards, like the motion of a rocking horse. The woman clung to the handle in front of her, trying to bear the shifting movement. Sadie increased the speed and the woman had to grab the handle behind her as well to maintain her balance, driving the dildo deeper.

Ben saw Sadie whisper something to Lola, who nodded and disappeared from view.

'Just a little faster, don't you think?' Sadie said mischievously, the man nodded, and Sadie obliged.

Ben looked up in agreeable surprise to see that Lola had slipped into the booth and was standing beside him. 'Sadie thought you might need some help with that,' she purred, looking down into his lap, a wry smile flickering over her ruby-red lips.

Without a word Ben unzipped his flies. It felt good to release the pressure building there. He stroked himself and let Lola take a good look. He liked that moment when a woman first saw what he had to offer.

'Mmm, that's some piece, baby,' Lola oozed sexily, and undid the broad metal zip at the front of her leather bask. She lowered herself onto Ben's erection in much the same way that she'd just lowered the submissive woman onto the dildo. He sighed deeply. He felt the warm muscles of her vagina tighten around him as she settled astride his lap, still allowing him a clear view of the naked woman beyond the mirror. Lola moved up and down, gripping him between her well-toned thighs. Over her shoulder he watched the other woman gripping the leather horse, her breasts bouncing as she began to abandon herself to the rhythm of the contraption. As if she read his mind, Lola fully unzipped the front of her costume and her superb globes sprang free, hard and needy. He stroked and pinched the fat brown nipples and eased his hips lower, driving even deeper into the tight channel. Lola gasped and clenched her muscles around his unyielding shaft.

Beyond the mirrored screen the wife's pained grimace had been replaced by a frown of impending pleasure. Ben saw the same frown forming on Lola's brow. He grasped her shoulders, thrust hard, her powerful body jerking up and down on his lap, her perfumed breasts nudging his face. His balls ached for release, but he let the force of Lola's orgasm rip through her first, and mewls of ecstasy coming from beyond the mirror signalled the beginning of the other woman's pleasure too. Her pale face was flushed and she arched her back, abandoning herself, all inhibition gone, prolonging every blissful ripple the leather dildo could offer. One final thrust and Ben exploded inside Lola, his own deep moans of satisfaction joining those of the two women.

Ben waited a few minutes before he joined Sadie in the salon; enough time for him to recover and for the couple to leave.

'That's pretty ingenious, Sadie,' he said, admiring the piece of apparatus. 'And thank you for Lola,' he added.

'I'm always pleased to serve,' she beamed. 'She looked pretty happy too, so I might get jealous.' She kissed him lightly on the cheek. 'Now what else can I do for you?' She lifted her skirt just high enough to tuck the brown envelope into her stocking top and indicated that he should sit beside her on one of the red velvet couches.

'I thought you might be able to help me with a story we're covering,' he explained. 'Did you read about that woman in Islington who makes Victorian corsets? The *Globe* did a piece about her a few weeks ago.'

'You mean old Gina Bent?' Sadie giggled her recognition of the woman in question. 'Calls herself *Georgina* Brentwood nowadays. You remember her, Ben? Used to work with me down the *Starlight Rooms*.' Sadie poured them both a glass of champagne.

Ben did remember the dark-haired Scottish girl who had worked as a stripper all those years ago. He never got close to her, as he had to many of the others. She always kept him at arm's length, treating him with the arrogant disdain that some working girls kept for non-paying acquaintances. Sadie had never been like that.

'Yeah, I remember,' Ben said, watching Sadie twisting the stem of her wine glass between delicate fingers. 'What happened to her?'

'Gina? Oh, she was a clever one. Found herself some toff to set her up south of the river. Quite a place, she had. Just a few minutes over Westminster Bridge.'

'So what happened? How did she get to Islington?'

'No idea, my lover. Last I remember there was some nasty smell of a scandal. Some business with an MP, they said. Almost another Christine Keeler. Never heard of her since. Thought she must've gone back to Glasgow until I saw that bit about her in the paper. A *school teacher?*' Sadie scoffed. 'They don't give lessons like hers in any school I went to! Mind you, she was a good seamstress; I'll give 'er that. Used to make costumes for all us girls.'

Ben struggled to remember what he could of the gossip that had threatened to bring down yet another government. It was over twenty years before and Sadie's proximity was not helping his hazy memory. He tipped down the rest of his drink and stood to plant a kiss on her forehead.

'Not going already, are you?' she asked.

'Work to be done, Sadie. And thanks, for everything. By the way, does the Ruskin Club mean anything to you?' Sadie shook her pretty head, and he stroked her upturned chin and left the room before he was tempted to stay any longer. 'See you soon.'

It was starting to get dark as Ben made his way along Dean Street. He was pretty sure that Bernie Peters would be propping up the bar by now. Bernie had been propping up bars for most of the last forty years. For the price of a drink he would entertain you with a mixture of trivia and intellectual anecdotes, dredged up miraculously from his alcohol-soaked brain. Once a successful journalist, he had long since been blacklisted by every newspaper in town. But with a little cajoling and lubricating Ben was sure he would recall the extra curricula activities of the MP and Georgina Brentwood.

He walked faster as the terrier-like excitement started to fill him, but at the same time there was a twinge of guilt. Gina Bent had been a tough nut all those years ago, so what had he gotten Jane Carter into? He must be getting soft - or old.

'Hello there, my old mucker!' Bernie was indeed settled in his usual place at the bar.

Ben bought some drinks and for a while they reminisced and caught up on old acquaintances. Ben bought a second round.

'Do you remember Gina Bent?' he asked, slipping her name into the conversation. 'Got herself mixed up with an MP.'

Bernie took his time, toying with his glass. 'Now why's everyone so interested in Gina suddenly?'

Ben was taken aback by his reaction. 'I didn't know they were, Bernie. I just saw Sadie and she mentioned her. Said she'd read she was living in Islington and calling herself Georgina Brentwood.'

'Georgina Brentwood, eh? There was some young fellow from the *Globe* sniffing round here a few weeks ago - asking questions about Gina Bent. He wanted to know about that business with Anthony Hazleton and a dodgy major. Rossetti Holdings - that was it.'

Ben stiffened at the mention of the arrogant and ambitious MP who'd brought about his downfall in television, but he let Bernie continue.

'The major was tendering for a government landfill site, and it turned out Hazleton was on the board. A junior minister in Defence, he was in those days. They thought he'd have to resign, but someone fixed it.' Bernie was warming to his subject.

'So how did Gina Bent fit in to it?' Ben remembered the broad strokes of the dubious transaction and was anxious to keep him on track.

'Rumour was that Hazleton had her set up, in one of their properties over the river. Half the cabinet were slipping over there between sessions. When the business with the landfill sites came out the opposition started to ask nasty questions. It looked like they'd uncovered a minefield. Then suddenly it all disappeared, and Gina with it. A big cover up. Must have come from high up, old boy. Higher than the likes of you and I can claim.' Bernie slumped heavily against the bar and indulged in a rare moment of melancholy.

'Ever heard of the Ruskin Club?' Ben asked, trying to revive his interest, but Bernie shook his head and ordered himself another drink.

Ben left the bar and used his mobile to call Lucy. One phone call and she'd be round at his place, dressed exquisitely in the way he liked best. He needed her with him. He needed to chase away the thoughts of Sadie - and Jane Carter.

As the cab drove along the Embankment he kept seeing Jane's face, framed with tawny blonde curls and her eyes shining with adventure.

Lucy knew where he kept his spare key and she was waiting for him, framed in the doorway of the bedroom. Her underwear was black, lacy and expensive. But Ben wasn't paying - *daddy* was. If she liked an older man occasionally, Ben was happy to oblige.

'Who's been a naughty girl then?' Ben pushed her down onto the unmade bed and flipped her onto her front, making her squeal briefly. 'Shut up, you little slut!' He ripped at her black lace knickers and swept the palm of his hand down across the alabaster cheeks of her bottom. She responded by climbing up on all fours and raising her buttocks to receive her punishment. Ben swung his arm without restraint, subconsciously punishing Lucy for the frustrations of his life.

Sadie, who he could never quite have - the ruined career. Somewhere there was Gina Bent. Then from nowhere came the innocent face of Jane Carter, taunting him with her radiant smile. He positioned the hot cheeks in front of him, and without warning plunged his erection into the girl's tight rear passage. He grabbed her shoulders and shunted her back against his groin, savouring the shock that spasmed through her body. He held her to him, pumping and rocking into her, until her body lost all resistance and started to move fluently with his.

She slipped a hand between her thighs and rubbed her swelling bud, until they came together, noisily and in perfect unison, and barely heard the shrill ring of Ben's phone.

He rolled off the bed and fumbled in the pockets of his discarded clothing.

'Ben? Is that you? It's Bernie.' Ben looked at his watch. It was after closing time. 'I just remembered something. The Ruskin Club, you said. Rossetti Holdings? Don't you get it? John Ruskin and the Pre-Raphaelites!'

'So what's the Ruskin Club's link to...?' The phone went dead.

Ben brushed away Lucy's renewed advances. 'Stay here,' he said, and she smiled contentedly and curled up on the bed to wait for him.

He pushed aside the empty coffee cups and booted up his computer, and it took him until dawn to begin to piece together the strands of the story. He searched for clues in the life of John Ruskin, the Victorian defender of the Pre-Raphaelite artists and writers. He read about the Brotherhood - the secret society these artists formed. He looked for what he could find about Rossetti Holdings. The minister, Anthony Hazleton, had once owned shares along with the mysterious major, a Harley Street surgeon and the younger son of a duke. Was there a connection between the company and Dante Gabriel Rossetti, the Victorian artist whose work Ruskin championed?

The hackles rose up his back when he found a reference to Ruskin's untimely death in his beloved home in the Lake District. The house was called Brentwood. *Georgina Brentwood.*

Something told him that Anthony Hazleton, the smooth talking politician tipped to be the next Prime Minister, was involved in more than a few avaricious property deals. He'd waited years for his revenge - now he needed hard evidence.

Lucy rolled over sleepily when he eventually returned to the bedroom. He slid under the covers and curled up with her, needing the comforting softness and warmth of her body.

What had he gotten Jane Carter into? He felt surer than ever that she hadn't really returned to Yorkshire.

Later, as Lucy gathered up the torn remnants of her underwear and dressed, preparing to leave for home, she said to Ben, 'Last night, on the phone, you mentioned the Ruskin Club...'

Ben raised himself on one elbow, totally alert and listening, all drowsiness instantly gone.

CHAPTER SIX

Sir John's First Test

Jane woke on the fourth morning of her stay at Dr Morris's house and lay stiffly on the bed. Her wrists and ankles were chained as usual, and her body encased in the cruellest corset. It came high up under her armpits and crushed her breasts. Matilda took pride in lacing it tighter every night and Jane's ribs ached relentlessly.

But these discomforts were nothing to the constant burning and itching that the doctor's treatments had caused to her buttocks. She shifted her hips in an attempt to find a cooler part of the sheet, but the relief was too temporary, so there was nothing to do but wait for the inevitable footsteps on the stairs.

At last she heard them and the doctor entered the room, followed by Matilda carrying the tray of milk and porridge. She wore a small white apron and a pair of the split drawers over her corset. As she leaned to untie Jane's bonds her bare breasts stood out starkly against the lace. A fine chain had been threaded through the rings in her nipples and joined to a collar at her throat.

'He's got a visitor come to see you this morning,' Matilda whispered as she led Jane down the stairs. 'Sir John himself. You must be special.'

Jane entered the room with more trepidation than she had felt for the last few days. Sir John turned to take in her semi-naked body, and instead of the hooded cloak he wore a supple leather mask that clung to the contours of his face. Only his lips and jaw were exposed, making his appearance even more intimidating.

'Display,' he ordered, his eyes glinting at her through the holes in the mask as Jane took her position obediently for his perusal.

'Turn.' Jane turned and allowed him to inspect her bare buttocks.

'Very good, doctor. You have not marked her unnecessarily. You are a skilled practitioner. You could give Lord Waterhouse some lessons. I fear his zeal, sometimes.'

Sir John settled into a comfortable armchair, as Jane was taken to the pulley. 'Now we must see how effective Ms Brentwood's treatment has been on our young charge.'

In spite of the penetrating stare of her new audience, she started to feel the familiar throb between her thighs. She closed her eyes before the blindfold was put in place, her mind already anticipating the pleasure to follow. She allowed her wrists to take her weight and breathed as deeply as the corset would allow, guiltily yearning for the first touch of the hard instrument. He kept her waiting longer than usual and she started to pant with anticipation, longing to hear the low motor start up, her belly swimming with unrequited desire. He didn't need the spreader any longer. She kept her thighs apart willingly.

Her mind had opened to the pleasure it was expecting and the first crack of the paddle caught her completely unaware. She reeled and threw her head back in confusion with the second blow, but it seemed more like a caress than a chastisement. She arched her back and raised her hips to seek the third and fourth. To her horror, she found herself wanting him to continue until the tension deep in her stomach was satisfied.

Instead the blindfold was ripped off and Sir John's masked face loomed down at her, his vivid blue eyes challenging her, before he reached down to sink his fingers into the soft flesh between her thighs. He lifted her easily off the floor until her face was close to his and she sat, perched like a bird, on his hand. He moved his fingers skilfully inside her, opening her, sensing how close her orgasm was.

When it came he pinched her nipples and the bittersweet sensations shot through her, mingling with the heat in her buttocks until she no longer knew where the separation came. She slumped forward as she felt her juices seeping down between his fingers.

'Congratulations, Dr Morris,' Sir John said, lowering her to the floor. I would say that you've been remarkably successful. That is the first time the two parts of the therapy have been reversed?'

The doctor nodded, and handed Sir John a hand towel to wipe his glistening fingers. 'In which case, I think she has earned herself a day of rest before she leaves you.'

Sir John lifted Jane's chin, and his lips spread in an approving smile. To her amazement she felt a small rush of pride and blushed, knowing she had pleased him. 'I hope you will be joining us for the May Day celebrations, Jane,' he said. 'They will coincide very nicely with the end of your training.'

Jane spent the rest of the day, and the next, in relative luxury. Although she was kept corseted at all times, she was provided with a pretty silk dress and elegant satin slippers. The split drawers now seemed the height of propriety and she revelled in the softness of the cotton against her bottom.

The doctor paid her no particular attention, and after lunch in the dining room, served by the still semi-naked Matilda, he allowed her free range of his extensive library. Jane spent the afternoon exploring the rows of leather-bound books, curling up in an armchair to read the collections of poetry and literature.

Sometimes a ring on the doorbell, and the sound of footsteps, interrupted her peace as visitors were led upstairs to the consulting rooms, and she recognised the sounds that followed only too well.

So she diverted her attention by looking at the vibrant paintings that covered the walls of the library, captivated by the women depicted in the pastoral scenes. A demure bride, her arms raised in supplication, a younger girl standing coyly with her arms behind her back, her golden hair tumbling over her bare shoulders.

Other paintings were more disquieting. In particular, a gas lit drawing room where a partly dressed young woman was attempting to rise from the lap of a man, who restrained her with his arm.

Once the doctor came suddenly into the room to fetch something, and found her transfixed by it. She looked away, as guiltily as the woman in the painting.

'I see this painting interests you,' he said. 'It's called *The Awakening Conscience*, by Holman Hunt.'

Jane blushed and felt his eyes burning into her, seeking her reaction. 'Thank you, doctor.' She breathed a sigh of relief as he left her alone again.

The more Jane read in the well-thumbed books, listened to the sounds echoing through the house, and gazed at the strange figures in the paintings, the less her former life held any reality for her. The Awakening Conscience. The title hung in her mind.

That night she awoke with a start when she felt the covers being pulled back, but before she had time to cry out a hand covered her mouth.

'Shhh.' Jane stopped struggling as she heard Matilda's whisper in her ear. 'Tomorrow morning they will take you away. But I told you I could give you greater pleasure than any man.' Jane could see nothing but the whites of Matilda's eyes and the glint of her teeth. She lay quite still as she felt a hand tugging at the hem of her nightgown, working the material up until it was gathered around her waist.

Then Matilda leaned lower and sank her mouth into the bed of soft, damp curls. She started to lap at the pink flesh, teasing and coaxing, then stopping, withdrawing, stroking and exploring intimately. She took the ripening girl to the very edge of her tolerance and left her teetering on the precipice. Her tongue and lips returned to entice again, on and on until they were together in another place, and when the time came Matilda held Jane's hips as if she were a precious goblet, and drank of her juices indulgently.

Then without a word, as Jane dozed, replete, Matilda slipped back down the dark stairway as silently as she had arrived.

CHAPTER SEVEN

Hunt Manor

The grandfather clock struck nine o'clock as Jane sat waiting in the hall. Matilda had dressed her with particular attention, under the doctor's watchful eye. He had used the time to remind her of the terms of her agreement.

She sat up a little straighter, stroking the soft silk of her elegant skirt. Was it false bravado she felt? What more could they ask of her? She had learned to accept the restrictions of the corsets, strangers had intimately and humiliatingly explored her, and her bottom had endured the sting of the leather paddle.

Dr Morris slid back the bolts and let in the bright morning sunshine. Paul was there, dressed as ever in his immaculate uniform. In front of him he held Bessie, her hair in messy disarray and her fleshy cheeks smudged with dirt.

'A delivery from Lord Waterhouse, sir,' Paul said respectfully.

'Take her straight upstairs,' the doctor instructed, and Paul urged the stumbling girl into the house. Her cloak fell open and Jane gasped as she caught sight of the torn stockings and livid stripes across her bare thighs.

'I urge you to cooperate with your training, Jane.' The doctor spoke slowly and moved close to her. 'You have witnessed the results of intransigence, but there is one thing you must know before you leave here. Your permission will always be sought before any full sexual activity. There is always a choice, Jane, and that choice is yours alone. Do you understand me?'

'Yes, Dr Morris, I think so,' she said, lowering her eyes demurely, but inside his words made her quake with renewed confusion and apprehension.

Paul negotiated the mid-morning traffic, and soon the black limousine was cruising on the motorway. Jane stared out of the window, trying to adjust her thoughts to the surroundings. Where was she being taken? She was tempted to slide back the window that divided her from Paul and engage him in conversation, but she remembered Matilda's warnings so they drove on in silence, Jane shifting her position occasionally to accommodate the stiff metal stays that held her in their vicelike grip.

When the car turned off the motorway she looked out at fields lined with hedgerows and trees. They must have been travelling for several hours when Paul made a sharp turn and the car bumped along a farm track, and came to a halt outside a deserted barn.

'Get out.' Paul pulled open the rear door of the car, and Jane looked around uneasily. It seemed Matilda had been right about Paul, but the open air offered more chance of escape than the confines of the car, so she raised her skirts and stepped out.

'Undress,' Paul ordered, and moved to stand at the front of the car, turning his back as she fumbled with the fastenings until her bodice was free. She paused nervously, uncertain whether to continue, but eventually she let the dress slip to the ground.

He glanced over his shoulder as he heard her gathering up the rustling folds of silk, and his eyes widened as he took in the sight of her, standing awkwardly in her split drawers, the sunlight shining on her bare breasts. 'Everything... the corset too,' he muttered.

Jane stood completely naked, the sunshine not enough to drive the chill from her. She stiffened as he walked towards her, his expression fixed in an enigmatic smile. When he stood in front of her and grasped her shoulders she shook beneath his hold. Was it trepidation or anticipation? Her mind raced in circles of confusion.

Paul backed the car out onto the road, and drove off. A few minutes passed before he slid open the window that separated them, Jane sitting with her hands modestly covering herself.

'I'm sorry,' he started hesitantly. 'That's how he wants you delivered.'

'How who wants me?' Jane asked, bemused by his apology.

'The major. Major Hunt, he calls himself.'

'*Holman* Hunt?' Jane didn't know why the name jumped into her head, and Paul jerked his head round to look at her, the car swerving dangerously.

'*Major* Hunt, I said. Why did you say that name?' he demanded suspiciously.

'I'm not sure,' Jane admitted, relieved as he regained control of the vehicle.

He closed the partition and they drove on. The landscape changed and ugly excavations enclosed by tall wire fences replaced the open fields. *Danger* and *Keep* out signs hung ominously at intervals along their perimeter, and Jane sat naked on the leather seat, the environment adding to her sense of foreboding.

Paul used his pass to open the set of electronic gates, the long, tree-lined drive beyond winding its way up to the front of an imposing Georgian mansion. It reminded Jane of a grand house outside York that she once visited with her mother and Aunt Judith - a jolting memory from another life.

Paul helped her from the car. The sharp gravel bit into the soles of her feet, but she barely felt the pain as he urged her forward. She hung her head and looked down, her nakedness overwhelming her as they entered the house.

'Miss Carter?' She recognised the voice at once and raised her eyes, and Mrs Morris, the homely doctor's wife returned her gaze. But instead of the cheerful expression that Jane remembered, her features were fixed in a look of subservient acceptance.

'On your knees, woman!'

Jane gasped and stepped back in shock as the major's burly form, in leather boots and riding breeches, strode towards them across the flag-stoned hallway. Mrs Morris scrambled frantically to the floor and began to crawl towards him, and Jane froze as she noticed the two heavy kitchen weights, attached by wooden clothes pegs to the woman's nipples, dragging cruelly at the pendulous flesh. She was naked except for a roughly fashioned rope harness that cut into her skin and separated her broad buttocks, and between her thighs a further weight swung as she moved.

'Get back to the kitchen,' the major ordered, swiping at her quivering bottom with his riding crop, before leading the way into a large drawing room, sparsely furnished with no traces of a feminine touch, faded rugs partially covering the stone floor.

The major used a silver paper knife to open the envelope Paul handed him, and Jane shivered as she watched him unfold the stiff, crested notepaper and start to read.

'I see that Sir John has already paid you a visit?' he observed, raising his eyes from the letter to fix Jane with a stare. 'I understand you have... particular charms.'

His ruddy face fixed in concentration as he lowered his eyes again and read on. 'Ms Brentwood has already prescribed treatment which has been successful - up to a point.' He glanced up to gage her reaction to the report on her progress. 'But the dear doctor has not attempted to go any further, it seems. He is a man of high principals who understands the female mind well.'

He threw the letter aside dismissively. 'Display!' he barked, and Jane responded automatically, noticing his sweaty body odour as he moved close, caressed her hair, and then ran his hand up her throat. He lifted her face by her chin until she teetered on tiptoe in front of him.

'So which is it to be, Jane?' he mused, as much to himself as to her. 'Where do you want to be taken first?'

She choked and spluttered as she realised his meaning, then he dragged her, resisting futilely, to a small two-seater couch. 'Lie on there,' he ordered brusquely, pointing at the coach, 'on your front or back - it makes no difference to me. I will have all of you before long. That is what you agreed to.'

Jane miserably lay back on the musty old piece of furniture as he started to open the front of his breeches. She couldn't believe what was happening to her, how fast, and the choice she was being told to make. But she lay uncomfortably on her back and turned her head away, not wanting to look at the loathsome man.

His rough hands parted her thighs and she heard his lustful grunt as he exposed her to his gaze. 'Please,' she whimpered, although she expected no mercy.

'It's your choice,' he said harshly. 'The doctor explained that, didn't he?' He took Jane's silence as an answer. 'Now lie still. It's not your first time, so stop being so prissy.'

His words lashed her as he eased his bulk over her, and she fought to contain her cries as the bulbous crown of his erection nudged at the entrance to her vagina. Despite her loathing for the man and what he was doing to her she shamefully felt herself moisten. The doctor's plug had done its work and however hard she tried she couldn't stop him.

His hands forced her thighs wider as he lowered his heavy frame onto her. The course tweed of his riding jacket irritated her breasts and his breath rasped against her shoulder. The major's cock swelled as it pushed its way into her, until he was rutting into the very core of her being, and she bit her lip as she felt her juices lubricate his path.

Before she could stop herself she even found she was raising her hips, seeking each aggressive thrust. He paused, a faint smile on his fleshy lips as he observed her compliance, then continued, staccato, rhythmic movements that jerked through her, his strength lifting her off the uncomfortable couch, slamming her back down again until she could stand no more. The unending friction provoked feelings that came from an unknown place deep inside her, and before she could stop it the waves rushed through her like a torrent. She heard his grunts of raw pleasure follow hers, and for a brief moment they were joined in ecstasy.

The major heaved himself up and stood over her trembling body. 'You really enjoyed that, didn't you?' The flush of her cheeks answered his question, and before she could find her voice he scooped her off the coach and sat in her place. He folded her over his lap and she felt the sticky dampness between them as her silky pubic hair chafed against his coarser covering. Her head hung down and her cheek brushed against the polished leather of his riding boots, then she sensed him raise his hand.

The first blow fell, the flat of his palm stinging her buttocks. She yelped but he merely chuckled in response. 'I think you deserve to be spanked for your wanton behaviour, don't you?' She tried to answer but the next blow fell, knocking the breath from her. 'Don't you?' he repeated.

'Yes... Major Hunt,' she managed, but he spanked her thoroughly and rhythmically anyway. Her bottom burned and the heat radiated through to her stomach, but despite her humiliation and the pain of the spanking, a low throb of pleasure pulsed inside her. Perhaps he was right and she did need a good spanking for her behaviour.

But she was relieved when it was over and he rang for Paul. 'Take her to the kitchens,' he said curtly. 'She needs some food and exercise. A few days in the stables should see to that.'

He stroked her hair back from her face with uncustomary gentleness. 'You're a pretty little filly, aren't you?' he said pensively. 'Spirited, too. I'm going to enjoy breaking you in fully.'

'Sit down,' a gruff male voice instructed Jane, and she crept forward towards a space at the end of the table.

'Looks like she could do with a good hosing,' another male said.

'That's enough from you, Tom,' the gruff one snapped. 'Get her a plate, you!'

Jane saw the doctor's wife shuffling towards her on her knees, and then as soon as she had delivered the plate she dropped onto all fours and crawled away.

Jane took the food she was given and risked a few furtive glances at her companions. There were five men, apparently ranging in age from a buck-toothed youth to the gruff man in his fifties. They sat at one end of the table eating greedily, leaning back in their chairs to belch and wipe the rich meat juices from their chins. They all wore breeches held up by broad leather belts, and waistcoats over their collarless shirts.

To Jane's horror Mrs Morris scrabbled between their legs like a starving mongrel bitch, gnawing the bones and eating the scraps of food they let fall from the table. A round-faced man with a bulbous nose offered her a tempting morsel from his hand, so she craned up and accepted it and he rewarded her with a slap across her ample bottom. The heavy weights pegged to her breasts swung cruelly as she scurried away.

Jane sat amongst the five women at the other end of the table. The succulent meats were not passed in their direction and they made do with bowls of thick dripping, mopped up by lumps of homemade bread. But it tasted good to Jane, after the monotony of her recent diet.

Was she really sitting dishevelled and naked, surrounded by total strangers? The other women mainly kept their eyes down and ate silently. She recognised some of their faces from the auction, particularly the tiny Oriental girl who looked as

49

uneasy as she felt. They were all dressed in the same strange uniform. Grey, horsehair corsets cut just below their breasts, and chemises of thin cotton barely covering them. Jane glimpsed the coarse brown linen of their lower garments, and noted that although the material was heavier than the cotton drawers, they were cut to the same crutch-less design. Around their waists they wore stout leather belts.

Just then the gruff man, who seemed to be in charge, grabbed hold of the Oriental girl as she tried to dodge past him. 'Hey, you, get the new filly togged up and bring her out to the yard,' he ordered her. 'And hurry up the rest of you; I want the hay barn filled this afternoon.'

Her name was Seihime; she whispered it to Jane as she took her to a dormitory behind the kitchens. The room looked grim, with two rows of narrow beds, each bed separated from the next by a low metal cabinet. A grey blanket lay neatly folded on each of the thin mattresses.

Seihime moved quickly, her dark eyes flickering anxiously. 'They brought uniform for you yesterday,' she said, reaching into one of the metal cabinets and producing a set of clothing identical to her own.

'I need to wash first,' Jane said, moving towards what she could see was a washroom at the end of the dormitory.

'No, no,' Seihime hastened in alarm. 'It is forbidden. They say when we wash.' She pulled Jane back towards the bed. 'Must hurry. Must not keep waiting. You call me Sei, yes?' She smiled shyly and Jane smiled back. Perhaps she had found an ally at last. Her English was not perfect but almost everything else about her was. Her delicate fingers worked the laces of Jane's corset loose, and as she concentrated on her task Jane could see her pert breasts, visible through the thin fabric of the chemise. Her skin shimmered like gold and her hair was as black as the night. Her waist was pulled narrower than seemed possible. She was a few inches shorter than Jane, and she had to reach up to slip the chemise over her head.

It hung to just below her breasts and was no protection against the discomfort when Sei closed the front fastenings of the corset. At the doctor's she had grown used to the stiff cottons and satins, and the first touch of the horsehair shocked her, irritating her bare skin. Sei worked with all her strength, tugging on the long laces, while Jane acquiesced and braced herself against the wall to help her gain more purchase.

'It feel better in few days,' Sei said sympathetically, and held out the linen lower garment for Jane to step into.

'Where he have you?' Sei asked suddenly, and Jane blushed and looked away, knowing that Sei must have noticed the dried evidence on her thighs. 'You have to tell me.' She was just as embarrassed as Jane as she passed the black leather belt around Jane's waist. 'I have to put discs to show.'

Jane looked inquisitively at the belt around Sei's tiny waist. Two metal discs, the size of old pennies, hung from a ring embedded in the leather. One was bronze and the other was silver. 'Where he take you?' Sei persisted.

'Here,' Jane pointed vaguely between her thighs, humiliation and confusion consuming her. 'He *took* me here.'

Sei attached a silver disc to one of the rings on Jane's belt. Then she gathered the drawstring around the neck of the chemise, until the material framed and held her rounded breasts perfectly. The outline of Jane's nipples could be seen through the freshly laundered garment, darkening the oatmeal coloured fabric.

'Come, I take you to the yard.' Sei took her hand and led her out through the backdoor into the comforting afternoon sunshine.

They walked together barefoot across the soft grass, and for a brief moment Jane relished her freedom. In spite of her inner turmoil the fresh air and sunshine invigorated her.

Sei stopped suddenly as they rounded a corner to an immaculate cobbled yard. Several horses nodded their heads contentedly over the stable doors that lined it on three sides. Sei pulled her back out of sight and whispered urgently. 'You know rules?' Jane shook her head. 'You must call the grooms *master*. No talk otherwise, just "yes master", "no master", "thank you master". You understand?' Jane nodded, her head spinning with all she was seeing and hearing. 'Except him,' Sei went on, her eyes narrowing as she nodded back towards the house. 'You call him *major*.'

'Hey, you two!' It was the bulbous-nosed man who caught sight of them first. 'You're wanted up at the hay barn.'

Jane hurried after Sei, but he grabbed hold of her wrist as she passed him. He pulled her against him and a grimy hand mauled her breasts through the thin material of the chemise. She felt the disgusting bulge in his breeches growing while his hand wandered down to check her belt.

'Just a silver, eh?' he sniggered as Jane struggled to break free, his breath foul.

'Let her go.' Another man, the one Jane thought was called Tom, had appeared in the yard and she was grudgingly released, her odious assailant savouring one last grope as his hands left her.

The soft ground felt good as Jane followed Sei and the newcomer up a narrow track that led away from the stables. At the end of it the other women were dragging heavy bales off a trailer and heaving them towards a barn.

It was a warm afternoon and the work was arduous, and very quickly Jane was sweating just as much as the others. It took all her effort to lift each bale and carry it into the barn. The others seemed much stronger than her; particularly a statuesque redhead who was able to lift a bale onto her shoulder, her large breasts thrusting proudly, her sweat rendering her thin chemise transparent.

Very soon it seemed that every muscle in Jane's body ached and resisted her efforts, the roughness of the corset agitated her abominably, and she panted for breath against the constricting lacing, but she didn't dare stop her labours or ease up in her endeavours.

The other women ignored her, but with barely half the task complete she could see Sei was struggling too. Jane was returning to the trailer having delivered yet another bale, when she saw Sei drop one and sink to her knees in exhaustion, and instinctively she stopped to help her new friend to her feet.

'Leave her alone, you!' Jane jumped as the man barked his rebuke. She hurried on and left Sei desperately trying to drag the bale towards the barn, but before she reached her goal the strings that bound it together snapped and the golden bundle burst onto the ground. Jane froze as Sei looked helplessly at the spilled straw in front of her, and the man rose and grabbed her by the arm.

Jane heard her strangled whimpers but she could do nothing to help her. She could only watch while Sei was frog-marched towards the barn. She heard the sound of the generator start and a clank of metal, and the grinding, winching sound that followed confirmed her worst fears. The man came out of the barn, wiping his hands on his breeches.

'Get back to work,' he snapped, dropping his hefty frame back onto the pile of straw that now offered a comfortable spot from where to monitor their efforts.

Jane felt sick at what she might find when she dragged the next bale into the barn, and rightly so, because Sei's delicate body was hanging by her wrists from the pulley that was used to raise bales into the loft area. Her linen drawers had been removed and her chemise torn away. Jane moved towards her but she shook her head and forced a weak smile. Jane was far from reassured, but turned and left the barn.

Sei managed to grasp the hook from which she hung, and her body tensed and stretched as she made an attempt to pull herself up to relieve the strain on her wrists. Absorbed in her weary efforts she seemed oblivious to the two watching her from the barn entrance.

'So it looks as if your little friend still has a bit of fight in her,' said the man. 'Another hour up there should settle her down a bit.'

He roughly held Jane's arm up behind her back as she gasped in shock, 'Another hour?' Sei didn't look as if she could bear another minute. Jane knew how it felt to have your arms held high like that, but at least she had always been allowed to keep some contact with the floor, however slight. Sei's eyes were sunk in shadowy pools of desperation and tears spilled down her golden cheeks.

'Unless you would like to earn her a reprieve, of course,' the man goaded, and Jane frowned in apprehension. What did he want from her?

'I'll take a silver,' he said, flicking the disc on her belt as he answered her unspoken question, and the significance of the silver disc started to become ominously clearer. She had noticed that the other women, apart from Sei who wore two, all wore three discs - one bronze, one silver, and one gold.

'I'm waiting, yes or no,' he growled in her ear, and his free hand lifted and started to fumble with the drawstring of her bodice. His rough fingers squirmed inside the neckline and found her nipples, twisting them, using them to drag her breasts free of the chemise.

Jane cringed at the thought of what he was proposing, but took another look at poor Sei, dangling helplessly from the hook, and said, 'Very well... yes... master.'

He let her go long enough to pull some bales into position. 'I'll fuck you from the rear,' he said crudely, 'even if I can't have your arse.'

Jane moved hesitantly forward, and stood by the low stack he'd made. He pushed her over it and kept one heavy hand firmly on the small of her back as he callously nudged her legs apart with his foot and wrenched open the slit in the linen drawers, leaving her rounded buttocks exposed, without the need to undress her further.

He felt for his target and she heard him spit onto his hand, then a surge of abhorrence rushed through her as he plunged his fingers into her sex and used his saliva to lubricate her. She gripped the bales tightly, the straw horribly rough against her cheek, her naked breasts, and her parted thighs. She closed her eyes and didn't move, even when she heard him loosen his belt and open his breeches, his breath shortening, low grunts rumbling from his throat.

He thrust himself into her without warning. She cried out, trying to stifle her gasp with her fist. His body weighed down on her, crushing her against the bales until she could hardly breathe. Her heart pounded and her ribs ached with every gasp. He rutted against her, oblivious to her feelings, ploughing his desires into her. But despite such uncaring treatment she again found herself trying to meet his rhythm, wanting him to find the place deep inside her, but his haste made it difficult. His hands squeezed between her and the bales and sought her breasts, cupping and using them to gain more leverage. Then he came with a series of long groans, spilling his seed into the core of her being. Tears crawled down her face and soaked into the straw as he withdrew, and Jane realised to her horror that they were tears of frustration; frustration born from his inability to prolong the act and give her the pleasure she craved too.

'Stay where you are,' he muttered, and she heard him start up the motor, the squeak of the rusty pulley, and the creaking of the rope as he lowered the hook.

'Nice tight little cunt, your new friend's got,' he said to the exhausted Sei as she flopped to the straw-covered barn floor. At least Jane had saved her from prolonged distress, but his next words made her cringe with hopeless dismay. 'Now you best lick us both clean.'

He sat down heavily on the makeshift bed of bales and drew Jane onto his lap, hooking her knees over his to hold her legs apart. He held her back against his chest and used his free hand to pull aside his breeches.

'Over here, you,' he ordered. Sei was crouched where he'd left her, rubbing her wrists to hasten the circulation back into the slender limbs, but she crept forward obediently, the cramps in her muscles marring her delicate features, and knelt in front of them. Jane struggled futilely as Sei pressed her face between their open thighs, but the man's hold on her was too strong.

'Keep still you little bitch, or there's always the pulley,' he rasped hoarsely in Jane's ear. 'You, get on with it,' he instructed Sei, his aggressive manner enough to persuade Jane to give up her struggles, and she watched as Sei licked and lapped between the man's thighs. Her dainty hands cupped his balls as she stroked her tongue over them, then Jane watched aghast as Sei opened her doll-like mouth and took him inside. The man's hot breath fanned Jane's neck and quickened as Sei carried out her task meticulously.

'Okay, that's enough for now,' he growled, his voice strained. 'Now sort your friend out,' he added, forcing Jane's thighs even wider.

Jane closed her eyes as she felt Sei's breath waft softly over her excited and tender flesh. She had no option but to submit and get it over with - for her and for Sei.

Then she'd seek an opportunity to speak to her new ally. Perhaps together they could plan an escape from the terrible place, and the loathsome people who inhabited it. Suddenly even the experiences at the doctor's house seemed preferable to what she'd gone through and was going through since leaving there.

Jane's thoughts drifted back to the last night in the attic room, when Matilda came to her, and despite her chagrin she felt the same sensations stirring inside her again. Sei's tongue felt different, but equally good. She used her teeth and lips to nibble and tease before she pressed her tongue deep into the wet channel. Jane gasped as Sei sucked deeply, sweeping her tongue around, drinking her freely flowing juices, Jane unable to resist the pure bliss the petite Oriental girl was evoking.

She tried to hold back, her mind racing as it sought distraction, but Sei's skills were too seductive. The man's hands molested her bare breasts and pinched her nipples. She felt the spasms clutching her, low down in her stomach. She could not delay her pleasure any longer and it flooded from her, anointing Sei's golden cheeks and chin. She slumped drowsily back onto the man and allowed the deepest waves of contentment to permeate her being.

The man left Jane and Sei alone in the barn, and Jane took advantage to learn a good deal about her new friend. She had arrived at Hunt Hall two weeks before. She was the new wife of a prosperous Far Eastern manufacturer. In his travels through Europe he'd met Major Hunt, to whom he supplied the heavy machinery for the landfill sites that surrounded the Hall. It was the major who introduced him to certain methods of possessing a female, and thus it was to the major that he sent his new bride for training.

When Jane looked shocked Sei insisted that her husband considered it an honour for his British client to undertake her education.

When Jane continued to look exasperated, Sei lowered her eyes and whispered demurely, 'But I love my husband. I want to please him, and so I must learn how.'

Jane's heart chilled as she listened to the doctor's policy being echoed by the lovely, innocent girl, and began to doubt that she had found quite the ally she'd hoped for. Nevertheless, as they made their way across the deserted yard back towards the house she tentatively broached the subject of escape, but the panic it induced in her companion only confirmed her reservations.

Sei stopped in her tracks and grasped Jane's arms, turning her towards her, her eyes wide with a strange determination. 'No escape,' she insisted. 'You understand? Not possible. You go when you are ready, but you must learn, like me.' Then she surprised Jane by giving her a warm, apparently affectionate kiss on the lips. 'And it is not all so bad, is it?' A flirtatious smile sparkled in her eyes.

By the time they reached the house the other women were stripped naked and in the dormitory's communal shower room. To Jane's surprise Mrs Morris, the doctor's wife, was amongst them, freed of the dreadful bonds and weights and looking very cheerful.

'Hurry up you two,' the tall redhead snapped at them, and reluctantly following Sei's lead, Jane took off her clothing and joined the others, just as two men appeared in the shower room, bizarrely dressed in long, white rubber aprons and white wellington boots. Jane wondered what on earth was going on now as the women huddled together protectively.

The men then unravelled two hoses Jane hadn't noticed before from wheels mounted on the wall, and Jane then realised what was about to happen, hastily looking around for somewhere to take cover. But as the first freezing jets of water erupted from the hoses the other women selfishly held her in front of them, shielding themselves from the full force. She struggled feverishly to get free as the water buffeted and stung her skin. The men laughed and jeered, one pausing long enough to throw bars of yellow soap at the tangled mass of womanhood.

Glistening limbs skidded against each other as they fought to avoid the stinging jets, but the men were adept at their task, and easily able to use the powerful fountains of chilled water to separate the women for individual attention.

'Get up!' one of them barked at Jane when she crouched in a corner to protect herself. She struggled to her feet and he aimed the full force onto her back, pinioning her against the wall, then directly at her buttocks, forcing them apart, biting at the tender area between. He made her turn, and as she raised her arms to protect her face she felt the torrents pummelling her breasts. Then down to her stomach so that she doubled over, the breath knocked out of her. She peeped behind her to see Mrs Morris kneeling on all fours while the hose was pointed at her parted thighs. Her head was thrown back and her eyes were closed. Sei was crouched over the central drain, rubbing one of the bars of soap between her legs.

At last the men switched off the hoses and the girls were allowed to dry themselves with towels the men handed out. Jane miserably traipsed after the others, damp and shivering back into the dormitory, and then copied them as they laced themselves into their night corsets.

Supper passed uneventfully, and Jane was pleased when the meal was over and they were allowed to crawl into bed. Jane was exhausted after what had been a very long day, both physically and mentally draining. Just as sleep was claiming her she felt warm breath against her cheek, and opened her eyes to find Sei close to her.

'I'm so glad you come here, my friend,' the dainty girl whispered. 'We learn together.' Sei planted an affectionate kiss gently on Jane's upturned lips. 'Goodnight.'

CHAPTER EIGHT

The Contest

Over breakfast the next morning they were given their duties. All the men wore clean white shirts, and the cooks seemed busier than ever with their steaming pots and hot ovens.

'He wants you ready to bring the horses round for his guests.' Tom spoke to the redhead, who smiled at being given such a trusted job. 'You can get yourself some boots from the tack room.' She preened with pride.

'You and you,' he pointed at Mrs Morris and one of the others, 'can help cook in the kitchen. The rest of you can get the tack ready. Make sure it's gleaming.' He got up from the table to leave, and then as an afterthought he said, 'The courtyard needs raking. You two,' he pointed at Sei and Jane, 'get yourselves some tools, and be quick about it. They're due in an hour.'

Jane saw Sei grimace and some of the others snigger, and thirty minutes later, as the loose stones dug mercilessly into the soles of their bare feet, she knew why. They both had a rake, and it was their task to rid the area in front of the house of the tyre marks and hoof prints that marred its gravel surface.

'I want this forecourt to look perfect for my guests.' The major had appeared through the front doors of the mansion, holding a delicate china teacup in one hand.

'You look like a diligent worker, Jane,' he acknowledged. 'We must put you to good use today. And you as well, Sei.' He produced a handful of the bronze, silver and gold discs he'd been jangling in the pocket of his breeches, and when he'd made sure they'd seen them he turned back into the house and they were left alone to finish their task.

'Sei, you have to tell me,' Jane urged, 'what exactly do the discs signify?' They only had a relatively small area left to rake and were able to work close together without being overheard.

'You have silver,' Sei said. 'It means the major take you in your vagina. Now the other men can too.' Sei kept raking as she spoke, and Jane lowered her eyes, recalling her violation in the barn.

'But you have a bronze disc and a silver disc,' Jane prompted.

'Yes. I make my choice. I earned the two.' Sei had a defiant edge to her voice that Jane hadn't heard before.

'How, Sei? How did you earn it?' Jane pressed her for an answer.

'I earn bronze disc because I take the major in my mouth, and the silver because I let him fuck my cunt as well.' Her bluntness shocked Jane, and seemed at odds with her delicate femininity. She stopped raking the gravel. 'I do it willingly because I want to learn to please my husband this way. You have no bronze disc, so I guess you have not sucked a man yet. It is a rare thing in modern day for pretty girl like you not to do it yet, so the major will want to make most of it.'

Jane stopped raking too and they stared at each other for several seconds, understanding each other, before they resumed their chore in silence. Jane's mind was racing, and the doctor's words on the final morning of her stay at his house came back to her.

'Your permission will always be sought... there is always a choice... that choice is yours alone.'

The significance of his words and the three discs was now clear, and soon she would be asked to make a choice. It seemed she must either surrender her bottom or her mouth, and both options filled her with unease. The humiliating memory of Ms Brentwood's finger probing her anus came flooding back, and she remembered being relieved that the doctor had made no further attempts to examine her there. Yet surrendering her mouth, the other option, the one that Sei had already accepted, filled her with consternation too. She couldn't forget the sight of Matilda kneeling in front of the doctor, the livid stripes of her recent beating streaked across her flesh, her lips stretched tightly around the erection that impaled it. Jane was surer than ever that she'd choke if she had to do the same thing.

'But you, Sei, you still have to earn a gold disc?' she pressed yet further. 'You have to let the major...?' Jane left her question hanging.

'Today I must make my choice,' Sei confirmed. 'I must earn last disc from the major. I will learn... for my husband.' Sei rested one hand lightly on her buttocks as if to protect them.

'Supposing you refuse?' The sound of a car approaching up the long driveway made Jane's question urgent.

'They give you other choice. Maybe worse choice. You must decide.'

As a black estate car crunched to a halt on the newly raked drive, Jane was momentarily confronted with the memory of Kurt priming the metal instrument and the crack of the bolt as he delivered the silver ring into Matilda's clitoris. Was that the ultimate choice on offer?

The major emerged again from the front door to greet his guests.

'Display,' he ordered Sei and Jane as he passed them, and the two girls dropped the rakes and raised their hands behind their heads.

Jane recognised the tall figure of Lord Waterhouse, and she also recognised the woman by his side. She was the first of Ms Brentwood's models to parade on the stage that night at the abandoned theatre. Then she had been dressed in a scarlet corset, now replaced by an exquisitely cut riding jacket of the same hue. Her lustrous brown hair was tied back under a veiled black top hat, and a cream silk stock hugged her throat, Jane's eyes widening as she identified the stock pin that kept it in place; three entwined discs, one bronze, one silver, and one gold, fashioned into a discreet design that nestled in the folds of the material.

The brass-buttoned jacket was cut tightly into her waist, the buttons repeated down the length of her skirt. Polished black leather riding boots peeped out beneath, encasing her shapely ankles and feet. A leather hunting crop gripped in one hand completed her appearance.

The woman looked at them haughtily from under her veil, and Jane would have done anything for the ground to open and swallow her up. Lord Waterhouse, too, was staring at them, fingering his goatee beard and stroking his own leather crop up and down his thigh.

'Good morning, Lord Waterhouse, I have some excellent mounts for you and your companion today.' The major looked admiringly at the scarlet-clad beauty as he greeted his guests. 'I understand you are accomplished at side saddle, Bridget?'

Over the next few minutes a fleet of cars delivered the rest of the guests. Jane, still required to stand as ordered, didn't recognise any of them but assumed that some had been present at the auction. They greeted each other politely, but only the men approached the major directly. The women held back, clustering together in small groups.

'I suggest that the fillies here for training go to the stables immediately,' the major announced when the greetings were done. 'The rest of us can take some refreshment on the lawn while we wait.' Two of the male grooms had appeared from the direction of the yard, setting up a trestle table and filling it with food and drinks. 'And I think our newest arrival could do with some exercise.' As he spoke all eyes turned on Jane. 'Get her tacked up, too.'

Sei was dismissed with a wave of his hand and she scurried away, her eyes wide with sympathy and warning for Jane. Four of the women stepped forward voluntarily, one of the male grooms grabbed Jane by the arm, and retained the grip as they were taken around the side of the house. The rest of the grooms were lingering in the yard, awaiting their arrival.

Amid murmurings and lewd comments the women were shepherded into a stable that housed a row of narrow stalls with wooden sides.

'Okay, ladies, most of you know the rules.' The head groom, the one called Tom, the one who'd taken advantage of Jane in the barn, seemed to revel in his role. 'Strip off all your clothes, including your underwear. No talking, and may the best filly win.' He stood, hands on hips, watching as the women each found a stall and started to divest themselves of their elaborate clothing. Jane had no option but to do the same, although she had rather less to remove than the others. She struggled with the laces on her corset, but once removed she let the linen drawers fall to the floor too. She waited, shivering in the cool barn, the wooden sides of the stall obscuring her from view.

She heard the groom's command to display working its way slowly towards her, and by the time it reached the woman in the stall next to her she could hear a creak of leather and a jingle of metal that followed it, and then the groom appeared before her stall.

A few paces behind him stood one of her fellow stable girls - and Sei. Over their arms, they held a variety of supple leather harnesses. The brass rings and bits that connected them glinted, even in the dim light.

'Display,' he ordered.

First he passed the belt of the harness around her waist and pulled it tight, positioning more straps around her breasts, before fastening a buckle behind her neck. Metal chains, with a heavy brass ring at the centre, trailed across each breast, and as he tightened the buckle at her back the rings pressed over her nipples. Before he secured the final notch he took each bud between his fingers, and pulled to check that they protruded to his satisfaction. Jane flinched but kept her arms high, the indignity affecting her more than the pain.

Before she had a chance to recover he tugged the strap that ran between her legs, and a third ring, like the ones holding her nipples erect, positioned itself precisely over her clitoris. She didn't make a sound, all too aware of the traitorous sensations he provoked when he touched her, but when he dipped a finger in a pot of grease and started to probe between her buttocks she could stay silent no longer, although her protests proved to be short-lived and futile.

Jane felt the full force of it but stayed quiet. Thankfully the doctor's beatings had prepared her well, and she was more distracted by her new restrictions and the indignity of the little tail that hung behind her. She could barely move her head to left or right, or lower it. The bit made her jaw ache and the leather straps cut into her, in spite of their suppleness.

A few minutes later they were taken into the stable yard to join the redhead. She was mounted on a magnificent animal, and was leading two other horses of similar quality. Each woman was lead by one of the male grooms, and it was the buck-toothed youth who yanked on Jane's rein as he positioned her in line.

The strange procession made their way to a small paddock that was overlooked by the lawn in front of the house. Tables and chairs had been set along its perimeter and the guests were gathered around them, sipping long, cool drinks.

The redhead rode over to the gate and the major, Lord Waterhouse and Bridget joined her there.

'The grey for you, Bridget; she's a favourite of mine.' She stepped forward to mount. 'Lord Waterhouse, I thought you might like to try out the chestnut. He just arrived a few days ago. Haven't ridden him myself. Fine animal, though. Excellent bloodline.' The chestnut snorted at the air and swished its tail in response.

'Attach them to the lunge lines and check their tack while you're at it,' the head groom said, and for the first time Jane noticed the mechanised lunging post that stood in the centre of the paddock, its long metal rails pointing up into the sky. One of the men lowered them until their ends formed a circle. The grass below had been worn away and wood shavings strewn on the bare earth to define the track. The young groom tapped his leather whip across Jane's buttocks to urge her forward, and fastened her rein to the end of one of the rails of the contraption.

'Great tits,' he sniggered crudely, tweaking her nipples until they strained further erect through the constriction of the brass rings. He couldn't resist checking lower, to where the third ring encircled her clitoris. But some strange pride welled inside her, making her refuse to reveal her turmoil to the lad. So she held her breath and felt close to fainting as he toyed with her engorged bud.

'I think we are ready to start.' The major had rejoined his guests, and Bridget had begun to circle the outside of the track. Her expertise as a horsewoman was obvious and she looked even more attractive than ever mounted on the fine beast. She looked down imperiously at each of the women as she passed them.

'Ten circuits in each direction,' the major pronounced. 'Gentleman can withdraw their fillies at each break and set the forfeit. But remember, I shall award more serious penalties for fallers.'

Jane took in the opposition. One was a young woman, but short and stout. Another looked fit but more mature than the rest. Two looked ready for the challenge, their heads held high, their muscles tensed. The rumbling motor had started and the rigid rail to which her bridle attached her forced her forward.

Bridget singled Jane out for extra attention during the first circuit. Each time she passed the woman wielded her leather crop expertly so that the plaited leather thong attached to its tip flicked Jane's flesh between the straps of the harness. Then just as Jane was beginning to find some sort of stride the tip glanced off a nipple, distended through the metal ring. Jane stumbled badly and the crowd applauded Bridget's accuracy.

In front of her the plump woman was already in difficulties, barely able to keep pace with the relentless turn of the mechanism.

Lord Waterhouse was having difficulties of his own. The chestnut was proving more spirited than he anticipated, throwing its head about wildly when its rider attempted to take aim at the women. Nevertheless, he managed some accurate strikes across thighs and buttocks before the major blew on his brass hunting horn to end the first round.

A stout man stepped forward, wiping the sweat from his brow with a garish pocket-handkerchief. 'That's enough for my mare, major,' he called out in a jocular voice.

The major seemed pleased by the early player in his entertainment. 'Ah now, Mr Woolner, I think she made a brave effort. A light forfeit, I think.' The audience murmured their approval as the woman was detached from the contraption, panting heavily as her groom jerked her bridle and led her to the edge of the paddock. 'A spanking by you with the rubber paddle, Mr Woolner?' he suggested. 'You decide the quantity.'

Until that moment Jane hadn't noticed the table displaying a variety of instruments, from which the major made his suggestion. But she had a perfect view as the audience cheered when the strongest looking groom stooped to heave the woman's ample frame over his shoulder. Her husband appeared to relish the opportunity to chastise his wife in public, removing his jacket and adjusting his embroidered waistcoat, before carefully drawing aside her horsehair tail.

He raised the paddle high and brought it down squarely on his wife's quivering behind. Mrs Woolner shrieked and babbled loudly behind the constraints of her bridle, demanding that her husband stop the indignity. The audience fell silent so they could hear her cries, and the rest of the six hard slaps he considered her due. Finally he dropped the tail and gave it a short tug to signify to the groom that he was done.

The audience applauded again as she was set on the ground, a pail of water placed in front of her, and her bridle loosened.

The mechanism began to turn in the other direction, and Jane found that if she maintained a steady trot she was able to bear the cuts of the straps and the way the tail tugged at the plug inside her. The metal bit in her mouth and the straps that kept her head held high were harder to tolerate, but it was the three brass rings, positioned over her breasts and clitoris, that caused her the most consternation. With every snatched breath her breasts swelled and her nipples jutted further through the rings that encircled them, the skin stretched tight as they fought release. She didn't have to see her clitoris to know it was in the same condition.

The chestnut was friskier than ever, and Lord Waterhouse struggled to control it as he drew alongside her. 'Step higher,' he instructed, and managed to flick his whip so that it curled around one thigh and snaked up between her legs when he snatched it away. She was relieved that his mount didn't allow him to linger, but Bridget was not far behind, determined to repeat her accurate strike on Jane's nipple.

She reined the grey in and raised the crop, flexed her gloved wrist, and swishing the three-foot long thong through the air to gain control, before she unfurled it. Her aim was perfect, the tapered tip wrapping itself around Jane's left nipple, and with immaculate timing Bridget whipped up the slack. For a few seconds she held Jane by her breast as firmly as if she were a fish on a hook, and it took all Jane's effort to maintain her gait before the thong loosened and unwound itself. Her nipple burned and throbbed fiercely, as her tormentor let out a squeal of triumph and rode on.

They must have completed six or seven circuits when a whoop went up from the crowd and the major sounded his horn. 'A faller!' he bellowed.

The machine ground to a halt and it was one of the fitter women being pulled to her feet. 'Mr Woolner,' the major said, 'would you select ten of our guests to join me in the paddock? Five men and five women, please.' The groom had brought the faller, a brunette, to the fence. The major handed him a coil of thick rope, and as the selected guests passed through the gate into the paddock he gave each of them an item.

One of the grooms threw a saddle blanket over the top rail of the fence and the girl was folded over it, so that she was bent double, her head and feet hanging freely on either side, her pale skin glistening in the sunlight. They tied her wrists to the lower rail, and her ankles likewise. When they were done, they undid the strap between her buttocks and roughly pulled out the horsehair tail. Her position revealed the tiny puckered hole and the pink lips below it, smooth and shaven, exposed and ready.

'Mr Burne,' the major said, 'your filly, you will commence.' One of the guests narrowed his eyes and walked to the trussed girl. Jane's heavy breathed eased, and she watched as he raised a leather whip above shoulder height. He lined up his stroke, it was a good twenty seconds before he took two paces back, paused, and then used the full force of his body to step in and crack the whip across his young wife's toned buttocks.

Jane let out a shocked squeal from behind the metal bit, but the girl accepted her punishment in stoic silence. 'That's what you get for disgracing me,' her husband said, close to her ear.

After that each of the other guests were free to administer their punishments on the girl. Some were severe, some cunning, some unexpected. A broad-shouldered man was armed with a heavy tawse, which he applied with great force.

A pretty lady made the tip of her delicate whip lick up the inside of their victim's thighs.

An elderly gentleman was helped forward by one of the grooms. He grasped the handle of a flexible leather whip, about five feet in length, and the years fell away when he curled it in the air and brought the heavy plait of leather precisely between the girl's parted buttocks. The tip arced up between her legs and she jerked and twisted wildly, despite the ropes tying her to the fence. The old man chuckled, knowing he'd found his target.

'Good shot, Uncle Eustace,' Bridget called out. It was obvious where she'd learned her skills.

By the time all strokes had been applied the girl's bottom and thighs were a mass of red and weals, but still she stayed silent.

The major seemed satisfied that the penalty had been paid, and Jane watched them throw a bucket of water over the girl's doubled form, before the machine started up again.

It was lighter now and turned faster, and the three that remained struggled to keep their stride. Lord Waterhouse seemed to have more control of the chestnut and was making good use of his whip. Bridget had lost none of her zeal, and with only three of them to concentrate on there was barely half a circuit when Jane didn't receive a vicious cut from one or the other.

So it was an enormous relief when the major blew his horn to signal the end of the round. 'Another forfeit! A wise decision, Mr Jones.'

It was the husband of the older woman who stepped forward to withdraw his entry. She was tethered next to Jane and as she panted desperately for breath, Jane could hear the rasping gasps deep in her throat and see how her breasts swelled against the rings. She, too, was shaved, and the pinkness of her clitoris stood out, perfectly framed by the matching brass ring that made up the triangle.

'Undo her harness,' Mr Jones told the groom.

'One full circuit of the track!' Jane flinched, terrified that the major's instruction was meant for her. But instead she saw that the girl beaten previously over the fence was kneeling, and that the woman due to pay her forfeit was mounted on her back. The redheaded, astride her equine mount, rode up to them and took hold of a long leading rein. She yanked on it, urging them forward, and the rider gripped her mount tightly between her thighs.

Jane felt every strain and arch of their limbs as they moved tortuously around the track. The redhead led them the longest possible route and Bridget took up the rear, flicking her whip so that it caught both mount and rider. As the crawling girl moved her limbs the horsehair tail swished obscenely from side to side. As they came closer Jane saw the livid weals turning shades of purple across her bottom. Her head was strapped high and her full breasts thrust forward, the puckered nipples protruding through the brass rings. Her face was etched with resolve, ignoring the cuts of Bridget's whip as she carried her burden, and her dignity, determinedly around the track. She would not dare to disgrace her husband for a second time.

'My lords, ladies and gentleman,' the major began pompously, when the lewd spectacle was over and the audience had shown their appreciation, 'we are ready for the final.'

The grooms seemed to know the drill. The one in charge of Jane untied her bridle while another cranked up the metal arms of the contraption. 'The last two fillies will run free until the first one falls, however many circuits that takes,' the major decreed. 'I'm sure we can rely on Lord Waterhouse and Bridget to keep them on their toes.' The blast of his horn cut through the vibrant excitement of the onlookers.

Jane's heart was pounding and her legs felt like lead, but one crack across her back from Bridget's crop convinced her to move off. Although the ache in her muscles burned with every pace it felt better not to have the metal bar dragging her forward. But the mounted riders cantered faster and faster around them, using their crops liberally on the two runners.

Jane sneaked an anxious glance across at her opponent. She looked unbeatable; her toned thighs shining in the bright sun, a stream of golden hair flowing behind her as she moved agilely round the track.

They circled several times, dodging the cruel cracks of the whip as best they could. The onlookers started to roar their encouragement and Bridget's excitement grew, her eyes flashing with adrenalin. Lord Waterhouse struggled to control the chestnut as the frenzy built, but still he wielded the crop high above his head, aiming less carefully but with more ferocity. One blow cracked across the back of the blonde, knocking her off the track. The crowd rose to their feet in excitement as she stumbled on the grass before regaining her balance.

Bridget successfully attempted the same trick on Jane, sending her lurching into the grass too. Only the consequences of falling kept her from crashing to the ground. The crowd roared louder and Bridget galloped away across the paddock, her cheeks burning with fervour, her skirt streaming out behind her, exposing her nakedness from above her riding boots to the tops of her thighs.

The mounting chaos was becoming too much for Lord Waterhouse's highly-strung mount. They were alongside Jane, his lordship's crop raised high when the horse plunged to one side and then reared up, pawing its hooves in the air. Its rider clung on for several seconds before he fell heavily to the ground. The horse bolted for freedom, scattering the grooms who attempted to catch it. Lord Waterhouse lay a few yards from Jane, groaning on the grass, winded by his fall. The horse's panic increased as it sought escape. The crowd's roars had turned to shrieks as it swerved and charged the fence, threatening to leap amongst them, then turned abruptly and headed towards Jane and its fallen rider.

Was it some kind of empathy with the terrified beast, or her own fear that made Jane reach out and catch hold of the flapping reins? Whatever her motives, the horse halted inches from Lord Waterhouse's prone body, and the relief of those gathered was almost tangible as the foaming animal stood snorting the air, rolling its eyes, jerking at the reins. Jane cooed as reassuringly as she could behind the restrictions of her own harness until it calmed and let her stroke its steaming neck.

'Very impressive, Miss Carter.' The major's voice cut through the shocked silence. 'I see you have a way with horses.' His relief was palpable as he strode towards Lord Waterhouse, now sitting up and gingerly nursing his arm. 'I shall declare the contest a draw. Has Dr Morris arrived yet?'

The doctor stepped out from the crowd, his black coat silhouetted against the midday sun.

CHAPTER NINE

Lunchtime Lessons

Ben Handford wiped his brow and stood patiently while Lucy fathomed out the complex entry system to the exclusive waterside development. As they took the glass-sided lift up to the fifteenth floor, Lucy raised the hem of her short pleated skirt. She giggled as she guided Ben's hand inside the waistband of her tight white knickers, and popped open the buttons of her cotton blouse. A light blush tinged her clear complexion and coloured her upper chest. The midday sun glinted on the river as it snaked past the Houses of Parliament, under Westminster Bridge, away towards the East End.

It had taken Lucy a few days after their last encounter to arrange their lunchtime assignation. 'My brother's gone to Norfolk and Ellie's in Paris with her lover...' She was calling from her office at a Chelsea PR company, and breathed sexily into the receiver, awaiting his response. She'd suggested it some weeks before, but Ben was getting too old for rushed lunchtime couplings, however exotic the surroundings. But now he needed to know if his hunch about her brother was right.

She closed the heavy door of the apartment behind them and wrapped her arms around his neck, panting softly with relief and anticipation. Ben held her to him, using the time to look around them. The palatial penthouse, with its expanse of white marble flooring, was certainly exotic.

'Come on, I'll show you the bedroom.' Her voice was sultry with pent up excitement as she skipped away from him to slide back a smoked-glass partition. It revealed a vast sleeping area, dominated by a huge bed. A striking headboard made from sleek, brown, animal skin covered the wall above, and matching rugs were strewn on the floor.

Otherwise the area was bare, inviting only one activity. Lucy had stripped to her underwear while Ben was still absorbing the minimal opulence of his surroundings. Despite his real purpose for agreeing to join Lucy in her lunch hour, she looked enticing, kneeling up on the bed, her thighs slightly parted, and reaching behind her back to undo the clasp of her bra.

'Keep it on,' he said, divesting himself of his own clothing. She sank back onto the sumptuous fur bedcover, her pale skin contrasted against it, and used the tip of her tongue to moisten her lips.

It was too much for Ben. He sprang at her, ripping at the delicate and expensive underwear, enough to expose her breasts and hard nipples. He ripped her white knickers so he could see the glistening lips peeping through, but he left the remnants clinging to her lithe body. He liked the sight of the aristocratic girl, her alabaster skin adorned in nothing but flimsy, tattered remnants of lingerie. She moaned, pretending resistance, clutching her breasts and covering herself coyly, but he knew her well enough by now. He knocked her hands away and she spread her arms obediently.

'So where are the toys?' he whispered in her ear. 'Show me.'

She pointed up behind her, and Ben flicked up a cleverly disguised panel in the headboard. The small computer flickered back at him invitingly, so he touched the screen, selecting an option at random, brass rings emerging silently through the sleek surface of the headboard.

His next selection made him look up at the beamed ceiling, as a chain and hook lowered over the bed. Lucy stretched out, watching his reactions eagerly, a light film of perspiration forming on her upper lip. Ben made another selection and part of the wall opened to reveal a series of drawers, purpose built with lined, green-baize compartments. Vibrators filled one shelf, restraints and stretchers another, clamps and smaller items the next. The instruments intended for corporal punishment had their own larger area, and Ben smiled wryly to himself. It looked as if this was going to be easier than he thought.

Lucy looked up expectantly at the hook, but Ben had other ideas. 'Turn around,' he told her. He selected a soft leather blindfold from the drawer, and she cooperated while he adjusted it over her eyes. She let out a long sigh as he took her wrists and snapped them into the rings on the headboard, wide apart and high enough that she had to kneel up at full stretch.

Ben looked in the drawers. He should find something to thoroughly distract her while he carried out his mission. He searched among the incredible array of vibrators of every shape and size, until he found one to suit his purpose. He tried it on his finger, testing its mechanism and power. It was the size and shape of a small gull's egg, operated remotely and designed to be held firmly in place by two flat metal clips.

Lucy mewled and squirmed with expectation when he pulled aside her torn panties and eased back first one lip and then the other, brushing aside the dewy web of moisture that had already formed between the fleshy lips. He attached a clip to each side, seating the egg exactly over the hood of her clitoris. He turned the motor on low and she fell silent, her nipples hardening. When he increased the power he saw the muscles in her buttocks tense. He turned the motor up to its highest setting and she arched her back, thrusting her buttocks towards him and moaning with pending ecstasy.

Ben couldn't resist. He'd never done more than spank a woman before, and even then only at their request. But at that moment he felt the blood pounding in his temples as he scrutinised the extraordinary range of canes, cats, whips and paddles. He chose a short bamboo cane and let it cut through the air a few times, before he brought it down across the perfect white flesh of Lucy's raised bottom.

He savoured the delicious sensation of power and the sight of the red slash the strike left behind. He raised the cane again, ignoring the babbled cries from his tethered victim. He found his target for the second time, and felt himself stiffening powerfully. Just one more. He must not be distracted yet. He had work to do.

Lucy's orgasm was already gripping her when he slashed the cane through the air for the third time. A trickle of golden liquid even ran down one thigh as she slumped forward, mumbling incoherently.

The clips held the device tightly over her clitoris. No amount of movement could dislodge it. Ben marvelled at its ingenuity. 'You want me to turn it off?' he leaned over her and whispered teasingly. She nodded her head, but Ben chuckled. 'I don't think so. I think you want a little more, don't you?' Lucy shook her head but already her hips were twisting as the next wave of pleasure engulfed her. She opened her mouth wide and threw back her head in abandon.

'I think I'll just leave you there for a while,' he told her, when she subsided temporarily.

Ben fumbled through his jacket pockets and extracted the crumpled piece of paper he'd brought with him. He left Lucy with reluctance, but after the information she'd given him a few days earlier, he needed to learn more about her brother's involvement with the Ruskin Club.

Lucy had only ever mentioned her older brother, Lord Kensal, with sibling disdain, which she extended to his American heiress wife, Ellie. However, Lucy wasn't averse to house sitting when they went to their chalet in Gstaad, or their estate in the Hamptons. That's how she discovered the attributes of the bedroom, but what she found didn't surprise or shock her. She and her brother had been raised at the family's ancestral home, a stately pile on the edge of a bleak Scottish moor. They had one thing in common: they both revered and feared their widower father, the duke, a strict disciplinarian. While he entertained his mistresses he expected his household to be run with military precision - and that extended to the nursery. Although Lucy had not elaborated further, her cheeks burned as she revealed the background to her aristocratic upbringing.

'The Ruskin Club?' he had pressed her. Whilst he didn't normally mind acting as father confessor, he was anxious for information.

'I don't know anything about it. Just some boring committee my brother's on. He goes off to meetings and stuff. Something to do with old paintings, I think.'

Ben suspected otherwise, but as he explored the huge space, sliding back more partitions to reveal several bathrooms and wet rooms and more sleeping areas, he wondered if he would find anything to help him. It was as if no one occupied the vast area. Not a magazine left open and half-read, or a scarf slung carelessly on the sumptuous white leather sofas. Just an endless maze of shimmering glass, everywhere he looked, affording him spectacular views across London.

He paused from his search and looked down at the Houses of Parliament, diminutive from his superior vantage point. Lucy's wails drifted from the far end of the apartment, building in intensity as the vibrator continued to deliver its relentless pleasure. He smiled as he touched himself, hardening as he moved his hand more urgently, thinking about the blue-blooded girl tied to the headboard, blindfolded, unable to escape her own lust. Fresh in his mind was her bottom; striped with the three livid marks he had delivered. He was tempted to return and stuff his erection between those alluring cheeks, but instead he wanked himself quickly, thrusting his groin forward, letting the jets of semen splash onto the pristine white marble floor. He stayed there slowing his breathing, naked and invisible to the masses, feeling more vital than he had in a long time.

His pulse quickened when he saw the short flight of steps, which led down to an area where at last he might find some clues. A leather chair was placed in front of a blank screen in one wall. As he sat down a desk and keyboard emerged from their hiding place. Ben shook his head in admiration as the screen lit up automatically, and then he began to search urgently. He couldn't keep Lucy in her present predicament for much longer.

He moved to the files marked *private* and found it almost at once. It was there at his fingertips... *Rossetti*. He clicked to open it. Lucy's squeals had developed a note of desperation and he frowned with irritation, as the machine demanded a password. Ben unfolded the piece of paper he hoped would hold the answer. *Burne*... incorrect. *Brentwood*... incorrect. *Hunt*... incorrect.

Sweat was beading on his forehead and his mouth was dry as he worked alphabetically through the list of names. *Morris*... incorrect. *Ruskin*... incorrect.

He thought he'd have to admit failure by the time he reached almost the last name on his list. Waterhouse. He entered it without conviction, but the document opened instantly!

Tension crept across his shoulders as he roughly scanned the contents. He clicked print and the pages began to emerge silently from a slot beneath the screen. The sounds from the bedroom had faded. He snatched up the sheets of paper, turned everything off, and hurriedly retraced his footsteps.

Ben found Lucy close to fainting. Rivulets of perspiration ran down her virtually naked body. The remnants of underwear clung to her and her blonde hair hung limp. She was moaning, her hips rotating slowly but instinctively, her mind unable to resist the quest for pleasure.

Ben found the remote and turned off the motor. He untied her, laid her down and removed the clips and blindfold. He rubbed the circulation back into her arms and called her name, but still she barely responded. Perhaps such sessions should be left to the experts, like Sadie, and the members of the Ruskin Club, the names of which he was convinced he now possessed.

He stuffed the printed sheets of paper into the pocket of his crumpled jacket and was relieved when Lucy began to murmur softly. He moved back closer to her, leaning over her, her utterances growing stronger until he was able to make out her words. 'Fuck me...' she breathed. 'Fuck me, *please...*' she repeated clearly.

Ben's erection resurged instantly and he sank easily into her wet sex. She took all of him, opening her eager mouth to his hungry tongue, wrapping her limbs around him, clinging to him, letting him rock himself into her, skewering her tight rear passage with a finger. Deep from beyond her consciousness came one final, silent flood of ecstasy, and Ben met it with his own.

Fifteen minutes later they were descending in the lift, Lucy completely revived, scrubbed fresh, and the neat pleated skirt and white blouse back in place. She had disposed of her torn underwear and asked him to rub ointment into the livid welts that crossed her buttocks. Only the sparkle in her eyes and the lustre of her cheeks might have revealed her recent tribulations to an expert eye.

'Does the name Waterhouse mean anything to you?' Ben asked casually as the lift descended.

Lady Lucy frowned and looked at him quizzically before she shook her head and raised one thigh, rubbing it between his legs. Her hands drifted across the front of his trousers. 'I'm hungry,' she purred, dropping to her knees in front of him. Ben let her lower the zip and wondered if the girl possessed some insatiable gene, bred into her by generations of lustful aristocrats.

'I'm hungry.' Lord Waterhouse lounged back on the wicker chair, his injured arm dressed in a blue polka dot silk sling, a stable girl kneeling at his feet, licking the traces of semen from his deflating cock.

When the excitement of the contest and the drama of Lord Waterhouse's accident had subsided, the cooks appeared carrying silver platters laden with delicious meats and fruits, and set them out on the tables. The stable girls were corralled to help serve the picnic - and whatever else the guests desired.

Meanwhile, Major Hunt deliberated on how best to display the two joint victors of his devilish sport. Eventually he asked the grooms to place two wooden chairs opposite each other and about a yard apart, on the raised stone terrace that bordered the lawn. Jane and the blonde goddess were then led across and seated directly opposite each other.

Ropes secured their waists and their hands were tied behind their necks. Their bits and head harness had been removed and they'd been allowed to dip their faces in the pails of cool water, but still Jane's physical discomfort was considerable. Her thighs burned and her feet ached from pounding the circuits of the track, but such worries were dwarfed by the rising panic she felt as the major approached them, jingling a bundle of fine chains in his hands.

'Well, my beauties, you ran well today,' he congratulated them, stroking their hair and patting their shoulders. 'We'll have to make sure you don't run off again while we enjoy our picnic,' he added, a sarcastic smile spreading across his ruddy face. His guests had gathered below the terrace, their glasses charged, eager to discover their host's intent.

Jane stiffened as he fondled her nipples, easing them further through the brass rings that encircled them. When he was satisfied he turned to the other girl and did the same. Jane's heart thumped in her chest when he unravelled the chains and she saw the metal clamps attached to the ends.

The guests drew breath as he again pinched Jane's left nipple and lined up a clamp. Tears sprang to her eyes as he tightened the screw over the swollen bud, and he watched her face intently while she struggled for self-control.

When satisfied it was firmly fixed, he stretched the fine links of chain towards her opponent sitting opposite, and the onlookers murmured in admiration as he began to attach the clamp at the other end to her left breast. The blonde lowered her chin and breathed deeply as the major tightened the screw, and by the time he returned his attention to Jane her right nipple was rigid, the areola dark and puckered. She didn't dare look directly at the woman sitting opposite her, although she realised that soon they would be inextricably united. Instead she looked around in search of any distraction while the major tightened the second clamp, only to meet the doctor's steady stare, and she was startled by how easily she returned it and the calming strength it gave her, creating a warm glow in the pit of her stomach.

The colour flooded her cheeks as the major crossed the second chain over the first and fastened the final clamp to the blonde's right breast. Then with the flourish of a magician performing his act he snapped a ring around the point where the chains crossed, and the guests gasped as they absorbed the vision of the two beautiful girls, their arms clasped behind their heads, their breasts pulled forward and joined by the two taut chains. If one or other moved just a fraction the clamps would wrench and stretch their nipples.

At first the blonde's eyes smouldered with hostility, but slowly they softened. Gradually they learned to gauge each other's pain, and when the major hooked a small weight to the central ring they had wordlessly formed a tacit bond beyond the fine metal links that joined them.

As the guests dispersed and the feast began, any modicum of control Jane might have managed was disturbed by the forced activities of her fellow stable girls. Their chemises had been removed and their breasts were exposed above their horsehair corsets. One was being used as a table and paddled by a young man if she arched her back and dislodged his plate. Mrs Morris was bent over a beer barrel, her wide buttocks spread and available for entertainment as the men waited to have their tankards refilled. Another knelt in front of the doctor, leaning forward to take small morsels of food in her mouth, which he transferred to his own, lifting her to him, cupping her breasts in his hands.

The bacchanalian feast continued well into the afternoon. They ate and drank greedily, the stable girls, including Sei, scrabbling between their legs, receiving slaps or scraps at random. Several of the guests clambered up onto the terrace and fed Jane and her partner in misfortune with morsels of food, or raised goblets of wine to their lips. They were both grateful for the sustenance, but less so for the movements such manoeuvres necessitated.

The major had piled a small stack of weights beside their chairs, and when the guests had enjoyed their fill of food they amused themselves by adding and removing them from the central ring. Each time Jane winced, moving her body forward to accommodate the shortening chain, but inevitably she would feel hands on her shoulders, or worse, pulling her elbows back, stretching her breasts and nipples - and her enforced collaborator's - to their limits.

But the major's test to find the ultimate victor was the most devilish of all. He sounded his hunting horn and Bridget bounded up onto the terrace, her dark curls tumbling over the upper slopes of her creamy breasts, exposed where she'd loosened her scarlet riding jacket, and knelt behind Jane's chair. The dark-haired beauty, who paid such a heavy forfeit earlier, was now re-adorned in her finery. She followed Bridget readily, and knelt behind the other sitting female.

'Open your legs.' Jane trembled at the major's directions, but the girl opposite held her gaze and they both obeyed in unison. Jane bit her lip as Bridget's hands crept round and felt for the brass ring that framed her clitoris, and watched the dark girl imitate her actions on the blonde.

'Wider.' Bridget's voice was raw with lust. She parted the lips and sought out the ripening bud with expert fingers. Jane shuddered but her stomach fluttered at the delicate touch. Opposite her the blonde was receiving identical treatment, her eyes swimming, the lids heavy as her pleasure started to consume her.

'Don't resist me if you want to win; it's an hour with the grooms for the loser.' Jane heard Bridget's whispered words and understood them with terrible clarity. Bridget's fingers were rubbing faster on her budding berry and the guests were crowding eagerly around the raised terrace. Jane looked up and saw that her opponent's eyes had closed completely, and she had ceased to be aware of the fierce tugging on their nipples. Both their breasts were swollen and full, pointing towards each other as their pleasure was so cruelly forced upon them. Jane felt the panic rising. The familiar waves were building inside her, but her inhibitions at such a public display held her back.

She heard Bridget whispering hotly in her ear. 'Do you *want* to be beaten? Do you? Do you want the grooms to double you? Hang you in the hay barn? Fuck your little cunt with their fat cocks? Is that what you want?' She rubbed harder and faster, emphasising her words, and for Jane the strangers around her seemed to dissolve.

All she sought was surrender. 'Go on... please, say more things like... like that...' she begged, falteringly, not understanding why the words excited her.

Bridget didn't hesitate. 'You're a bad girl... a very bad girl,' she hissed. 'And they punish bad girls worse than the others. They'll burn your little arse with their paddles... make you grovel like an animal while they fuck you... one by one...'

The images filled Jane's mind, and the heat rose from the pit of her being. The point of release was so close, yet out of reach. She snapped her eyes open. Her opponent's face was scarlet, her breath coming in short bursts. Jane closed her eyes tight. She was back in the doctor's surgery, the device vibrating on her clitoris.

But it was the caress of his leather paddle, which she knew must follow, that made the orgasm well up and burst - and then she heard Bridget's triumphant shout as she raised her hand in testimony to their joint victory.

Jane slumped forward and felt the tug on her nipples as her opponent threw herself back and succumbed to her own pleasure.

'We have a winner!' The major joined the foursome on the terrace. He loosened the screws and Jane let out a low sigh as the blood flooded back into her nipples. 'My filly, I'm afraid! I shall decide on her reward later.'

The grooms were already untying the ropes and helping the loser to her feet. Her tanned thighs trembled and her full breasts heaved, her eyes downcast. Jane wanted to reach out and comfort her, overcome with contrition at being the inadvertent cause of her fate.

'So I must thank you all for attending and look forward to seeing you at Sir John's May Day celebrations,' the major addressed his guests. 'You can take her away now,' he added to the burliest of the grooms, who didn't delay in stooping to haul the blonde girl over his broad shoulder and stride off towards the stable yard. His quarry hung limp, her breasts squashed against his back, her slim body bent double, her hair sweeping low in unison with his stride.

Jane shuddered at how nearly their fortunes might have been reversed, and the consequences had she not allowed herself to conjure up images and sensations. But her skin crept with shame when she recalled how Bridget's lewd suggestions, and the memory of the doctor's paddling, had provoked such explosive pleasure.

The party was dispersing. Jane searched the gathering and identified Doctor Morris's figure, stooping to get in one of the waiting cars. Paul, ever the perfect servant, stood smartly on the gravel drive holding open the door, and Bridget then climbed in elegantly, and a little reluctantly, beside the doctor.

'Lord Waterhouse will be staying the night,' the major informed the cooks as they cleared away the debris of the food spread. 'I feel obliged to find ways to repay him for his injury.' He looked meaningfully at Jane, stroking his chin as he pondered the thought. She returned his gaze, steadily. Winning the contest had filled her with a new concoction of fear and boldness, which both confused and infused her.

Ben Handford didn't return to his office after he parted from Lucy. He walked up the Kings Road towards Sloane Square station with new vigour. He enjoyed the warmth of the sun on his back and the knowledge that, in his pocket, he possessed some vital clues that would reveal the membership and activities of the Ruskin Club.

Sadie was working when he arrived at her establishment, so he was shown into her infamous viewing booth and treated to the delicious scene of two young women tied to a padded whipping stool. They could have been twins, certainly sisters, dressed in matching silk shifts raised to their waists. Their torsos were tied to the upper step, and their bare bottoms held high as they knelt on the lower one. They pleaded for mercy while a sinewy gentleman, old enough to be their father, chastised them alternately. Sadie, dressed in a figure-hugging navy uniform and starched white apron, winked at Ben through the glass screen while the heavy leather tawse found its targets.

Ben didn't mind, for once, that it was several minutes before she joined him. His personal experience with Lucy at Lord Kendal's apartment had enlivened his curiosity for such pursuits, so by the time Sadie sat beside him and uncorked a bottle of his favourite wine his cock was hard again.

When she leaned her head on his shoulder and rested her hand between his thighs the freshly laundered smell of her starched uniform filled his senses. He stared ahead, motionless, as she fondled him and deftly unzipped his trousers, not daring to do anything to make her stop. It had been some years since Sadie had shown him the attention he craved from her.

He closed his eyes and listened to the sounds coming from beyond the glass screen, the thwacks of the tawse and the choked entreaties that followed each one.

He breathed sharply when the softness of Sadie's lips closed around his erection. She licked the length of him from all angles. She traced every contour, wrapping her cat-like tongue around him. The blood swam in his head and he was transported back thirty years to a dark Soho courtyard and a headstrong girl, kneeling in front of an earnest youth. That night Sadie had revealed an elixir that Ben had never quite recaptured.

He was coming close, the orgasm rising in him like a volcano. The gulfs of sensation clenched at his being as he sank back into the sumptuous velvet couch. He felt the first hot jet exit him and splash against the palate of her mouth. He laid a hand lightly against her throat, and felt the bob of her Adam's apple as she swallowed the stream that pumped from him.

Ben stayed still, revelling in the blind aura of peace that enveloped him, wanting to keep it forever. After a few moments he opened his eyes to find Sadie dabbing the corners of her mouth with a fine lace handkerchief. She smiled at him, her face shining with pride and affection. 'Did you want something...' she purred, 'apart from...?'

'Waterhouse?' Ben pressed her. 'Ever heard the name?' Sadie shook her pretty head and helped him to adjust his clothing. 'Kensal? Lord Kensal? Does that name mean anything to you?'

Sadie chuckled. 'What, the son of the demon duke? His ol' man brought him to me when he was still a schoolboy, before I found easier ways for a girl to earn a living. I remember the first time he brought 'im; gangly lad, dressed in 'is striped blazer. I was 'is reward for scoring a century!' Sadie took a long swig off her drink. 'Happy days. Eton College versus Harrow School, at Lord's, if you don't mind!' She pronounced the last sentence with mock precision.

'You're incorrigible, Sadie,' he laughed. Sadie had more clients among the upper classes than any house in Soho, and his hunch that she would know Kendal looked like paying off. 'When did you last see them?'

'Haven't seen '*is grace* for a while. He doesn't get to London much since they chucked 'im out of the Lords. And the young 'un? Well, he was a vicious little bugger.' Sadie's expression darkened, and for a second her composure slipped. She took a packet of cigarettes from the pocket of her starched apron and Ben lit one for her. 'Married that heiress... Ellie Furstenberg. Haven't seen him in years, except on the society pages.' Her rosebud lips closed over the cigarette and she inhaled the smoke deeply into her lungs, her perfect breasts straining the buttons of her starched uniform. 'But he buys plenty of my stuff.'

Ben scrutinised the instruments that hung on the walls with more attention than usual. His mind shot back to the green-baize drawers at the penthouse and their array of similar objects.

'You said you sold one of your vaulting horses to a major in Norfolk...?' Ben hadn't lost his knack for recalling apparently insignificant detail when he was onto a story.

'Oh, him?' Sadie perked up. 'Funny you should mention the major. Kendal introduced him. Major Hunt, he calls 'imself. Not 'is real name, I'm sure, but you know I never deal without an introduction,' she added primly.

Ben smiled to himself and nodded his approval at the wisdom of such a precaution.

'Never met 'im, mind. He sends the driver to collect and pays cash. Nice young lad, quite a dish. Paul, that's 'is name. Always stays for a glass of bubbly.'

CHAPTER TEN

The Major's Horse

After Paul and the other drivers pulled out of the driveway, Jane was taken back to the stables, un-tacked and left naked and tethered in her stall. She stood shivering with terror, listening through the slatted walls of the wooden barn to the terrible cries as the grooms extracted their reward from her former opponent.

At last their triumphant roars subsided and the woman fell silent. Jane heard the other stable girls being instructed to lay down their tools and return to the house, and the crunch of heavy boots as the head groom came back for her. He led her across the deserted yard, her feet sore on the cobbled surface, into a vacant loose box strewn with fresh straw. He tied her hands to a ring high on the wall, intended to hang the horses' hay nets, and her heart leapt when he fastened a black rubber apron around his rounded stomach and approached her with a hose. He kicked aside the straw to uncover a drain in the concrete floor and turned on the tap at the wall.

'Now stand easy.' Her skin crept as he ran a rough hand over her face and down, mauling her breasts and tummy. 'He wants you groomed thoroughly tonight.'

The water stung as he aimed the jets at her sensitive flesh. It hurt most where the whips of Bridget and his lordship had fallen, and he gave these areas particular attention.

The bar of saddle soap, which he worked over her body and massaged between her thighs, gave off the rich, pungent odour of glycerine, and suddenly she was a young girl back on the farm in Yorkshire, helping the men rub down the horses after a day in the fields.

Her eyes closed and she let the rope take her weight, almost swooning as she let the man lather and wash her. The jets of water splashing on her belly began to soothe her and she complied instinctively when he opened the fleshy lips of her sex and doused the hidden pink flesh. But her eyes shot open when he poked the rubber hose inside her. She looked down with horror and cried out, begging him to stop, but he ignored her pleas, stroking the drum of her belly he'd created with satisfaction.

Then just when she thought she might burst he pulled out the hose and the water gushed from her, splashing into the drain beneath. She was still reeling from the release when he moved behind her, and helplessness besieged her when she felt the tip of the hose probing between her buttocks, and she squealed in anguish.

'Stop your noise - it's got to be done,' he warned her, and brought a heavy hand down across the clenched and squirming cheeks of her bottom. The blow shuddered through her and her stomach churned as, with the help of the glycerine bar, he eased the rubber hose into her tight rear channel. The sensation of the cold liquid flooding into her was yet another shock. Her eyes widened as she tried to accommodate the strange pressure. He held the hose firmly, kneading her hardening belly with his other hand. She squealed in panic as she swelled beneath his fingers, much more than she had done when he filled her from the front, and she begged openly for him to stop the terrible treatment. The feelings were unbearable, the overwhelming heaviness soaking into her thighs, the ache weighing low. The tears fell freely when he felt for her clitoris and found it hard and sensitive, waiting for his touch. She heard his mutter of approval and whimpered for release - of she knew not what. Finally he was satisfied that she'd taken enough and he eased the hose out of her. In spite of the terrible pressure straining for escape, she used every ounce of willpower to clench her buttocks tight, too ashamed to let go.

He carried on soaping and hosing her between her thighs, knowing she would be compelled to open herself before long. He rubbed the glycerine bar against the little bud of her clitoris and pressed his fist into her swollen belly until she could stand no more. Her orgasm overcame her and the ring of her anus relaxed, the contents cascading down her thighs and swirling around the drain at her feet.

The man stood back, enjoying her indignity and abandon as she was forced to empty herself in front of him. He watched as she expelled the liquid, every heave and push causing more surges and contractions that merged and seemed never-ending.

He kept the hose on her for several more minutes until she had evacuated herself completely, and she hung limply from the metal ring, spent and humiliated.

He cut her down and made her kneel in the soft straw while he rubbed oil into her body. When he was done he plaited her long hair and put a collar and leash around her neck. He helped her to her feet and lifted her chin, holding her away at arms' length, and she blushed with shame as he admired his work.

'Wake up, I have to dress you, they nearly finish dinner.' Sei shook Jane urgently from the depths of her sleep.

After her shower the groom had taken her back to the house, but instead of delivering her to the dormitory, he led her naked upstairs and along a dark landing. She didn't think her legs would carry her another step, and he had to tug on the leash when they reached the end. He urged her into a brocade-draped bedroom and allowed her to lie down on the softest feather mattress. She must have fallen into a deep sleep at once, and now she struggled to remember where she was as she rubbed her eyes.

It was dark outside and she guessed she must have been asleep for several hours. The events of her extraordinary day flooded back. Nothing in Dr Morris's examination room had prepared her for what she'd endured since her arrival at Hunt Hall. Sei was already loosening the laces on a white satin corset, and urging her towards the foot of the bed.

By the time the groom came for them they were dressed identically in the corsets, black stockings and laced, heeled ankle boots. Around their waists they wore the leather belts, and Jane shuddered again at the implications of the discs that hung from them. How soon before she would be expected to earn a new one?

Although her limbs were stiff she had a curious, floating lightness about her as she followed the man back through the dark house. When she and Sei were delivered into the dining room Major Hunt and Lord Waterhouse were seated at opposite ends of the long table, lolling back, replete from their late meal. They cradled crystal brandy glasses in their hands, and one of the stable girls stood by to replenish them from a fine crystal decanter.

'Lord Waterhouse, as my guest, you should choose your mount.' The major was in jovial mood. His ruddy nose was tinged purple and his fat neck strained against the collar of his shirt.

'You're a gentleman, sir!' Lord Waterhouse took a swig from his glass and let the fiery liquid slowly trace down his throat. 'The winning filly, I think. See if she can do me a service twice in one day!'

He had removed the sling from his injured arm, but used it gingerly to unfasten the buttons of his trousers, and Jane's anguish heightened as she was shoved roughly in his direction.

'Mount.' Jane had time to exchange one quick glance with Sei, who dutifully climbed onto the major's lap. His lordship's penis was standing vertical and erect, and Jane stared openly, compelled to confront its gnarled length. He dipped a hand languidly into a china butter dish that remained from their meal, and crudely started to caress himself while Jane watched, abhorred, as the yellow unguent oozed and melted between his fingers and coated his cock.

Through the tears that clouded her eyes she crept forward at his beckoning, and timidly straddled his thighs. She nearly gagged as he seized her chin and sought her mouth, the strong taste of brandy lingering on his reptilian tongue as it probed between her lips while he filled his palm with another scoop of the soft butter.

A twisted smile creased his face as he pressed his hand between her parted thighs and rubbed it over her sex. 'Ride me; I've heard you're good,' he muttered, his cock nudging threateningly against her buttered lips as he forced her to lower herself. He hardly had to shift his hips for her to be powerless to resist the penetration, and in moments she was impaled on his erection.

He fucked her hard and furiously, lifting and plunging his hips, ramming his full length into her without heed or mercy, and with each thrust he spanked her buttocks with his greasy palm. Her breasts, held outthrust by her corset, brushed against his chest, the nipples sensitive and swollen from their earlier punishment. She had no alternative but to grip the back of the chair behind his shoulders and meet each upward thrust, riding on thighs toned by a lifetime of sportsmanship.

Despite the frenzied onslaught she heard the grunts and rhythmic moans coming from the other end of the table, the major screwing Sei with equal verve.

After several minutes Lord Waterhouse drew back his lips and bared his teeth. Jane felt his body tighten in a way she was learning to recognise, then winced in pain as he drove his greased fingers between her buttocks, plugging her rectum, and released his ejaculation into her, in long, powerful eruptions.

'Dismount and change ends,' the major instructed almost immediately. 'Time these fillies earned themselves some new discs.'

Jane slid from the lap of her most recent submission, her mind numb with turmoil and her legs trembling. Sei was already moving unsteadily towards her, her golden body glistening with sweat, her eyes averted. The doctor's words drifted into Jane's head again, and she feared that at any moment she would have to make that choice of which he spoke.

Her heart pounded when she saw the thickness and power of the major's erection, apparently undiminished by his fun with Sei. 'So, Jane, what's it to be?' He held out two discs, one bronze and one gold, but both options repulsed her equally. The major shuffled the discs. 'Come on, make up you mind,' he said impatiently.

She hesitated, frozen by the enormity of what she was being asked to decide upon, and as her fingers trembled above the two discs lying on his broad palm, he finally lost patience and pressed the gold disc between them.

'Excellent choice, young lady!' he bellowed enthusiastically, grabbing her arm and roughly pulling her to him, a slow smile of satisfaction spreading across his ruddy face. 'Turn round and bend over the table,' he said more intimately, just loud enough for her to hear, taking it upon himself to then brusquely spin her round and press her down onto the polished wooden surface.

'Pass me some rope,' she heard him say to the serving girl, who still stood dutifully by, the decanter of brandy at the ready.

76

Through sparkling tears Jane saw Lord Waterhouse was already passing a length of rope over Sei's back, binding her to the table, too. She was struggling weakly, no match for her captor.

Jane then felt the major grab her ankles, and whimpered helplessly as he spread and fastened them to the table legs. This couldn't be happening to her. She must stop him. The earlier ignominy of the butt plug and tail, and the humiliation of effectively being given an enema by the hose had been awful enough, but to let a man penetrate her there was unnatural... it was awful.

But despite her dread she felt too weary to fight when he pulled the ropes tight across her back, crushing her breasts against the tabletop, securing her there at his mercy.

Then, bizarrely, the two men charged their brandy glasses, basking in the moment, taking their time to prepare for the task ahead with relish.

'You made your choice,' the major eventually loomed over her, 'now not a sound or I'll whip you until you quieten down. Do you understand me?' It was a rhetorical question, neither needing nor receiving any response from the trussed girl.

The men continued to sip their drinks, in no hurry now their prey was firmly tamed and secured.

'I had my man give them both a thorough hosing,' the major proudly informed his accomplice. 'He's a particularly diligent chap. Takes great pride in his work.'

'Excellent,' Lord Waterhouse said approvingly. 'My father was a firm believer in the treatment. Kept a brass syringe in the butler's pantry for years. Used it on recalcitrant housemaids. "Best way to purge them of obstinacy", he always said to me. Kept one up in the nursery too. My young sister, Lucy, was a fairly hot-headed creature...'

'How is your sister?' the major asked, his amiability belying the decadence of the scene. 'I hoped you might persuade her to join us. And your charming wife, Ellie?'

'I fear they don't share our subtle artistry, major.' He raised his glass and the clink of crystal chimed. 'Here's to chaste and unsullied orifices, and the Ruskin Club!'

The major repeated the lewd toast and they drank deeply.

Jane's desperation increased when the major mirrored his friend and scooped up a handful of butter and prodded a finger at her puckered opening. Her position allowed her just enough latitude to raise her head, but it was no comfort to see Sei staring back at her, eyes wide in anguish as her buttocks were similarly prised apart. She felt the major's bloated helmet nudging at the ring of her anus, and in spite of her resolve she cried out for him to stop, attracting several hard blows from his heavy palm on her parted buttocks.

'Long held inhibitions learned in childhood, I'm afraid,' the major said conversationally. 'I'll fetch the cane, if you like.' But his lordship didn't answer. He had already positioned himself behind his victim, his eyes ablaze with unbridled lust.

The major breathed close to Jane's ear and she gulped back her sobs, overwhelmed with her shame and helplessness. 'You'll learn to like it,' he told her before placing both his hands on her fevered buttocks and easing them wider apart. She tried to breathe evenly as she felt his fat penis pressing resolutely at the opening to the narrow channel, her worries compounded by the sound of Sei's sobs from the other end of the table, followed by Lord Waterhouse's cruel and triumphant snigger.

Jane's turn to sob came seconds later as the major stabbed forward, bursting through her tight ring, plunging himself into her in one long thrust. Pain spasmed through her insides, but he stayed firmly lodged deep within, pinning her to the unyielding wooden surface. Her muscles tightened involuntarily, shocked by the intrusion, and she could feel his girth blocking her tight passage.

Gradually he started to move, and very slowly the shafts of pain began to disperse, her consciousness struggling with a newfound desire to embrace it. The major's grunts seemed to come from far away as he gripped her hips and ploughed into her pinioned body. The salty smell of his sweat filled her nostrils with its pungency, and her pleasure rose from some undiscovered place, confusing her, surprising her with its fullness. She knew he was coming too; she could feel him pulsing inside her, gripped in her tight rear channel. She felt the weight of his heavy balls against her as he discharged himself and she swooned with the power of her own orgasm, abandoning herself, wantonly, freely, all inhibition crushed.

He slumped heavily on top of her, and for the second time they breathed in unison as their mutual pleasure subsided.

Jane wearily raised her head and saw Lord Waterhouse, his lips drawn back, beads of sweat glistening on his forehead, thrusting mercilessly into Sei's diminutive frame. Sei had spread her arms and her dainty hands gripped the sides of the table, the knuckles white with effort. He tugged on her thick plait of black hair so that her head reared up awkwardly. Jane tried to interpret her glazed expression. Was it despair or bliss her new friend was experiencing?

At last his rhythm slowed, and then he brought the flat of his right hand down on her right thigh, and Sei grimaced as he spanked her and pumped his semen into her vanquished bottom.

A knock on the heavy oak door cut though the ensuing silence. 'Come in,' the major responded, and Jane wondered how long the groom had been lingering outside, listening to their ordeal, waiting to enter.

'There's a telephone call for you, Major Hunt. A gentleman says he's got something you'll want. Needs to speak to you urgently.' Despite her position, still bound tightly to the table, Jane's pulse quickened.

'What, at this time of night?' the major snapped, clearly irritated but nevertheless intrigued. 'Tell him I'll be a few minutes. And untie these two. Take them back to the blue room. They can sleep there tonight.'

Once untied Jane stood up stiffly and the room spun as she sought her balance. Her thighs ached from being held apart by the ropes, and fiery shafts pulsed in her bottom. But it was her mind that was racing, distracting her from her physical discomfort. *Tell them you've got something they'll want.* Weren't those the exact words Ben Handford had used?

Jane and Sei washed each other gently, pouring fresh water from the heavy jug into the porcelain bowl, dabbing sensitively at the areas that had received the most punishment.

Afterwards they lay down naked on the soft feather mattress, pulling the covers over themselves, grateful for their privacy and comfort. Jane could not have taken the stares of the other women in the dormitory, or the lumpy horsehair mattress against her exhausted body.

Sei tugged Jane onto her side and nudged the cheeks of her enflamed buttocks into the cooler well of Jane's stomach. Her skin felt soft and fresh and Jane wrapped her arms protectively around her new friend. Their shared adversity bound them together as firmly as any ropes or chains.

'Did he hurt you badly?' Jane whispered softly.

Sei tilted her head slightly before she answered, and Jane caught the flicker of a smile on her parted lips. 'I earn my third disc. Now my husband is very happy.'

Jane smiled back. This was a strange and confusing world of conflicting values and unrepressed emotions that she had entered. The colour rushed to her cheeks as she recalled her response to her own treatment on the table, and she buried her face in the cool linen pillow.

And Ben Handford? Could it really have been him on the telephone? Her thoughts churned on long after Sei fell asleep in her arms, but eventually exhaustion claimed her too.

Ben Handford put down the phone in his deserted office and allowed himself a smile of satisfaction. He reached for the bottle of whisky he kept in his desk drawer. He deserved it, he told himself, as the first hit burned his throat.

It hadn't been easy but with morsels about private collections and secret auctions, the major became less belligerent, and eventually agreed to send a car to take Ben to Norfolk the following afternoon. Ben chuckled to himself. He was convinced that access to Hunt Hall would help him to piece together the covert activities of the Ruskin Club.

He ran his eyes to the bottom of the list he had obtained from the computer of Lord Kensal - alias Waterhouse. The names read like a copy of Who's Who and Debretts combined. Apart from MP's from both sides of the House, they included a world famous cellist, an international property tycoon, an Oscar winning film producer and a clutch of distinguished lawyers, bankers and theologians.

His finger rested on the very last name - his ex-boss at the corporation, and against it the pseudonym Thomas Woolner. That was another personal score he had to settle, very soon. In his own quest for revenge he momentarily forgot young Jane Carter, but then she came back into his thinking. He looked at his watch. The pubs would be closing, but there was always a drink at Sadie's. He grabbed his jacket and left the office.

79

CHAPTER ELEVEN

The Folly

Jane stood where she'd been told, in the centre of the cobbled yard, trembling with embarrassment and apprehension. The bright morning sun felt warm on her back. She wore nothing but the horsehair corset and a pair of polished leather riding boots that snugly encased her calves.

Two discs - one silver, one gold - now hung from the leather belt around her waist. The grooms, who had noticed the addition, sniggered and leered in her direction as they went about their work.

Earlier the redhead had woken her by heaving back the heavy drapes. Jane had squinted as the room filled with sunlight and looked around for Sei, but she had vanished.

The redhead wrenched spitefully at the long laces of the corset, making Jane gasp with every tug. When she was done she disdainfully threw down the leather boots and left Jane to put them on herself.

'Display,' the head groom instructed, and all the women ceased their toils around the yard and laid down their brooms and rakes. Dutifully they raised their arms and clasped them tightly behind their necks. They stood like statues, their feet set slightly apart, their breasts thrust out under the thin chemises. Jane obeyed too, except with no chemise or drawers she was much more vulnerable to the men's stares, and despite the warmth of the morning a shiver ran through her when the major strode into the yard.

He headed straight towards her, ignoring the coy glances and downcast expressions with which the other women hoped to impress their master.

'Let's see if you ride as well as you're ridden, shall we?' he said. 'I need to take a look at the folly.' His eyes narrowed and he ran his tongue over his fleshy lips. Jane's heart was pounding, but she met his lascivious stare with all the boldness she could muster.

And she still held it while the grooms led the horses from their loose boxes, and when she was told to mount the chestnut was already snorting the air and rolling its eyes.

She had no option but to afford the groom a perfect view of her nakedness as he gave her a leg up. She landed lightly on the leather saddle, but the horse was riled and it took Jane several seconds to settle it, the major watching her intently while she gathered the reins and stroked the horse's neck to calm it.

Major Hunt set a furious pace from the moment they clattered out of the cobbled yard. The redhead fumed with envy as Jane passed her, clearly livid that she had apparently been so summarily dismissed as their master's favourite.

The young thoroughbred chucked its head and fought the bit, shying at the hedgerows as they set out across the fields towards the distant woodland. Jane was more used to riding ponies across the Yorkshire moors, and she struggled to control this much more powerful animal, gripping the leather saddle desperately between her naked thighs.

They galloped on, faster and faster. The major looked back several times at his young companion, but spurred his mount forward relentlessly, Jane's anxiety compounded by the thought of where the fearsome ride might lead. The folly? What new ordeal might that entail?

They had crossed several fields before the chestnut ceased to fight her. At last they found each other's rhythm and she gave him his head. The breeze buffeted her bare skin and her exhilaration built. By the time they pulled up at the edge of the wood Jane was panting heavily, her cheeks flushed, the perspiration running freely between her heaving breasts. The horses stamped the ground impatiently, sweat pouring from their flanks and foaming between the leather straps of their bridles.

The major unlatched the gate, his eyes appraising her erect nipples and travelling down to where her naked flesh brushed against the leather saddle. She didn't dare look down herself, knowing a mixture of elation, tension and friction had caused the bud of her clitoris to swell shamefully between her parted thighs. As they rode into the wood it chaffed against the raised pommel, throbbing more with every pace.

The major set off purposefully into the dense woodland, barely adjusting his speed to the new terrain. Jane had to duck the low branches but she couldn't avoid the young saplings that tangled in her hair and whipped and stung her naked breasts and thighs. She was forced to ride low in the saddle, every muscle tensed with effort. But the chestnut moved with newfound confidence, and to her consternation the regular thud of its hooves on the mossy earth reverberated through her.

Her heart was in her mouth as they rode deeper into the wood, accompanied by the rustle of creatures skittering through the undergrowth as they disturbed the natural peace.

Jane saw the clearing from some distance, but it wasn't until they had almost reached the perimeter that she could see the shafts of sunlight glinting on the blue-black flint. The major tugged roughly on his reins and brought his horse to an abrupt halt, and Jane pulled the chestnut up beside him.

For a moment the light blinded her, but gradually she focused on the extraordinary sight in the centre of the clearing. A vast, circular tower rose into the sky, towering high above the tree canopy. Jane blinked with astonishment at the Gothic structure, hidden in the centre of the deep wood.

'One hundred and thirty feet tall,' the major proudly disclosed in response to Jane's bewilderment. He wiped the back of his hand across his forehead and breathed heavily, while Jane took in the rough flint walls and the small slatted openings that formed irregular windows in its surface. It seemed to have no definable purpose and looked like an illustration from a child's history book.

Jane looked back as the major dismounted and motioned for her to do the same.

If she was to dig her heels into her horse's flanks and gallop back the way they'd come she was sure she could outpace the major, but any thoughts of escape were swiftly crushed as he grabbed a firm hold on the chestnut's bridle.

'Dismount,' he said threateningly, as if he had read her thoughts.

He tethered the horses at the edge of the clearing and picked several of the newer, lower branches from a young birch tree. Jane's heart sank as he stripped away the leaves and tested their suppleness by swatting them against the leather of his hunting boots. She should have taken her chance when she had it, and when the major shoved her towards the small wooden door at the foot of the glowering edifice she stumbled on the rough ground, her legs weak with trepidation.

The building was no less intimidating inside, and Jane recoiled as the dank smell filled her nostrils. Her eyes adjusted slowly to the dim light. The walls appeared to slope inwards, climbing endlessly, open to the sky at their summit. A single shaft of sunlight beamed down and lit the spiral staircase that wound its way up.

'Start climbing,' the major ordered brusquely, his hand in the small of her back urging her forward. She shivered in the gloom and moved reluctantly, but he used one of the freshly picked birch switches to encourage her. So she started to climb the stone steps tentatively, while he kept his hand planted against her back, urging her to move faster.

The staircase was steep from the very start and twisted sharply. She held the wall and tried to climb as quickly as she could, barely daring to look up, where the spiralling steps ended at a narrow wooden gallery. She faltered, tears pricking her eyes at the prospect of such a perilous climb, but the major cursed her, the stinging birch across her buttocks forcing her onwards.

She tried to move faster to get out of his range, but he pursued her with alarmingly agility. He slashed the switch across her buttocks and thighs with increasing accuracy, and used it to increase her distress with every tortuous step. When one switch snapped he replaced it with another. The tears ran down her face, the steps a blur as she strove to climb faster, onwards, higher and higher, chased by her rabid pursuer.

They must have climbed half the distance towards the balcony when he stopped her, grabbing her arm and spinning her round to face him. His florid face was parallel with her stomach and she felt his hot breath against her. He reached into his pocket and produced a bronze disc, and held it in the palm of his hand. He too was panting from his exertions and no words were needed for Jane to comprehend his meaning. He replaced the disc in his waistcoat pocket and pushed her roughly on up the winding staircase.

But this time he didn't use the switch to encourage her. She felt his clammy hand on her burning bottom, and before she recognised his intention he slid an index finger up into her vagina, almost disturbing her balance. Shamefully her own moistness, compounded by the effects of the ride, eased his path. She managed a few more steps before she felt his thumb nudging between her buttocks. She tried to move higher out of his reach, realising his purpose, but her thighs were leaden and he ignored her protest as he plunged his thumb into the tight ring. She felt herself lifted helplessly, skewered on his hand, his assistance in propelling her up towards the open sky both sorely needed and acutely unwelcome.

He snatched his hand away just as she reached the top of the stairway and she tumbled, breathless, onto the rough wooden slats that formed the floor to the narrow gallery. The major stood over her, his beady eyes burning down into her.

'Have you made your decision?' Jane didn't answer, silent sobs wracking her exhausted body. The sound of creaking twine echoed off the flint walls as he used a long hooked pole to lower a rope ladder from the very top of the building, and fear overwhelmed her when he hauled her to her feet.

'Start climbing,' he instructed her coldly, and every muscle in her body trembled as she placed one foot on the first rung. It slipped and the ladder swung perilously. She estimated that there were about twenty rungs leading up to the opening, and with each one she groaned inwardly, her mind racing, struggling to maintain her hold, her heart beating frantically, aware that success would bring dubious rewards, and failure just wasn't worth considering.

The major placed one heavy boot on the bottom rung and watched from below. Jane no longer cared that he was afforded an open view of her privates as the rope ladder swung hazardously with her weight; her fears were far more immediate as she completed her perilous ascent.

Jane dragged herself on to the cold stone roof. She gulped at the fresh air as well as she was able, but the horsehair corset was drenched with sweat. She longed to tear at the laces and let her lungs expand fully, but she could hear the creak of rope as the major climbed up to her. She crawled desperately towards the edge and propped herself up against the fortressed wall. The top of the tower was no more than twenty feet across. Weeds and nettles poked up between the cracks of the stone flagging. Her heart thumped and her throat burned from the dust she'd inhaled. At any minute she would be asked to decide.

The major's fleshy cheeks were scarlet with effort when he emerged from the tower. He too took in deep breaths of air, his broad chest expanding, spreading the buttons of his tweed riding jacket. When he had recovered sufficiently he bent and began winding the handle of a rusty apparatus to the side of the opening. It may have looked old but the mechanism was well oiled and slowly a square wooden platform was winched across, until it covered the opening.

He turned on her, enjoying her wide-eyed astonishment. They were entirely alone in the centre of the woods, one hundred and thirty feet in the air, closed off from the world. There was no escape, and she struggled to her feet as he approached her, steadying herself between two merlons of the stone battlements.

'Would you like to see the view?' he mocked her, grabbing her shoulders and twirling her round. Jane reeled and fell back against him. The view was extraordinary. The woodland foliage formed a skirt around the tower and the fields they had galloped over were like patchwork. In the distance Hunt Hall, with its stables and outbuildings, were scaled down to the size of a doll's house. Under other circumstances she would have appreciated its dramatic beauty, but her head spun with dizziness, the nausea rose in her throat and she felt close to fainting.

'So what's it to be, Jane?' he asked, grabbing her hair as the breeze caught it. His voice was low with desire and she could feel the protrusion growing in his breeches. She couldn't, not now. Her throat was parched. She gagged involuntarily at the thought, but to her horror he interpreted this as a decision, releasing his grip on her, fumbling for the buttons on the panel of his breeches.

'No please, I can't,' she cried out as she doubled over, supporting herself between the stone parapets.

'This is no time for coyness.' His strong arms dragged her back, and she found herself crouched in front of him, his livid cock exposed and inches from her face. She could smell the saltiness as he stroked the length, pulling back the foreskin to reveal the smooth head. She shuddered as he pulled her to her knees. Her stomach churned and her lips were dry when he nudged against them. Her jaws seemed paralyzed and, try as she might, they would not open to allow him entry. She sensed his impatience, panic overwhelming her. The memory of Matilda reared in her head, her lips stretched as she tended the doctor, and she just could not face doing the same for the musty old major.

'Open your mouth,' he commanded, poking a finger between her lips as he would a young horse. She resisted in the same way, turning and tossing her head, fighting his attempts until he gave up.

'Very well, if that's your choice,' his voice rasped with unconcealed frustration, 'turn around.'

But he didn't waste time waiting for her to obey, his need urgent as he lifted and draped her in the embrasure between the two merlons, her breasts crushed against the stone, her hips and shoulders wedged between the flint-work, her toes attempting to make contact with the roof.

She managed to free her arms, but he swiftly fastened them behind her back with his belt, then he penetrated her before she had time to resist.

She cried out at the hurried invasion, and far below she saw the chestnut raise its head and heard it neigh. The major thrust into her several times, lubricating himself, his thumb probing at the tiny puckered entrance just above. She heard him grunt as he withdrew, and moments later he found his target and sank into her bottom without ceremony, the shock searing through her brain.

He gave her no clemency, thrusting vigorously in and out of her tight rear passage. Her breasts rasped painfully on the sun-warmed stone, her head unsupported beyond the battlements, her fear acute as she looked down at the drop beneath her, only his clamped grasp on her hips preventing her from tumbling over the edge.

As he began to penetrate both channels alternately she tightly closed her eyes, trying to block out the dizzying vista below, every muscle of her body tensed with fright. She wished she'd overcome her resistance and opened her mouth for him. Nothing could match the distress of her current predicament. He was sliding in and out of her with ease, establishing a rhythm that he increased and decreased at will, perilously jerking her back and forth, seemingly in no hurry to conclude his pleasure.

Perhaps it was the danger of the situation that caused the waves to build inside her, to lap through her stomach. The major's grunts altered to a guttural sound from the back of his throat, and she felt him tighten his grip on her. With each thrust the sensations grew until the danger overwhelmed and drove her into a black hole of sub-consciousness, where adversity met ecstasy. She seemed to float off the stone as his power roared through her - so she was unaware, until she felt herself slipping, driven forward by the power of his orgasm, that in his passion he had momentarily released her hips. A split second later he grabbed at the laces of her corset and fell over her, trapping her against the stone, relief and release conjoining them. She couldn't be sure, but she thought he planted the briefest kiss on the nape of her neck.

They lay there for some time in silence. Jane dared to open her eyes and look down at the peaceful idyll far below. The horses were resting in the shade of the trees, their tails swishing occasionally to rid themselves of flies. In the distance she saw a car winding its way up the long drive towards the Hall, and she was reminded of her own ignominious delivery, after Paul had made her strip naked in the deserted farmyard.

The major must have noticed the car too, because he roused himself and freed her wrists. He lifted her off the battlements and set her down on the roof. She rubbed the circulation back into her wrists while he stood over her, fastening the panel of his breeches, threading his belt back into them, and pulling on his leather riding gloves.

Her relief was enormous. Although she dreaded the descent, at least she had satisfied his lust, for now. She crawled towards the wooden platform that covered the opening, every inch causing distress to her ravished body.

'We're not finished yet,' he said dispassionately when she had practically reached her goal.

Jane's heart sank. What could he ask of her now?

He had produced some ropes from somewhere and was motioning her towards the platform. 'Lie on your back,' he told her sharply, and she had no alternative but to comply. She was not surprised when he spread her out on the wooden slats and fastened her wrists and ankles to the metal handles at each corner. She heard him rooting at the weeds and brambles that grew from the flint-work and the corners of the rooftop, her anxiety building, trying to predict what new torment she would be required to endure.

His bulky frame cast a shadow over her supine form. She looked up at his silhouette against the sun and saw the nettles, grasped in his gloved hand. He dangled them over her and she tensed with sudden, unwanted childhood memories of Sunday morning walks to church, stumbling home along the overgrown bridleway, dressed in ankle socks and pleated skirt, trying to keep pace with Aunt Judith.

The major trailed the nettles over her thighs and she gasped as the minute hairs on the surface of the dark leaves stung her bare legs, just as they had done all those years before.

He let the tougher storks linger on her inner thighs, a wry smile twisting the corners of his mouth when she flinched at their caress. He teased her, biding his time until her nipples stood from the perfect globes of her breasts.

He took a fresh one before continuing, and Jane cried out as he stroked the new leaves around the circumference of each breast, fighting her bonds frantically as the vicious weed made contact with her naked flesh. He was clearly practiced at such a mode of torment and enjoyed delaying the moment before the nettles released their venom on the hardened buds. She begged fervently for him to stop as he inched closer, alternating between each breast, twisting the stork against the puckered skin that surrounded his ultimate goal.

'Help me, help me,' she cried out to some imaginary saviour when the leaves assaulted her nipples.

He let her suffer while he replenished his supplies, the light breeze fanning her skin, irritating the clusters of tiny blisters already forming.

She heard the creak of wood as he knelt between her widespread thighs. Her head lolled to one side and her tears dripped onto the slatted surface. She no longer had the energy to beg. The tip of a fresh nettle taunted the fine hair between her thighs and she held her breath. A leather-covered finger parted her sex and he traced the weed carefully over the lips. He waited for her reaction before twisting it, releasing the venom into her most delicate flesh. Her body arched and her eyes stared. He held her down, closing the tender lips over the nettle, making sure the sensitive flesh received every last drop his devilish botanic weapon had to offer.

Jane was still writhing in agony when the grinding mechanism lurched into action and her tethered body moved with it. The wooden platform slid back to reveal the opening.

'I have some business to attend to,' he told her. 'Perhaps some time spent reflecting on your obstinacy will mellow your resistance.'

Despite the terrible stinging driving her to distraction, Jane was appalled to hear his heavy boot as he placed it on the first rung of the rope ladder. Surely he didn't intend to leave her there?

The rope groaned threateningly under his weight, and Jane listened fearfully to his retreat; fears compounded when she heard him reach the bottom of the rope ladder and cross the wooden gallery. She imagined his bulky frame then descending the long, winding stairway.

Several minutes passed before the sound of horse's hooves drifted up through the silence. She listened to the crack of the major's crop and the rustle of foliage as he drove his horse back into the woods. She was entirely alone, exposed to the elements. Suddenly her teeth chattered, the inflammation between her thighs heating her body, while the breeze cooled it. The ropes secured her to the wooden platform and prevented her from soothing the awful sting where the leaves had tormented her breasts and clitoris. How long would he leave her there?

The corset had dried and gripped her tighter than ever, the horsehairs tormenting her flesh where the nettles had been unable to penetrate. The only sounds were the birds flying above her, skimming the top of the tower, surveying the intruder tied helplessly to their rooftop home. The desperateness of her situation overwhelmed her when insects began to crawl over her, seeking succour in the salty residue of her sweat, and although there was no one to hear she let out a wail of anguish - the only form of protest left open to her.

If the chestnut thoroughbred had not responded to her cry she may never have found the courage to escape her bonds. But the sound of his neighing reply from far below filled her with new strength. She was not entirely alone, after all.

Jane tugged at the ropes around her ankles but it only served to tighten them. It took several painful attempts, the rope burning the delicate skin on her right wrist, before it finally slipped free of the knot. Her heart leapt with joy and her spirits surged with renewed resolve as she wrenched at the other ropes.

Her limbs felt weak as she stumbled towards the parapet but her elation kept her from falling. She snatched a handful of dock leaves that sprouted up between the stones, and the relief as she rubbed them vigorously between her thighs and over her swollen breasts was intense. Her clitoris needed particular soothing and she ground the leaves against it, their healing properties easing the stinging throb and replacing it with another kind. She closed her eyes and rested one hand lightly on the stone wall, the orgasm rising from deep within, growing unhindered, rounded and full, until it released against the bed of wet leaves pressed between her thighs.

When Jane opened her eyes a new perspective met her gaze. Alone for the first time in weeks the reality of her situation induced her natural defiance. How had she allowed all this to happen to her? Why had she not resisted enough that first night?

The blood pulsed in her temples. She'd found out all she needed to know about the Ruskin Club and its fiendish members. She no longer cared about their proposition.

She hurried to the far side of the parapet, where the view contrasted strongly with the rural idyll to the south. In the distance, on the far side of the woods, the land had been excavated. Ugly black pits dotted the vista and high metal fences divided them from the lush green hedges. But the depressing sight did nothing to quash Jane's mood. She was remembering her journey there, with Paul, the *Keep Out* signs, and she knew the direction she must take to reach freedom. The road could not be more than a mile away and the chestnut would carry her there with ease.

She allowed herself an excited whoop of triumph, exalting in her echo, before she began her descent.

She swung her legs down into the opening and flailed around, seeking the rope ladder, but in vain.

Finally, with her arms trembling from the strain, she heaved herself back up onto the platform and stared down into the gloom. When her eyes adjusted she saw the ladder, a crumpled heap of rope and rungs, lying on the balcony twenty feet below, way beyond her reach.

Jane slumped back on her haunches, buried her head in her hands, and wept with despair at the major's final heartless act. She was as trapped as ever.

Ben waited in the drawing room, planning his approach. He looked around at the austere furnishings that gave few clues. The journey to Norfolk had been equally unrevealing. The driver, a smart young chap in a liveried uniform, was uncommunicative, but Ben had established that his name was Paul. He decided against questioning him on his visit to Sadie, for fear of revealing his hand too early.

He crossed over to the French windows. In the distance a flame-haired girl was exercising a horse, her breasts thrusting forward under a thin shirt. The animal seemed to be attached to a contraption that turned automatically in a wide circle.

The crunch of hooves on the gravel drive signalled the major's return. A groom appeared at once and grasped hold of the reins for the portly major to dismount. The sweat sprang from his brow and his nostrils flared as much as the horse's as he slapped its haunches heartily, dismissing the groom.

'Everett, did you say your name was?' The major grasped Ben's hand and shook it vigorously. He slung his tweed riding jacket carelessly over one of the couches to reveal the dark patches of sweat staining his checked shirt. Ben nodded, leaving his host to take the initiative. 'You said you knew of a *Rossetti?*'

Ben smiled to himself. He was dealing with a greedy man, and in his experience greedy men gave themselves away. He hedged, admiring the house, the location, testing the major's patience. He teased him with talk of overseas clients, millionaire collectors who didn't ask questions. The major's eyes narrowed and his brows furrowed. Ben threw out more bait, watching his opponent try to gage his measure, like a boxer - his cheap suit and scuffed city shoes worn particularly to mislead.

'Okay, Mr Everett,' the major interrupted with derisory emphasis, 'what's your price?'

Ben paused dramatically before he answered. 'My price, Major *Hunt?*' He savoured the moment, letting the major splutter, his face turning puce with anger and suspicion at the open use of his pseudonym.

Jane threw down the short ropes that had been used to tie her to the hatch and kicked them away petulantly. Even with the addition of the leather belt there was no way they would help her lower herself to the safety of the narrow wooden gallery.

She scratched the stinging rash the nettles had left, her ribs aching within the constraints of the corset, so she tugged at the laces to loosen them. She couldn't be defeated now. The taste of escape was burning too fiercely, too close, to turn back. She reached behind her and pulled at the cross lacing. The afternoon breeze carried the fresh woodland scent and she inhaled deeply as her ribcage relaxed.

Then the idea came to her like a bolt. She wrenched madly at the horsehair garment until it fell free from her body. She laid it out flat on the wooden slats; the continuous lace was at least three yards long and the steel-boned panels added another eighteen inches to its length. If she could loop it over the supports intended for the rope ladder, it might be possible to lower herself to the platform...

With renewed optimism Jane crawled towards the opening, her hands shaking with excitement as she anchored her makeshift means of escape.

She held her breath and lowered her weight through the hatch. The corset stretched and creaked alarmingly, but she entwined her wrists around the thin cord and hung, panting, her legs swinging in the air as she dangled. There was nothing for it but a quick descent, and if she fell she prayed she'd land on the narrow gallery, and that it would support the sudden impact of her weight.

She must have lowered herself over half the distance before her hands began to slip. She held on for as long as she could before the laces slithered through her grip, then dropped and thankfully landed on the wooden balcony, just feet away from the top of the spiral staircase. A few feet to the left and she would have fallen through the gaping well of the tower. She shuddered at the consequences of that.

Jane ignored the blood that trickled from her grazed knees and descended as swiftly as she dared. Her feet slipped on the stone steps and her muscles tensed with the effort, and it was only when she reached the bottom and joyfully burst out into the light and warmth of the clearing that she considered her nakedness. But modesty was not going to prevent her now. Her recent trials had inured her to that, at least, and she would deal with it when the time came.

The chestnut pricked his ears forward in welcome, and she buried her head in the silky softness of his neck, filling her nostrils with his sweet, comforting smell.

The woods seemed thicker than ever. The afternoon sun was fading and little light penetrated its dense canopy. The chestnut stumbled on the unbeaten path and the low trees snatched at Jane's nakedness. But still she urged the horse forward, murmuring her encouragement, to bolster her own spirits as much as his.

She tried to formulate a plan. If she could just find a barn, and perhaps a sack or something to cover herself with. If she could even find a telephone... but who would she ring? Even as her mind raced she tried to imagine how she would explain the time of her disappearance, but she banished such thoughts from her mind when she reached the edge of the woods. For now her problems were more immediate.

She turned right and headed up the hill, just as the chestnut laid its ears back as if sensing danger. Fairly soon a foul chemical stench filled her nostrils, making her want to retch. At least she knew she was going in the right direction.

From the brow of the hill the wasteland of black craters stretched out ominously. She reined the chestnut in, considering her options, then heard the low hum before she saw the traffic - cars and lorries like toys in the distance, flowing freely, busy people living their ordinary lives. At last she was so close to rejoicing in freedom.

As she galloped on through the bleak, deserted landscape, she began to realise how much she'd changed since the night she visited Ms Brentwood at her Victorian villa. How easy would it be to go back? Had she changed too much? Had she understood too much about the links between pain and pleasure, danger and desire? She tried to chase such thoughts from her mind, avoiding the real question: how much of what she'd learned had she come to enjoy... maybe even to need?

Clouds had formed and the light was dimming by the time Ben was driven away from Hunt Hall. A good day's work, he told himself. It seemed that on top of everything else the Ruskin Club were involved in international art theft. But the major's reaction to his pseudonym was revealing. Ben had kept him dangling for a while, watching the veins in his neck pulse and swell. Then he'd mentioned his old friend, Gina Bent. He was bluffing, but it rattled the major considerably. He couldn't wait to be rid of him, but he couldn't resist the sniff of a stolen painting, either.

They eventually made arrangements to view it in London the following week. Slowly but surely, with what he'd learned at Lord Waterhouse's riverside penthouse, Ben was building the background to a story with enough strands to bring down the Government and most of the British Establishment.

They had turned out of the long drive onto a narrow lane when they were overtaken by a battered Land Rover. It squeezed alongside them and the passenger opened his window.

'Runaway!' he shouted against the rushing wind. 'It's the new one! Escaped from the folly!' His rough, country accent was charged like a huntsman caught in the thrill of the chase. Ben's driver nodded his acknowledgement and glanced nervously in his rear mirror to assess his reaction.

Jane was within minutes of freedom when they caught up with her. She had tethered the chestnut to a rusty caravan used by the site workers and was inside, rummaging through bundles of greasy overalls, when she heard the vehicle pull up outside. She froze as heavy boots came closer, sucking at the sticky mud. The chestnut whinnied a warning but it was too late. She was trapped, so she hunched into a ball and awaited her inevitable discovery.

The head groom and the buck-toothed youth were her captors. The youth carried her over his shoulder, like a fallen deer, and slung her roughly into the back of the open-topped Land Rover. He tied her feet and ankles together while the older man mounted the chestnut. Thoughts of escape were a shattered dream as she lay bumping painfully against the dirty metal floor, while the vehicle careered down the narrow lane back towards the Hall.

At last they slowed and she was able to get herself into a sitting position.

'We got her!' the boy called out exultantly.

Jane's eyes widened in horror and she ducked down out of sight when she saw the occupant of the car, his hand raised in acknowledgement.

Ben Handford? What was he doing there? The phone call to the major? Could he be part of the conspiracy too? Had he known all along? After all, it was him who encouraged her in the first place. In spite of her misery her mind was working frantically, piecing together all that had happened to her. Whatever was to be her fate they wouldn't beat her, and if she had to complete her training, so be it. She'd show Ben Handford. If the Ruskin Club fulfilled their promise she wouldn't need him or his tacky job. Her ambition burned in that moment, as brightly and blindly as it had in the attic of her Yorkshire bedroom.

CHAPTER TWELVE

Jane's Banishment

Despite her nakedness and dishevelled appearance, Jane displayed herself proudly at the major's command. She met the fury in his eyes with a boldness of her own. A fire burned in the open grate and the flames lit the blemishes on her pale skin.

'You have proved your resourcefulness,' the major hissed, and she smelt the sourness of his breath on her cheek. 'Nevertheless, I am disappointed in you. You showed particular promise.' He gripped her hair, spitefully twisting it in his fist, and pulled her face to his. 'You will pay for your betrayal.'

Jane flinched as he tugged cruelly at her scalp, straining her onto her toes. 'Take her to the stables. The men can have her tonight, and tomorrow I want her out of here. She's caused enough trouble.' He kept his eyes fixed on Jane while he addressed the groom, his voice cold with anger and suspicion. His words sent an icy chill through her and it took all her resolve not to beg for mercy as the groom led her away.

The cobbles dug painfully into her bare feet. The groom held one arm high behind her back and frogmarched her out into the chilly night air, and her courage ebbed when he lifted her over his shoulder and set off up the track leading to the hay barn. He must have felt her heart beating against his back as she recalled the events that took place there on her first day at Hunt Hall.

Once inside the groom wasted no time in attaching her wrists to the pulley, but when he grabbed her ankles to secure them too she wriggled and thrashed in futile protestation. But he was not interested in her compliance, grunting to himself as he completed his task. He slapped her bottom dismissively before he left her alone.

Jane hung in the darkness, trussed, alert to every element in the night air. The pulley creaked as she tried to shift her position to relieve the wrenching in her arms and thighs. She must have been crazy to think she could outwit them. The image of Ben Handford kept rearing into her vision. If she had escaped it seems it would have done her little good. She didn't know who to trust any longer.

The clanking of crates and loud, uncouth voices drifted along the track. Jane's flesh crept and her mouth was dry as they came closer, the beam of their torches darting about in the darkness. She screwed her eyes tightly shut as the men entered the barn, but she couldn't ignore the crude comments as they surveyed their quarry, and when they cracked open their beers and toasted their fortune, Jane heard the female giggle above their deeper tones. Her heart plunged. The statuesque redhead, who the men addressed as Ruby, had been included in the party.

And she was the first to shake a bottle and hold it under Jane's vagina, aiming the foamy liquid up into her, giggling at Jane's attempts to avoid the frothing jets. They used her as a plaything, shining their torches on her, swinging her body like a pendulum until her head swam with dizziness. Perhaps there were eight or ten of them, Jane couldn't tell as they splashed the beer over her, wiping it away with their calloused hands, groping her breasts and bottom and thighs. All the time they swigged from their bottles, lubricated inhibitions turning them into a pack of hungry animals. Then at last they cut her down.

She lay for a few minutes on the barn floor while they nudged her with their boots and settled themselves on hay bales. Two of them fastened leather cuffs to her wrists with a short chain reaching to her knees. The redhead clipped a collar and leash around her throat and pulled the buckle tight. She took great delight in her role, dragging Jane amongst the group. The cuffs and chains made it impossible for Jane to do anything but remain on her hands and knees like a shackled bitch, and that's how they treated her. They ran hands crudely over her body and reached down to maul her breasts, and the more she vainly struggled to avoid the foul molestation, the more they whooped with laughter and the more intense they became.

When they tired of tormenting her and began on a second crate of beer, they slit the twine on a fresh bale and kicked the straw out to create a makeshift bed. Jane resisted when Ruby tried to drag her to it, but a forceful slap across her buttocks from one of the men propelled her forward. Ruby rolled her over onto her back and lowered herself, spreading her toned legs on either side of Jane's upturned face. She wriggled her hips seductively, raising herself on her elbows and knees and tossed back her mane of red hair. Jane was compelled to look up at the ripe, plump lips shimmering in the torchlight, the hair shaved away so that the pink interior was revealed.

The men gathered round in a circle, and when Ruby was satisfied that her audience had admired her thoroughly, she lowered herself onto Jane's face, grinding her hips while Jane gasped for breath, struggling to be free of the moist pungency.

Jane was horrified by the taunting jeers of the unruly men, their booted legs encroaching, closing around her, and the writhing redhead squatting on her mouth.

'Be quiet, you lot.' The head groom's voice sliced through the mayhem. The men fell silent at once, and Ruby lifted herself just enough for Jane to take in a full breath. 'Line up, and remember, she's a two disc now. Ruby can take care of her mouth.'

Jane cried silently to herself, all vestiges of her remaining courage rushing from her, understanding their intentions at once.

Ruby pulled back her shoulders, her full breasts heaving, the dark nipples taut above her corset. Her eyes shone in the torchlight, as green as a cat's, ablaze with cruel anticipation.

The scuffling of the men's boots as they took up their positions was the only sound breaking the eerie silence. Ruby took Jane's nipples between her fingers and closed them like pincers. Jane gasped as she stretched the tender buds to their extremities, only releasing her grip when Jane started to lap tentatively between her thighs. Until that moment Jane's only experience of performing such intimacy had been the night when Ms Brentwood visited her at the doctor's. But that was different. There had been an element of compliance on her part, although perhaps she had not been fully aware of it at the time. And there had been no threat of what was to follow, or a crude audience to judge her.

She licked and lapped, her tongue finding the hard nub of Ruby's clitoris. She concentrated on it, feeling the heat against her face as the other woman's passion welled, and when she drew back for a moment Ruby's eyes were glazed with needy desire, her face flushed and burning. Jane buried her face again and jabbed her tongue at the swollen bud, working fervently as it pulsed and swelled. But if she thought her zeal would distract the men and earn her a reprieve, she was wrong.

They held her knees wide, and when they pressed her arms to the floor the cuffs and chains raised her hips so that both her sex and her anus were entirely vulnerable.

She lost count of the times she was screwed, their ejaculations filling her vagina and rectum. From time to time they threw a bucket of freezing water over her, cruelly reviving her to take more punishment. They turned her several times, but whatever her position she was forced to drink the juices from the rampant redhead while they penetrated her. Her torment continued until the full moon lit the barn - until she no longer knew what was happening, her face and hair soaked with her own sweat and Ruby's juices.

'I don't know what else you done to upset the major, but he's certainly in a hurry to get you out of here.' The buck-toothed youth pulled her to her feet. The cuffs had been removed but the collar was still attached around her neck, the leash clipped to the ring on the wall of the loosebox. As the dawn rose one of the men had carried her there from the barn, cradled in his hefty arms, close to unconsciousness.

The youth unclipped the leash, threw a rough linen shift over Jane's head and tied her wrists loosely but firmly behind her back. An engine ticked over in the yard.

The youth tugged urgently on the leash and she felt every bruise and ache as she was led from the stable.

'Get her in the back,' the major growled. He stood by the muddy Land Rover, his face tight with anger as the youth lifted her unceremoniously into the rear of the vehicle. She slumped in a heap on the dirty metal floor, tears glistening on her face as the doors slammed.

The vehicle shifted when the major climbed heavily into the driver's seat. 'Hand me the leash,' he instructed the youth, and when it was passed through the sliding partition that separated the driver's cab from the back section he clipped it to the steering wheel. He gave Jane just enough slack to half-lie, half kneel before he rammed the vehicle into gear and drove off at speed, across the uneven cobblestones.

Jane bumped painfully from side to side as the major sped along the country lanes. The thin cotton shift was little protection from the chilly morning wind that blew through the canvas roof of the vehicle. She shivered with cold and fear. Where was he taking her? Was it just her attempt to escape that had angered him so much?

They drove for several hours, the lanes replaced by a motorway and then by the grubby, crowded housing on the outskirts of a city. The bumping motion of the vehicle and the stench of the farmyard that filled her musty, windowless compartment made her nauseous. The traffic roared past them and the major swore when he was forced to break suddenly, tossing her around like a rag doll, the collar biting into her throat.

Her knees and elbows were red and sore as she tried to raise herself into a position that gave some sort of relief. She caught a glimpse of a river reflected on the windscreen, warehouses on the far side, people strolling in the sunshine. The reality of her own ignominy welled within her and she longed to wipe away the tears that wetted her cheeks, but the bonds around her wrists prevented her.

The chimes of Big Ben reverberated, jangling Jane's fractured nerves with their proximity. Nevertheless, she counted them. It was still only nine o'clock. Her heartbeat increased and beads of sweat broke out on her brow.

When the major swung the Land Rover south, across Westminster Bridge, she felt sure they were approaching the end of their journey, and she was proved correct when he steered the Land Rover down a sloping ramp and punched a code into a security machine. Jane's angst built as a vast metal grill rose to allow them entry and the interior of the vehicle was plunged into darkness. When the major reversed the Land Rover into a parking space she curled into a ball on its metal floor, shaking with fear.

Jane lay limply in his arms as he carried her a short distance to a goods lift. They would have made a strange sight, him in his tweed riding jacket and breeches, and the dishevelled girl dressed in nothing but a thin cotton shift, but no one challenged them. As the mechanism lurched into action Jane kept her eyes tightly shut, her cheek pressed against the major's chest, listening to his low, steady breaths as they rose towards their destination.

She forced herself to look when the bright light penetrated her eyelids. The morning sun splintered on the glass walls, blinding her momentarily. The major's riding boots resounded on the marble flooring as he strode across its expanse, and dropped her onto an enormous white leather sofa. He pulled a bone-handled hunting knife from his breast pocket and used it to cut the ropes around her wrists. She froze when he turned her on her back and held the blade close to her throat, his eyes sunken into his fleshy face. She flinched as he cut into the neck of her cotton shift and held her breath as he ran the knife down, slitting the material apart, exposing her breasts, the tip of the knife grazing her stomach, slicing down between her thighs until the garment fell open, exposing her nakedness once again.

'Tell me what you know about John Everett,' he demanded. Jane stared up at him blankly. He asked her again, unbuckling his leather belt as he spoke.

Jane's mind raced in confusion. Everett? She didn't know anyone called Everett. She shook her head desperately, too petrified to speak, her breasts rising and falling, the nipples crimped with panic.

'Very well, perhaps I need to jog your memory. Turn over.'

Jane quaked with terror. None of the beatings she'd received so far had been delivered with such menace. 'Turn over!' His lips curled in an ugly snarl and his normally florid cheeks were drawn and pale. Jane rolled onto her front. 'Pull up your shift.' The thin material clung to the backs of her thighs as she fumbled for the hem, gathering it up in her trembling fingers, exposing her naked thighs, taut with apprehension.

She heard his breathing shorten when she drew the hem over the swell of her buttocks, and held it around her waist. The soft leather of the sofa creaked under the weight of his knee as he knelt beside her. She lay meekly, beyond resistance when he took her wrists and pinned them above her head. The flash of his leather belt, doubled in his hand, caught the sunlight that filtered through the vast area of glass. 'Open your legs.' She moved her thighs apart, and tried to prepare herself for the punishment.

She heard the hiss of the belt as it swept through the air. The major's aim was perfect, and the first blow landed across her buttocks and exploded in a shock of pain. She had no time to recover before the belt cracked down across her thighs. The ferocity of the impact made her body arch and rear, but the major's powerful grip around her wrists prevented any avoidance of her fate. The burn spread quickly across her punished flesh, much deeper into her consciousness. The next stroke sliced through the air and landed on her left buttock, and she sighed a long, low sob into the leather sofa. She heard the next few blows echo around her, as if they came from somewhere else. She stopped writhing to evade his strikes and lost count of their number. Her whole world seemed to fall away until she was conscious of nothing but the steady, unrelenting pounding the major was inflicting. Each strike jerked her hips hard into the sofa, and she felt the wetness forming beneath her. All pride had evaporated and she no longer cared about its source. The shafts of pain were all she understood, concentrating on their intensity until they blurred and shifted, turned and seeped. The final strokes fell like fire, lighting her insides, desperate, ecstatic surges wrenching at her being.

95

'So is that punishment enough?' Jane's eyelids flickered open and she tried to raise herself onto her elbows. 'I'll ask you one last time. *John Everett?*'

She shook her head, her mouth slack and unable to form words, punished and satiated in equal proportion. She lay motionless and conquered, her buttocks and thighs burning while he surveyed her.

'All right, for now I must believe you,' he decided. 'That was a thorough thrashing that would elicit the truth from a more practiced woman.' Some of his anger had subsided. He pulled her to her feet and she felt the hardness under his breeches and the heat of his breath as she slumped against him.

He lifted her easily, and carried her to a large bed. She lay absolutely still while he eased himself into her, burying his hands in her hair. He took her gradually, pushing himself deep into her with slow, rhythmic motions, and despite her dislike of the man, her body began to sway and move with his. Unaware of her actions she raised her legs and wrapped them round the major's back. He held her fevered buttocks in his cupped hands, absorbing their heat while she rocked with his movement, taking him deeper, urging his orgasm from him.

He must have let her sleep for a while, and when she awoke he was standing over her.

'You'll stay here until Lord Waterhouse returns from his trip to continue with your training. You could do with some recuperation.'

Jane propped herself up on her elbows, and looked around in confusion. He leaned forward and tilted her chin so she was forced to look at him. 'It's a shame if you've brought us trouble, Jane. I would have enjoyed our rides together.' His voice was husky and his eyes had lost their hardness. He ran a hand down her throat and cupped a breast, squeezing it. 'And even don't think of escape this time. This place is a fortress.'

She heard the echo of the front door slam closed behind him and lay back on the bed. She closed her eyes, wriggling her scorched buttocks into the luxurious fur covering and fell back into the deepest sleep.

When Jane awoke it was dark. Where was she? She struggled off the bed, attracted by the city lights that shone through the glass. As she crossed the spacious acres of white marble her astonishment built. The space contained almost nothing but the two long white sofas, one of which had been the sight of her recent beating. The only other substantial piece of furniture was a huge mahogany coffee table that sat between them.

From the window Jane looked down at the night traffic, crisscrossing the bridges and Big Ben, standing tall beside the river. Her mind was still groggy and her body ached as she tried to assemble her thoughts. She turned back to the apartment and began to explore. To Jane it seemed more like a futuristic airport lounge than a home. Smoked glass partitions divided the space, but try as she did they would not move, and the solid front door was similarly unyielding.

Apart from the capacious central area she could only find access to a small galley kitchen, the bedroom and the luxurious bathroom beyond. The splendour of the large bath and gleaming fixtures made her draw back. She turned the chrome lever, and instantly warm jets cascaded down from the ceiling. She leapt aside in alarm, before she saw the drain in the centre of the floor carrying the water away. She stepped into the steamy flow of water, and let it soothe and calm her weary body, lifting her face, drenching herself, using the scented soaps between her thighs and over her reddened buttocks. She stayed there for a long time, before she returned to the bed to sleep again.

Ben had spent most of the afternoon in Sadie's viewing booth, drinking her wine and watching an eclectic procession of her clients. Behind the glass panel Sadie had a young woman, her hair cut short, like a boy, doubled over a padded leather stool. Her wrists and ankles were tied to the struts and she was whimpering softly.

Ben needed a diversion and Lucy was away in Gstaad, enjoying the last week of the ski season with her wealthy sister-in-law. He needed to forget Jane Carter's desperate face, staring at him from the back of the Land Rover. He'd tried hard to convince himself he was mistaken, but in his heart he knew he wasn't. He should have told the driver, Paul, to stop the car immediately.

Why hadn't he?

He wiped the beads of sweat from his brow. Because he wanted to break the story in all its glory, that's why. This was his pension and he wasn't going to have it spoiled for anyone - not even Jane Carter. If she'd survived over two weeks she could handle another ten days... surely? After all, whatever was happening to her couldn't be as bad as the chastisements Sadie's clients endured - and paid for, he reassured himself.

A tall woman, dressed in an expensive suit, was choosing an implement from the array that adorned the walls of Sadie's chamber. She purported to be the guardian of the girl attached to the stool, and Ben shifted in his seat when she selected a double-ended dildo of extreme proportions.

Sadie presented her with a pair if thin latex gloves, which she smoothed onto her elegantly manicured hands, before she approached the girl. Sadie moved beside the stool. She held a phial of warm oil, from which she poured, letting its contents trickle down between the girl's buttocks, lubricating the path of the dildo.

The girl's tearful eyes opened wide as she felt both ends of the implement nudging against her. Ben was mesmerised by his perfect view of the trio gathered around the stool. The woman's haughty expression was replaced by an intense frown of concentration, her lips parted, the tip of her tongue poking out. The girl's face was contorted and the colour rose in her pale cheeks as she tried to tolerate the duel invasion. And Sadie, as pretty and cool as ever, helpfully held apart the girl's buttocks to afford her client easier entry.

Ben watched as the dildo sank deep. The girl's slim body didn't look capable of absorbing its immensity, but she writhed as much as her position would allow, until both ends had disappeared. Her eyes were watery pools and her cheeks were flushed when the woman began to work the dildo in and out of both channels.

Ben downed the last of the bottle and smiled, exonerating himself from guilt. He was in no doubt that the girl was finding pleasure in her humiliation. Jane Carter was okay. She could look after herself. As the girl cried out in ecstasy and the woman smiled with satisfaction he convinced himself that he was right.

Jane didn't know how long she was alone in the strange, exotic apartment. She slept for long periods and woke to find herself in darkness or with light streaming through the panes of glass. At first her dreams were punctuated with the faces of her seducers and she woke, wet with sweat, her heart pounding.

She would rise and ate meagrely from the supplies she found in the small kitchen, but drink thirstily, driven by an instinctive desire to flush her body clean.

She stood for hours under the shower, and afterwards she would inspect her body, twisting and turning in front of the mirror. After a while the blemishes faded and her dreams became filled with more sensual memories. She dreamt of Sei and imagined her cradled in her arms, as she was on their last night together. One night it was Paul who came to her in a dream and she woke, wondering if she would see either of them again.

During the day she gazed out at the view - Big Ben and the Houses of Parliament with the miniscule figures milling on its waterfront terrace. Sometimes her loneliness overwhelmed her and at others she revelled in her solitude. Gradually she began to reflect on her captivity since that night at the abandoned theatre and slowly she began to put it into perspective.

Jane was watching the lights dancing on the water, her breasts pressed against the cool glass, when she heard the sounds. She spun round, her hands flying to cover her nakedness, darting for cover behind one of the leather sofas. Crouching low she saw the three women enter the apartment and dump a heap of fur coats and expensive luggage unceremoniously onto the pristine marble floor.

'Open the champagne, Lucy.' Jane crouched lower as the click of high heels approached, and one of the women draped herself onto the leather sofa, just feet away. 'I need a drink. Gstaad's a disaster without snow,' she drawled in an American accent.

'I love this view!' another of them said, as she crossed over to the window. A cork popped and Jane froze as they whooped excitedly. Her discovery could only be a matter of time.

Jane deduced from their conversation that they had abandoned their trip due to the early thaw. Ellie, the bossy American, seemed to own the apartment, so she must be Lord Waterhouse's wife. And Lucy, who was serving the champagne, appeared to be his sister. '*I fear they don't share our subtle artistry.*' Jane recalled his lordship's scornful comment to the major, on the subject of his wife and sister, with a shudder. If only she could cover herself before she was exposed in front of the three fashionable and sophisticated females.

It was the third woman that revealed Jane's hiding place when she turned from admiring the view. 'Well, well,' she said, 'something your husband left behind, Ellie?'

The American sat up sharply and peered behind the sofa. Her perfectly plucked eyebrows arched at the sight of Jane, naked and unable to hide herself. Her exquisitely painted lips parted in a wicked smile. Even the acuteness of Jane's embarrassment could not prevent her admiring the raven-haired beauty who unwound her elegant limbs from the sofa.

'Looks like coming home early was an even better idea than we thought.' Ellie's voice was husky and her hand as cold and smooth as ice on Jane's chin when she raised her unexpected guest to her feet.

CHAPTER THIRTEEN

The Apartment

In the time she spent alone with the three, before Lord Waterhouse's return, Jane witnessed indulgence of unimaginable proportions. Once she had recovered from her initial embarrassment, the arrogance of her hostess made Jane's blood boil. The men and women she'd met during her captivity had never treated her with the cursory derision that Ellie employed. She hauled Jane onto her lap and held her there, apparently unfazed by finding a naked girl hiding in her apartment. She toyed with her nipples while she dictated her requirements to her sister-in-law.

Jane watched Lucy, a willowy girl, not much older than her, with flaxen hair and pale features. She moved athletically, a smile flickering on her lips, obeying with youthful insouciance. But there was nothing casual about the third woman's desire to please her hostess. Her name was Kate and she was small, with a rounded figure and dark hair that framed her face in a neat bob. She reminded Jane of the head girl at her school, eager to please, cool, efficient and precise.

'I guess you're something to do with the Ruskin Club, are you?' But Ellie didn't wait for Jane to answer before she launched into a derogatory tirade on her husband's absurd secret society. 'So English,' she scoffed. 'Just an excuse for organised corruption of repressed women. He thinks I don't know about it, but my kind of money buys spies in every quarter.'

Ellie drank deeply from the glass she'd been handed, allowing some of its contents to dribble between Jane's breasts. 'But hanging out with a cabinet minister does him no harm.'

Kate picked up immediately on Ellie's indiscretion. 'Who? Not his friend Anthony Hazleton, surely? He can't be involved in anything, can he? They say he's tipped to be prime minister.'

'Anyway, enough, I feel like a party. Send out for some fruit from Grassini's. I'm going to take a shower with my little friend.' Ellie swept from the room, beckoning for Jane to follow.

When they returned Lucy and Kate had transformed the sterile splendour of the apartment. The partitions Jane had been unable to move now stood open, revealing spacious areas, some for eating, some for sleeping and some for relaxing. Huge church candles mounted on wrought iron stands bathed the spaces in soft light. Music with an insistent melody and a low drumbeat drew her to one particular place, partly concealed by a magnificent carved screen. Behind it they had conjured up an Eastern palace, with plump floor cushions embroidered in earth-baked ochres, reds and oranges. In the centre a brass burner, set on a low wooden table, had been lit and steam rose from the heavy copper pan it supported. The rich, sweet smell of dark chocolate wafted from the surface and filled the air.

Lucy and Kate wore elegant silk dressing gowns. Kate held out a similar one for Ellie to step into. Only Jane was left naked when the buzzer sounded.

Lucy answered the door and Jane caught a glimpse of the waiter, carrying an enormous silver platter piled high with exotic fruits and berries. Instantly her old inhibitions returned and she darted for cover behind the carved screen at the thought of being seen naked by the intruder from the ordinary world. But Ellie wasn't going to allow her a second hiding place. She took Jane's hand firmly and pulled her towards the cushions, pushing her down onto them just as the waiter reached their strange encampment. He set down the platter and the colour rose in her cheeks as she hugged her knees to her breasts, desperately trying to cover herself, but he had already seen enough to ignite his Latin blood. His golden skin glowed against the whiteness of his shirt and his deep black eyes simmered with passion.

'That'll be all, Alviso.' Ellie dismissed the handsome young man with a perfunctory wave and he backed away, lingering as long as he dared to take in the extraordinary scene. Although she didn't relish whatever game it was that Ellie had in mind, Jane breathed a sigh of relief when she heard Lucy close the front door behind him.

The smell of the bubbling chocolate pervaded the space, sickly-sweet and full of portent. Jane's stomach churned with unease as the women poured more wine. They handed her a glass and she drank from it deeply, letting the cool liquid soothe the dryness in her throat.

Lucy was the first to select a plump strawberry, kneeling to dip it into the copper pan. She twirled it until the chocolate coated the surface, before she popped it in her mouth. But instead of biting into it she held it between her teeth and crawled towards her sister-in-law. Ellie lay back languorously, her robe partly open to expose one perfect breast, the nipple hard and dark. Jane stayed hunched on the edge of a cushion, sipping her wine while Lucy transferred the strawberry from her mouth to Ellie's, who chewed it slowly, savouring it while the others watched like courtiers awaiting the approval of their queen. When she swallowed it Kate sipped some champagne and knelt over her friend, Ellie parted her lips and allowed Kate to dribble the foaming liquid into her mouth. Jane watched while they pandered to their spoiled hostess, feeding her delicious chocolate-coated fruit, washed down by the wine, all delivered by their servile mouths.

Ellie's robe gradually slipped open more, to expose her other breast and the smooth slope of her hips. The tension grew and Jane knew it wouldn't be long before they would demand that she be included. She accepted a second glass of champagne gratefully.

'Okay,' Ellie's voice was thick and satiated from her feast, 'enough.' She pulled open her robe completely and spread her legs, her tawny thighs shimmering in the candlelight, and stroked her stomach. 'But I'm not full yet.' She closed her eyes, a smile of expectation lingering on her sensuous mouth.

The music seemed to build and the drums pounded louder in Jane's head, as Kate selected more berries from the platter, taking great care in inspecting their size and quality. When happy she knelt between her friend's parted legs, and Jane stifled her gasp as Kate gently parted the damp lips and inserted the first berry. She watched transfixed as Kate pushed the berry deeper and picked up the next, and the next. Ellie rolled her head from side to side and moaned with pleasure. As the berries filled her and their juices ran down between her thighs Jane saw the inner pinkness, as ripe as the fruit being prised between the fleshy lips.

When Kate had wedged the last piece inside her she turned to Jane, her eyes ablaze with exhilaration. 'Maybe you would like something to eat?' She waved her hand theatrically over Ellie's reclining body. Perhaps it was the effect of the alcohol, or the hypnotic rhythm of the drums and pipes that made Jane abandon her inhibitions so easily, and without coercion. Before she could stop herself she was buried between Ellie's thighs, breathing in the sweet scent of the fruit, her tongue searching, teasing out each piece that Kate had so meticulously inserted, the flavours delicious, luring her back for more. She felt Ellie's muscles starting to contract around her tongue as her orgasm flowed out of her with raw, uninhibited intensity.

'I'll admit they teach you well at the Ruskin Club,' Ellie eventually sighed. 'We must return the complement.' Her blue eyes caught the candlelight as she looked at Jane's juice-coated face and let her gaze drift down to her breasts, the nipples stiff. Jane blushed at the frankness of her stare, but was unable to quell the fluttering in her stomach. 'Come here.' Ellie drew Jane onto her lap and turned her so she was seated between her parted thighs. She reached round and cupped Jane's breasts, squeezing their plumpness, pinching the stiff nipples. Jane closed her eyes and let her head nestle against Ellie's naked shoulder, breathing in her heady perfume.

She felt the heat and opened her eyes, to find Kate kneeling in front of her, a cake syringe filled with melted chocolate poised over her breasts. 'Keep still,' Kate warned, squeezing the syringe for a second time. Jane struggled to avoid the oozing flow but Ellie held her breasts, hugging her so that escape was impossible. She gasped each time the hot liquid met the coolness of her skin but Ellie squeezed her breasts harder, keeping them taut and swollen. Jane held her breath and tried to tolerate the insistent heat as Kate encased each nipple with the chocolate, pausing to let it set before she applied another layer.

The music was building to a climax when Kate beckoned Lucy forward. She knelt in front of them, her pale blue eyes wide with lust while Ellie offered her Jane's chocolate-coated nipple, as if it was a delicate morsel. Lucy leaned forward, her gown falling open to reveal her pert breasts, and accepted the gift her sister-in-law offered.

The sensations Lucy triggered as she feasted on the sweet coating were too much for Jane. Ellie's perfect breasts pressed against her back and Jane moaned when a hand crept down to touch the bud of her clitoris. When her head fell back tingling champagne, delivered from Kate's lips, rewarded her. She shivered with undisguised pleasure as Lucy teased each fleshy nub in turn, licking away the coating to expose the flesh beneath, and Ellie's fingers eased back and forth between her thighs. She was powerless to defend herself from the treatment she was receiving from the three women, and her orgasm was unstoppable, flooding her in long, flowing surges. She arched her back and heard the sound of her own cries before she fell into a well of unconscious bliss.

The rest of the night descended into an orgy of sensual indulgence. They discarded their robes, and with them their boundaries. The wine flowed and the music pounded on, driving the frenzied lovemaking of the four women, their limbs entwined, writhing as one.

'Miss Carter!' Ms Brentwood's voice cut through Jane's dreams, jerking her awake. Her head throbbed and her vision was blurred but she couldn't mistake the tall figure looming over her. She attempted to scramble to her feet but slipped on the residue of the previous night's indulgence. She looked around wildly. Where were Ellie, Kate and Lucy? There was no sign of them.

As if she read her thoughts, Ms Brentwood strode through the apartment, searching for further perpetrators of the mayhem. Jane trembled with cold and fear, unable to hide her dishevelled nakedness. For all she'd experienced during recent weeks, the presence of Ms Brentwood reduced her to the naïve country girl she'd been before she fell into the clutches of the Ruskin Club.

'You are a disgrace.' Ms Brentwood spoke sharply and Jane bit her lip to stop the tears that threatened. 'Yet again you have caused trouble. It seems you've learned little from your time with us, except how to indulge yourself.' Ms Brentwood indicated the chaos with a sweep of her hand, and although Jane knew she wasn't really responsible for it all, guilt overwhelmed her. She couldn't deny she had become a willing and enthusiastic participant in the excesses of the previous night. 'Go and wash yourself. Then you can clear this up before Lord Waterhouse returns from the Isle of Man. And be quick, he's expected shortly.'

Jane soaped herself hurriedly under the shower, rinsing away the remnants of fruit and chocolate that clung to her hair and skin. She wrapped herself in a towel and padded back to find Ms Brentwood, who had removed her severe-fitted jacket and was fastening the tapes of a starched white apron around the defined contours of her waist.

'Over here,' she snapped, producing a tape measure from her apron pocket. 'You have further defied my rules by removing your corset.' She snatched the towel from Jane's grasp and proceeded to measure her, just as she had done that first afternoon in the dining room of her Victorian villa. 'As I suspected,' her voice was edged with triumph, 'the improvement is not nearly great enough. You will be kept tightly laced until you are delivered to Sir John. I only hope that three days is enough to achieve the proportions he demands.'

Jane miserably placed her palms at shoulder level on the glass window, while Ms Brentwood prepared the corset. She gazed out at the view in front of her, and tried to compose herself. Soon enough she felt the stiff cotton garment start to hug her torso. She breathed in as Ms Brentwood tugged harder on the laces. The garment was cut high across her breasts and they swelled above it, her nipples crushed beneath its strictures. Ms Brentwood grunted softly as her exertions increased. The colour rose through Jane's body and her eyes began to widen as she held her breath, but still the laces tightened more. Ms Brentwood passed the tape measure around her for a second time, and continued, not yet satisfied by the reduction. By the time the torture stopped Jane was so tightly bound that she thought she'd faint. Her ribs ached as never before.

'Now fetch the cleaning equipment from the kitchen and get to work.' Jane lowered her arms and stumbled across the expanse of marble floor. Her head spun as she ran water into the bucket and found some soap and rags. It was terrible to be trussed up again, for the first time since she had removed the horsehair corset to aid her escape from the tower.

'Down on your hands and knees,' Ms Brentwood commanded, and Jane sank awkwardly to the hard marble, splashing some water from the bucket as she did so. 'You clumsy girl!' Jane hadn't seen the cane behind her back, but she heard the swish and felt its bite as Ms Brentwood swiped it across her bare buttocks. 'Now get to work.'

Her tears welled and dripped unchecked onto the floor as she scrubbed as vigorously as she could, but as diligent as she was she struggled to satisfy the exacting standards demanded of her, and Ms Brentwood admonished her continuously. She gasped and panted, dreading the next hiss of the thin cane whipping through the air, wincing with pain when it made contact with her flesh. With every move her breasts were forced against the metal stays. But still she strove, scrubbing and mopping and bearing the lines of fire that crossed her buttocks. Ms Brentwood showed no mercy, using the cane adeptly, but at last she lowered the implement and declared the task complete.

Having completed her tasks Jane was left standing, displayed as she'd been taught, in the centre of the main room with her back to the front door, and that's the sight that welcomed Lord Waterhouse.

'Ms Brentwood, what are you doing here?' he asked, clearly surprised by the sight that greeted him.

'I'm afraid Sir John had to send for me,' she explained. 'He suspected there were some inappropriate activities taking place in your absence, and I'm afraid he was proved correct. As you see, I have already administered some punishment for it.' Ms Brentwood circled Jane, stroking her capable hands over her starched apron, her knowing eyes darting between her and Lord Waterhouse.

His brows were furrowed in perplexed anger when he moved into Jane's vision. The tension in the room was palpable. Surely he must know it was his wife that instigated it all? Should Jane speak out and defend herself? There was a warning menace in his narrowed eyes and pursed lips that kept her silent.

'Well, Ms Brentwood, I'm pleased you're here; I'd like you to see my new purchases.' He seemed anxious to curtail any further surmising on the night's activities. 'Ah, Paul, put the package down here.' Jane heard the driver's footsteps and her heart plunged. Why did she hate him witnessing her humiliation, when she'd learned to tolerate the presence of others? 'And you, Miss Carter, turn around.'

Jane teetered awkwardly, keeping her hands locked behind her neck as Paul set a wooden box, over five feet in length, onto the mahogany coffee table between the two white leather sofas. His deep brown eyes caught hers, before she lowered her head to avoid his gaze. Her breasts heaved as she bit back her shame.

His lordship was breaking open the seals on the box and Ms Brentwood perched on the edge of a sofa to watch him. The way she held her back stiffly and spread her apron, decorously over her knees, was in sharp contrast to how Ellie had sprawled back into the luxurious leather the previous night.

'When I was at school my housemaster was an expert in the application of the Harrow spray birch,' Waterhouse went on. 'It was he who introduced me to the only Manx craftsman remaining since the abolition of corporal punishment on the island, in the sixties.' He was warming to his subject, discarding the straw packaging carelessly. 'He made birches for none other than the chief constable of the Douglas police, and he's made these up for me, in time for our May Day celebrations. I think they will meet with Sir John's approval, don't you, Ms Brentwood?'

Jane almost overbalanced when he produced the first of his purchases with a flourish. He held it high in the air and swished it back and forth. 'A genuine Manx birch, made in the Isle of Man!' Even Ms Brentwood shifted uncomfortably at the potential of the implement.

'It certainly looks capable of inflicting a very sound birching.' Jane detected a note of disapproval in Ms Brentwood's response.

'Indeed. The twigs must be soaked in water for several hours to have their full effect.' He dug into the box again, and produced several more of the frightful instruments. Each one consisted of three or four stout birch rods, over a yard long and as thick as a man's finger. The rods were lashed together with strips of bark to form a handle, and the rest of their vicious prongs tapered away and spread out at the tip. 'He only uses the finest birch and waits for it to mature to the point where it is thick enough to create the necessary weight, but still flexible.' He handed one to Ms Brentwood, and she fingered the rough handle before she tested it gingerly, flicking her wrist, assessing its qualities.

'Perhaps you would assist me in soaking them, Ms Brentwood.' He shot Jane a meaningful glance as he spoke. Ms Brentwood concurred and followed him, her face fixed in an enigmatic grimace.

Jane was left alone with Paul. Hesitantly she lowered her aching arms and folded a hand across her breasts with absurd coyness. She closed her legs too. He

104

didn't look at her directly and busied himself clearing away the straw packaging.

'I don't think I would be able to...' She spoke falteringly, terrified by the prospect of what might happen to her when the birch was soaked for a sufficient time. She remembered the sting of the single twigs the major had used to chase her up the narrow staircase of the tower. The multiple and much heavier branches would be intolerable.

'You'll be okay.' He glanced back to see that they were still alone. 'He won't dare use it on you.'

'How do you know?' Unconvinced she implored him for an answer, but it was too late. They both heard the footsteps returning, so Jane hastily raised her arms and parted her thighs, as was expected of her.

'That's all for now, Paul,' Waterhouse said. 'Wait downstairs in case you're needed.' Paul scooped up the empty box and obeyed his instructions with evident reluctance, and Jane's heart sank as he retreated.

'I need to wash and rest after my journey,' Lord Waterhouse said to Ms Brentwood, ignoring Jane. 'I'll leave you to deal with Miss Carter.'

When they were alone, Ms Brentwood produced a large leather valise and Jane shuddered at its familiarity. It was the same bag she'd been loaned on the night of the auction, and a large part of her discovery and downfall. Ms Brentwood settled herself on one of the sofas and beckoned Jane to her.

'Over my knee.' Ms Brentwood smoothed down the crisp white linen of her apron. 'Come along, I'm not going to hurt you,' she added firmly, when Jane hesitated.

'Yes, Ms Brentwood.' Jane frowned and lowered her arms.

The apron felt cool on her breasts as she lowered herself over Ms Brentwood's lap. She heard the low intake of breath as she exposed her bare thighs and the naked curves of her bottom. She felt the slow stroking as Ms Brentwood ran her fingers over the raised weals she had inflicted with her cane, and then soothed their heat with the flat of her palm.

'Relax, Jane.' Her voice was warm and coaxing, but Jane remained mistrustful, tense and unsure of her motives. The stroking continued, down her creamy thighs, massaging her tired muscles, gently kneading her buttocks. Jane breathed in the smell of freshly laundered linen, evoking memories of her childhood. How often she had stood, ironing Aunt Judith's crisp linen blouses, not daring to leave a crease for fear of earning her wrath. Steadily resistance left her, and she allowed herself to hang limp, accepting Ms Brentwood's caresses.

'Good girl. Now I need to apply some ointments to prepare you for your final days. It's for your own good.' She produced a series of bottles and jars, which she set out on the table in front of her. Jane regarded them with apprehension from the corner of her eye, but stayed still.

Ms Brentwood must have worked on her bottom for over an hour, leaving Jane both exhilarated and exhausted in equal proportions. Some of the potions she applied made her skin burn, the heat penetrating deep. The next would be cold, and Ms Brentwood held her still until she adjusted to the contrast. She alternated the treatments until Jane's mind confused the sensations. She seemed as absorbed in administering the treatments as Jane was in receiving them, and Jane began to forget the threat of the birch and longed for the healing therapy to continue.

Ms Brentwood prepared to leave as soon as Lord Waterhouse returned from his rest, wearing a silk dressing gown. 'I have an appointment at five o'clock,' she said, folding her apron into the leather valise.

'Paul will drive you,' he told her.

'Thank you,' she accepted. 'I will return tomorrow to check her lacings and apply more therapy. And I should remind you that Sir John demands that all the May Day participants to be in unmarked condition,' she added with an unmistakable note of warning, before she let herself out of the apartment.

Lord Waterhouse paced the floor, his fists clenched, attempting to control his irritation. Jane watched him from the sofa where Ms Brentwood had left her and desperately tried to assemble her thoughts. From her limited knowledge of men of his kind, they were not used to being thwarted in their actions, and certainly not by a woman. But it was clear, even to Jane, that it was Sir John's displeasure that concerned him.

'Get up,' he rounded on her. 'Don't imagine she's earned you a reprieve,' he hissed acidly as Jane rose. 'Follow me.' He strode in the direction of the main bedroom and Jane trailed helplessly in his wake.

He had already lowered a pulley from the ceiling in the centre of the room, and Jane recoiled with dread when she saw the bar that hung from its end. Her gaze was only distracted from the fearful sight when a portion of the wall glided open. Since she'd been there she hadn't known of the secret compartments, and she stared at them incredulously as their contents were revealed. He was behind her, his fingers closed on her arms, and propelled her to the bed. She fought for breath when he threw her down on her front and pressed her into the soft fur.

'Was my wife here last night?' he demanded, and the first slap across her buttocks came as she tried to answer. The next blows came fast and she writhed, feeling the heat as he imprinted his palm alternately on each cheek.

'Stop, please... I'll tell you...' she begged as coherently as she could, but he continued until she sobbed openly. When he released her he asked again and she nodded, wiping her tears with the back of her hand.

'And my sister, too? And that prissy friend of theirs, Kate?' Jane confirmed what she was sure he already knew. 'But you didn't tell Ms Brentwood?' She shook her head and the panic raced through her as he fastened a length of rope to each wrist and hauled her to her knees. Perhaps she'd been foolish not to speak out. She would never fathom the strange rules and hierarchy that existed in the Ruskin Club.

He lifted her easily to where he'd prepared the pulley. He snapped her wrists into the clamps of the bar, her arms held wide apart. His gown fell open, so that his naked body brushed against her as he worked. She turned her head away as she felt his arousal swelling against her.

He hoisted her off the floor by operating the pulley remotely from a touch-pad at the head of the bed. Her legs flailed in the air but the more she struggled, the more her arms wrenched at their fastenings. It only took a few minutes for her strength to be defeated and she hung limp, at his disposal. He opened her legs and shackled a metal stretcher between her ankles. She groaned, consumed with dread. Was he preparing to use the birch? Would he heed Ms Brentwood's warning?

Jane forced herself to watch him. At least for now he seemed temporarily distracted as his fingers moved over the display of instruments, deciding and selecting from the different compartments. His expression remained emotionless as he lifted and fingered each one, turning it, assessing its suitability. From her position, Jane could see the foreboding array of chains, whips and clamps.

'Some adornment, I think,' he mocked, steadying her by seizing one of her breasts, causing her to cry out with pain. When he released her it was only to hold the clamps in front of her face where she was forced to look at them. The diamond clusters that encrusted their surface sparkled in the light, but their dazzling beauty disguised their viciousness, as Jane soon discovered.

He prolonged the moment before he attached them, stretching each nipple to its extremity, a cruel smile twisting his face, watching her discomfort. He kept his eyes fixed on her as he let the clamps close around her nipples. With each one she gasped and held her breath while the stabbing bursts gripped her, and she waited until they faded slightly before exhaling shakily. She looked down at the diamonds encasing each nipple and the thin gold chain that joined them. They looked too beautiful for their purpose.

His lascivious gaze bored into her. The spreader kept her ankles apart, but not sufficiently for his next decoration, so he knelt between her thighs and adjusted the spreader until she thought she would split in two. She shuddered as he examined her and didn't hear him reach for the second set of clamps. He held them up, as before, for her view. They were about three inches long, with flat sides lined with rubber, so they gripped each lip when they closed on them. Through the centre of each there was a single screw, and Jane winced as he turned them until she was held open - entirely at his mercy.

He left her hanging there while he went to the bathroom, and when he returned she shrieked with undisguised alarm. He was brandishing the birch, droplets of water dripping from its tapered tips as he circled her. From his open gown sprouted his erect cock.

'They only used these on boys on the island.' He spoke with a malicious lilt and stroked the birch up over the back of Jane's widespread thighs. The muscles in her arms and legs burned with pain as the T-bar swung gently, but they were forgotten when he brought the birch up between her legs. The vicious implement dragged at the tender inner flesh, rendered entirely vulnerable by the metal clamps. She tried to contain her fear, sensing that her cries provoked more cruelty and certainly no clemency. Still he went on, his breathing becoming heavier, sometimes uttering low sighs of satisfaction when he felt her flinch and twist against the flexing wood.

At last he stopped, but only to move in front of her, to apply the same treatment to her breasts. The tips of the birch snagged the clamps on her nipples and she couldn't prevent herself crying out.

'So, shall I beat you or fuck you first?' He pressed the handle of the birch under her chin. Jane's heart raced and she shook her head - it seemed Paul was wrong, and the man knew no boundaries. 'Answer me,' he demanded. The tears rolled down Jane's cheeks as he lifted the birch high in the air and brought it crashing down onto the fur bedspread. Droplets of moisture showered as it landed with a fearful crack that filled the empty apartment.

He turned back to her, his eyes ablaze, and seized her chin in his fingers. 'So is it the birch first? I'm not frightened of marking you.'

'No, please,' Jane's mouth was as dry as bone but she had to answer him. 'You can... fuck me... first.' The colour rushed to her face as she forced the words from her lips. Nothing that she'd encountered so far compared to the potential brutality of the birch and she would do anything to delay its use. In fact, she doubted her ability to endure its viciousness, particularly in Lord Waterhouse's ferocious hands.

In seconds he had removed the stretcher, but he stood in front of her and held her legs to keep them apart. He tugged her and the bar lowered automatically, and she felt herself descending onto his standing erection, inevitably and unavoidably. The clamps that rolled back her lips provided no protection and she let out a sob of distress as he guided himself into her, inch by inch. She locked her thighs around his waist to relieve the burning in her shackled arms, but it only drew him deeper. When he was fully embedded he locked off the pulley.

He fucked her harder and more thoroughly than the major or any of the men in the barn on her last night at Hunt Hall. He took her with a cold precision, pounding his cock into her, inflamed by her cries, continuing until she softened and allowed him more. He took the gold chain that connected the diamond clamps between his teeth, so that with every movement her entrapped nipples stabbed with pain. Every fibre and muscle of Jane's body was tense and wracked with sensations as she tried to adapt to his ruthless pounding. At once all her focus shifted to the needs of her tiny bud and she ground her hips, throwing back her head, her mouth opening wide. She didn't care if he witnessed her abandon as she gasped through her orgasm, grinding her clitoris onto his hardness, seeking it out for her own pleasure. She felt his hot fluid erupting into her, and for a moment his strength was hers.

He chewed distractedly on the gold chain while he recovered, and Jane felt the tugging on her nipples but the pain had turned to a dull ache. Although she felt him sliding out of her, the clamps holding back her lips kept her strangely open.

As her mind cleared she remembered his threat - the sequence of his demands. The birch was lying across the bed, and all her former fears returned. At any minute he would be sufficiently revived to take it up, and she cringed as she recalled the brutality with which he had slammed it down on the fur cover.

The buzzer jerked him into life. He retied his robe and strode angrily from the bedroom. She heard Paul's voice on the intercom. 'A letter for you, your lordship, from Sir John.'

Her heart pounded and her mind raced. By the time he returned to the bedroom his face was white with fury as he read from the crested notepaper. He threw it down with disdain, and walked over to her. She flinched when he reached between her thighs, to where the clamps held her open. His fingers reached inside her, seeking their mingled juices, and she recoiled when he held them up.

'Lick it,' he said thickly. 'You may be spared the birch for now, so I must find other more ingenious methods to secure your obedience.' Jane opened her mouth meekly and lapped the palm of his hand, sucking like a kitten on the tips of his fingers, her first taste of a man's seed, sweetened with her own juices.

Ben had followed the car as it drove back along the Embankment. He'd watched Gina Bent climb out urgently, at the members' entrance. She hadn't changed much in the twenty years since he'd last seen her. The pieces of the story were now in place, and what a story it was. All he needed to do was to set up the final scene, and if his hunch was right this was his chance.

He saw the glass-sided lift in which he'd ridden with Lucy descending the outside of the building, and the dark figure of the chauffeur standing tall against the late afternoon sun. And Jane Carter? She'd soon be free, he convinced himself. The taste of revenge was too sweet, and too close.

CHAPTER FOURTEEN
May Day Celebrations

Lord Waterhouse may have resisted testing his new purchase on her, but it did not prevent him from making her days in his luxurious penthouse prison as arduous as any during the four weeks of her captivity. He specialised in her humiliation, and for the majority of the time he kept her tied or suspended in whichever position he decided to penetrate her next. He took delight in making her watch as he made his selection from the armoury of inventive tools at his disposal on the green baize shelves. His ardour seemed inexhaustible, and even when he dozed he kept her doubled on the pulley, ready for when he awoke. He kept her tied while he fed her, like an animal, or worse, made her kneel and fucked her from behind, forcing her to eat from the floor as he did.

Afterwards he commanded her to squat, his eyes burning into her as she delivered her own pleasure. While he ordered her to lick up the droplets of her own juices from the cool marble, he nudged the chain that joined her nipples with the toe of his boot.

The only time he removed the clamps was when he took her to the bathroom, prior to Ms Brentwood's daily visits. He'd let her shower, the blood rushing back into her tortured, aching buds, causing more pain than when they remained in place. And every day Ms Brentwood would lay her over her lap, rubbing in her potions until Jane's buttocks were silky smooth and as unblemished as they had ever been.

Lord Waterhouse lurked moodily in the background, pensively rubbing his goatee beard, until she left. But Jane endured his callousness with stoicism. However harsh his treatment, he never beat her after that first afternoon when he spanked her so brutally, and for that, at least, she was grateful. And he never insisted she deep-throat him. He allowed her that in exchange, he told her crudely, for keeping her mouth shut about the unexpected return of his wilful wife.

'Are you all right?' Paul was watching her in the rear-view mirror, his brow creased in a frown of concern as they drove along the river. 'He didn't use it on you, did he?'

Jane shook her head, her eyelids drooping with tiredness, and wriggled uncomfortably on the leather seat. The car stuck in traffic around Trafalgar Square.

'Where are you taking me?' she asked nervously, hugging the cloak tighter around herself, her only covering apart from the corset. Ms Brentwood had tightened the laces daily and it held her like a vice.

'You know I can't tell you that.' The note of regret in his voice was unmistakable as he manoeuvred the car into the relative freedom of the Mall. 'But it's nearly over, I promise. And I was right about the birch, wasn't I?'

Now it was Jane's turn to frown at his unexpected reassurance. She had to know, finally, if he was friend or foe. His handsome face turned towards her as he pulled across the lanes of traffic and into the darkness of the underpass. 'Ben Handford... do you know him?' she asked cautiously. 'I work for him. He was with you. My name's Jane Carter...' Suddenly she needed to confide in him.

'Shhh, Jane, please,' he interrupted her before she could tell him more. 'You don't need to tell me these things. I can't help you. In two days you can put all this behind you and get on with your life. We both can.' He spoke insistently. 'And for the record, I don't know your Ben Handford,' he added.

Jane slumped in the back of the car, unconvinced. She felt deflated and confused by his latest rejection, and they continued in silence as the car travelled west through the evening rush hour traffic.

'Put on the blindfold and pull up your hood,' he told her quietly as they drove down a wide tree-lined avenue, where the cherry blossom still clung to the trees and wisteria drooped across the facades of the imposing white stucco houses.

He let her take off the blindfold and lower the hood when the car came to a halt. He ushered her from the back seat, and as her eyes adjusted she looked around the underground garage, converted from a cellar. As they waited by the metal grilled lift, a spicy aroma wafted from the racks of musty bottles that lined the cavernous cellars beyond. *In two days you can put all this behind you and get on with your life*. She clung to his words for courage, repeating them in her mind. Just two days. What more would she be expected to endure? And would they fulfil their part of the bargain?

The lift creaked into action, slowly moving upward, and when it shuddered to a halt Paul drew back the heavy gates and she felt his hand in the small of her back, pushing her gently forward.

'You'll be all right.' His lips brushed her cheek when he whispered in her ear, and a sudden surge of pleasure raced through her. She was blushing when she stepped, barefoot, in to the black and white tiled hallway. Then she blushed for a different reason when, with a murmured apology, he lifted the cloak from her shoulders. He couldn't disguise his desire as he beckoned her to follow him.

With every step her astonishment grew at the opulence that surrounded her. A sweeping staircase led up through the centre of the house and paintings crammed the whitewashed walls. They began at eye level and hung, in regimented tiers, all the way up to the high ceilings above. The distinctive and haunting sound of the cello drifted down, and Jane recalled the inspired dark-haired stranger who had played that first night at the theatre. Was she there too?

Her heart was in her mouth by the time they reached the drawing room, and Sir John turned as they entered. The same intimidating black mask that he'd worn when he visited her at the doctor's disguised his face.

Beside him Jane recognised the imperious and exquisite beauty who had provided the finale to the auction. That night she'd been dressed only in a rough horsehair corset. Tonight she was rather better dressed, in an elegant silk gown that swept the floor and accentuated every curve of her figure.

'Display.' Sir John spoke offhandedly as he approached. He arrogantly pinched Jane's swollen nipples between finger and thumb before moving behind her.

'Lord Waterhouse kept his word, I see.' He stroked a hand over her rounded, unmarked buttocks approvingly. 'But did he comply with my other request?' Jane bit her lip and stared blankly ahead, not understanding the question. 'Don't be coy, Miss Carter. Did he make you fellate him?' he qualified tersely.

'No sir,' Jane shook her head insistently, and the woman turned away, conveying a lack of interest.

'Excellent. Another source of virgin purity for our May Day events. An added bonus I had not expected. I shouldn't have doubted his lordship's integrity or restraint.'

So that was why she'd been spared that particular trial, Jane thought, although she had been spared little else. Her discretion regarding his wife's nocturnal visit had been no more than an added incentive.

'Take her upstairs.'

Jane felt a hand on her arm. She hadn't noticed Bessie enter, but the sullen girl led her from the room as Paul stood aside, his eyes fixed to the floor, to let them pass.

As they climbed the grand staircase the strains of the music grew louder, and when they reached the second floor Bessie wheezed, 'You're in here with Anna,' shoving her into a room and slamming the door behind her.

The music stopped mid-chord. The heavy drapes blocked out the afternoon light. Jane crept forward into the darkened room. 'Anna?' she called out softly.

'Yes, I'm over here.'

The voice came from one corner, and Jane saw her in the shadows, the cello resting between her parted thighs. 'I'm Jane. Shall I open the curtains?'

'It's not allowed,' the voice came back. 'I'll light a candle.'

Jane listened intently to Anna's story. She was a poor but clearly talented musician from a small Baltic state. In spite of her burgeoning reputation she was badly paid for her art. To earn some extra money she had worked, briefly, as a translator for a visiting British trade delegation.

A few months afterwards she received a letter, offering her the opportunity to join a London orchestra. She spoke even more softly as she described how, after the night Jane had seen her play at the theatre, she was brought to the vast house. During that time she had never left the confines of the room they were in, and Jane's anxiety grew as she realised how easily Anna's fate could have been hers.

'And what did they do to you?' Jane looked away in embarrassment at her own question.

'They haven't touched me... I never see anyone,' Anna replied. 'Only that woman, Ms Brentwood. She comes most days.' Jane didn't press her for details but found out soon enough why Anna had been saved from further attentions. 'They are preparing me for tomorrow. I am to be the Virgin Queen of May. After that they say I'll be free to take up my position with the orchestra.' Anna's eyes filled with tears and she grasped Jane's hands tightly in hers. Jane wept too, for the beauty of the girl's untouched innocence.

That is how Matilda found them, in the corner of the room bathed in the light of the candle, their arms entwined. None of the magnificent woman's defiance or energy appeared crushed since Jane had last seen her. She strode across to them, her ebony limbs glistening below her white corset, and greeted them effusively.

For the next hour they compared their experiences. Matilda made the two younger girls stretch out on the four-poster bed and climbed between them, her muscular arms enveloping them, coaxing their stories from them.

'But it wasn't all bad, was it, Jane?' Matilda asked, with a low chuckle, when Jane finished describing her perilous escape from the tower. 'You were learning pretty fast at the doctor's house.' Jane felt the heat of her cheek burning against Matilda's strong shoulder.

'Well, maybe you're right,' she muttered, to reassure Anna, but also because it was the truth. Seeing Matilda again reminded her of how good a woman's tongue felt when it probed the bud of her clitoris and how readily her senses had begun to fuse pain and pleasure. As she lay in the crook of Matilda's arm she tried to count the metal rings that jostled for space in the woman's distended nipples, but it was difficult.

As Matilda shifted position her long thighs parted, and between them Jane saw the cluster of new silver rings that pierced her clitoris. The shocking sight consumed Jane with a final burst of determination. She had come this far; if

Matilda could withstand the demands of the Ruskin Club, so could she.

'But why do you let them treat you like that?' Anna asked meekly.

'We all have our reasons, honey. I'm sure you do too. Ain't that right, Jane?' Jane nodded and nestled deeper into Matilda's shoulder. 'Now rest; we'll need our strength later,' Matilda added, and closed her eyes.

Was it only a month ago that Jane had asked the same question, and Matilda provided the identical response?

Jane dozed fitfully. Anna was so perfect, with her tumbling curls and porcelain skin, and her nature so gentle and sensitive. What devious scheme did the mysterious Sir John have for his Virgin Queen? And for her?

They were entwined on the bed when Bessie brought them identical black satin corsets, silk stockings and high-heeled court shoes. Only Anna was provided with a white shift to cover herself. Jane and Matilda both tried to bolster Anna's confidence with deserving compliments while they laced each other. Her small breasts rose flawlessly above her corset, and the darker skin formed perfect circles around her unsullied nipples. Where the triangle of hair had been removed from between her thighs, the olive skin was as silken smooth as the rest of her body.

Matilda helped her ease the shift over her head, but the diaphanous material did very little to hide her.

Bessie led them back down the imposing staircase and across the tiled entrance hall. Sir John and his consort were waiting for them in the drawing room, and to Jane's consternation Lord Waterhouse had joined the party. He lounged nonchalantly on a brocade sofa, enjoying her dismay.

Sir John stood in front of the fireplace and clicked his fingers in the direction of the new arrivals. As one they dutifully raised their arms and stood with their legs slightly parted. Jane looked anxiously at Anna, fearful that she hadn't understood the unspoken command, but Ms Brentwood had instructed her well.

'We have devised a small contest for this evening, a prelude to tomorrow's entertainment, which I hope Anna will find instructive.' Sir John addressed the room with cool authority. 'Jane, your reputation precedes you, and Stephanie would like to put it to the test.'

The haughty beauty rose from the armchair where she'd been hidden from view, and flashed an arrogant smile. 'And Matilda,' he continued. 'Your tongue has been well appreciated by both sexes in your time with us.'

Jane's head felt light with dizziness as she watched Sir John arrange the scene. By now she should have been used to their games, but still the trepidation overwhelmed her.

Stephanie held up her lustrous mane of hair, and allowed Sir John to unfasten her gown. It cascaded at her feet and she stepped out it, proud to exhibit her splendour to a new audience, and Jane had to concede that even Ellie could not surpass her all-pervading aura. Her full, firm breasts perched above her lace-trimmed corset, and her already narrow waist was inched tighter by her lacings. Below she was naked and her hips flared out voluptuously. High-heeled, black patent shoes edged her pelvis forward and enhanced the magnificence of her long thighs, toned calves and slim ankles. Her skin glowed with a radiance that Jane envied, although she heard Matilda snort beside her.

Sir John sat Anna on the sofa beside Lord Waterhouse, and guided Stephanie to a highly polished wooden chair. Its clean lines and grained surface matched the discreet elegance of the room. Without any hesitation or embarrassment Stephanie sat down and spread her legs, hooking her knees easily over the smooth arms of the chair. Jane gasped and Matilda shifted audibly, confronted with the luscious pink interior of the proud beauty's most intimate part, with not a hair to veil its nudity.

Lord Waterhouse had a perfect view from the sofa. He tugged on his beard with his sinewy fingers, his clean-shaven upper lip taut with expectation.

'You will begin with Stephanie.' Sir John addressed Matilda. 'Come and kneel here.'

Matilda crossed the room slowly, her head held high, and knelt in front of Stephanie's chair. 'And you, Jane, will kneel beside her for now, and observe.'

Jane moved forward, trying to imitate Matilda's swaggering manner, but with less success. As she knelt beside Matilda the heady scent of Stephanie's sex filled her nostrils.

'When you've evoked Stephanie's orgasm you will hold it on your tongue, and Lord Waterhouse will assess its quality and quantity. After that you will elicit Jane's emission for comparison.' Sir John spoke evenly, but his eyes glinted through the holes in his mask. The leather was supple enough to see the muscles of his jaws, clenching repeatedly while he waited.

Matilda placed her hands on Stephanie's parted thighs and moved her head forward. Jane watched, transfixed, her mind and senses churning. Could she win this extraordinary contest? Quality and quantity? She resented her naivety all over again.

Stephanie's head was thrown back and her lips parted, a frown of concentration marring her perfect brow. Matilda sucked and licked until Stephanie's breathing became shallower and her nostrils flared when she inhaled. A film of moisture formed on her upper lip and Jane saw colour start to tinge her flawless skin. The atmosphere in the room was taut with tension and Jane shared in it. Matilda withdrew for the merest pause before she plunged down for the final time, her tongue lashing energetically, luring Stephanie's release.

And when it came Stephanie grasped the arms of the chair, her knuckles white with effort, and let out a long deep hiss, fearsome in its intensity. Jane felt it vibrate through her own body, like sparks flying, lighting and arousing her senses. She watched in wonder as Matilda withdrew her tongue, and in the centre, on the purple-pink surface, she nursed a small pool of creamy fluid.

She skilfully held it there as she crawled on her hands and knees the short distance to the sofa, her neck arched and her tongue protruding. Anna sat bolt upright beside Lord Waterhouse, her hands folded in her lap, as Matilda approached them. Her nipples jutted through the thin cotton shift and her cheeks

114

burned with embarrassment.

'Very impressive, Stephanie.' Lord Waterhouse leaned forward to inspect the precious cargo. 'But I think you may find that your prowess is under threat tonight,' he taunted her. 'You may swallow now, Matilda.'

Matilda licked her lips and looked at him disdainfully as the cream slid down her throat.

Sir John helped Stephanie to a more comfortable armchair, where she lounged back and looked condescendingly at Jane. A conceited smile flickered on her full red lips, but didn't deign to respond to his lordship's jibe.

Jane crawled up onto the hard wooden throne, still warm and damp from Stephanie's pleasure. Matilda had resumed her position and took hold of Jane's legs, to help her ease them over the arms of the chair. She was shorter than Stephanie and had to spread her knees wider. The whites of Matilda's eyes shone and her ebony skin glistened, as she tried to soothe Jane's unease with her expression.

'Begin,' Sir John said when he was ready, and a shiver rippled through Jane's stomach as she felt the hot breath on her thighs. She closed her eyes and resolved to exclude the room and its other occupants from her consciousness.

The tip of her friend's tongue parted her lips as dexterously as a finger, and immediately sought her clitoris. It was already as hard as a berry and Matilda swiftly moved lower, prolonging and provoking the building waves. Jane's mind swirled with images as she raised her hips and wriggled, begging silently for Matilda to return to her clitoris. She felt the throb in her nipples as the blood filled them, itching and imploring attention. Before she knew it her hands were there, pinching her own tender flesh. She squeezed hard, until it hurt and she cried out, oblivious to her pride, driven by desire.

Matilda sensed the crescendo and used her tongue to draw back the hood and flick mercilessly over her clitoris. The orgasm flooded from Jane, she felt Matilda's tongue curl, and from the depths of her pleasure she remembered the terms of the contest.

Her eyes flickered open when she heard the murmurings from her unwanted audience. Matilda still knelt in front of her, her tongue offered up, a testament to their joint feat. The cream flowed over it like melting honey, in spite of her efforts to contain it. Then slowly, so as not to spill it further, Matilda lowered herself onto all fours and began to crawl.

But the bitter taste of potential defeat must have been too much for Stephanie's conceit, for before anyone could prevent her she raised a shapely calf and drove the toe of her high-heeled shoe viciously into Matilda's nearest buttock. Matilda spun round like a wounded animal to confront her attacker, rearing up, ready to strike. But before she could lunge at her foe Sir John seized her arms. She struggled valiantly in her efforts to break free. Lord Waterhouse joined the fray, and it took both men to wrestle the powerful woman to the floor and secure her arms behind her back.

Stephanie thrust out her breasts to assert her superiority. 'I declare myself the winner!' she announced jubilantly, while Jane cowered on the chair and Matilda snarled in indignation as they waited to see whether such blatant cheating would be rewarded.

Sir John paced the room several times before he passed judgement. 'In the absence of an opportunity for comparison, I declare Stephanie the victor,' he finally decreed. 'What is your wish, my dear?'

Stephanie wasted no time in delivering her demands. 'My wish is to take your little virgin to the cellar, and tie her to the walls while I test Lord Waterhouse's new birch on her.' Her large eyes turned on Anna, and her announcement sent shockwaves rippling through the room.

Jane didn't dare look across at the sofa. She remembered how Lord Waterhouse had slammed the birch branches down onto the bed, and it was too terrible to consider the awful implement striking that smooth, untouched flesh.

There was a long silence before Sir John replied, with a distinct tremor in his voice. 'Really, my dear, I think you ask too high a price.'

Stephanie prowled the room, thwarted in her desires. 'Well, Sir John, I am prepared to defer to your reservations provided you will allow me an alternative.' She hovered over Jane's cringing frame. 'I would like to see my opponent punish her careless servant instead. After all, it was her inability to control her temper that caused the evidence to be spilled.'

Matilda seethed with uncontained anger and fought her bonds, but Stephanie tossed her head and turned away.

Jane insisted that she couldn't comply with Stephanie's pitiless option. Whatever pain she had suffered, she'd never considered inflicting it on others, and the notion seemed abominable. Yet she had to protect Anna from the terrors of the cellar, too.

'If you refuse to perform the task there is one further option.' Jane lifted her head expectantly, to meet Stephanie's sneering smile. 'Lord Waterhouse can test the birch on you himself.'

Whatever was to occur was considered too extreme for Anna to witness, and when they reached the hallway she was taken away, her face pale and her lips trembling. The cellar venue was the only point that Stephanie had conceded, and the rest of the party continued to Sir John's study, where Lord Waterhouse supervised proceedings.

The long box that carried the birches lay ominously on a side table. Jane had regretted her decision even before the words left her lips, but it was too late. Her limbs felt like weights and her skin crept with shame at her own cowardice.

They had bent Matilda over a large wooden desk, and Stephanie was holding her down while the men roped her arms and ankles. From the instant Jane sealed her fate, Matilda had fallen into compliant sullenness. She lay still and tamely allowed them to part her thighs and raise her hips, high enough to part her bottom cheeks and expose the pink lips below.

Lord Waterhouse lifted the shortest of the bound birches from the box, and shook the residue of water from them. He held them up proudly. Four stout sticks, over three feet long, were bound together at their thicker ends. 'Cut from the finest Manx woodland!'

Jane cowered as he extended the bark-bound handle towards her, but there was no escape. All eyes were on her. Her arm shook as she grasped the rough handle.

'Four strokes was the minimum Corlett prescribed for errant boys,' Lord Waterhouse stated knowledgeably.

'Four strokes it is,' Stephanie replied, settling herself in a leather armchair.

They had to push Jane forward, her legs almost giving way beneath her, until she stood just a few feet from Matilda's pinioned body. How could she have agreed to inflict such awful punishment on Matilda in order to spare herself? The tears started, almost blinding her, but through them she saw Matilda raise her head as much as she was able. She looked straight into Jane's guilt-wracked eyes, understanding radiating from hers.

Sir John gave the command and Jane lifted the heavy rods in the air. She heard the intakes of breath as she held them there until her arm ached. She saw Matilda steel herself, and from her own experience she knew that the waiting was the hardest part.

The birch fell, almost with its own weight, and landed squarely across Matilda's buttocks, spraying them with flecks of water. Jane cringed in alarm at the natural force of the blow, but Matilda didn't flinch.

Jane raised the birch for a second time and didn't hesitate so long. Consequently it fell faster and she felt the jolt resound through her own body. Red weals were already appearing on Matilda's buttocks, but she stayed silent. The shards of bark pricked Jane's palms as she gripped the handle.

Two more and it would be over.

The sweat trickled down between Jane's breasts.

'Continue, and with more force now you have the feel,' Lord Waterhouse instructed. 'Or I will have to complete the sentence myself.'

His warning spurred her to end Matilda's suffering as soon as possible. In Lord Waterhouse's hands the weapon would be too fearsome to contemplate, so Jane was privately grateful for her traitorous decision, as she felt the birch flex above her head. If she could aim accurately for the fleshiest part of each buttock she might cause the minimum amount of pain.

She brought the weapon down as hard as she dared, but its design was too clever. Its shortest length flexed between Matilda's buttocks, and her gasp was masked by a shrill cry of excitement from Stephanie. Incredibly Matilda lifted her head and looked back at Jane's appalled expression. The whites of her eyes blazed against her ebony skin and she moistened her lips with the tip of her tongue. The tongue that had so recently given so much pleasure.

Jane raised the birch for the fourth and final time. The livid stripes crossed both cheeks, transfixing her. She could see the cluster of rings that lined the lips below. They were like a magnet to her, and in that moment some madness overtook her. The birch descended heavily and all four of its tips gathered, whipping into the valley between Matilda's buttocks, biting at the sensitive flesh and snagging the silver rings attached to it.

As Matilda struggled to absorb the viciousness of the blow, Stephanie snatched the birch from Jane's grasp. 'Now suck her!'

She pushed Jane to her knees, and too startled by her own actions to hesitate, Jane buried her head, determined to earn Matilda's forgiveness and desperate to soothe the anguish she'd inflicted. She licked the burning flesh, running her tongue over it, blowing to cool it, and astonishingly Matilda responded, raising her hips, facilitating Jane's access to her. Jane's nostrils were filled with the rich sweet scent, and she plunged her tongue deep into the tight entrance of Matilda's vagina.

It felt good to be repaying the torment she'd caused - so good she didn't want it to end, Matilda's juices coating her face and filling her senses.

They spent their last night of captivity in the dormitory that had been prepared for them. Matilda held Jane in her arms, comforting her, when it should have been the other way round. When Jane begged forgiveness Matilda took her hand and placed it between her thighs, breathing softly, while Jane gently fingered the cluster of silver rings.

She listened patiently while Jane confided that in all the weeks at the doctor's, at the major's, and the time with Lord Waterhouse, she had avoided accepting a man into her mouth. Matilda chided her lightly for her reticence, until Jane confessed her reasons.

It was watching Matilda having to endure, that first afternoon at the doctor's house, that held her back. Matilda stroked her hair and reassured her, then very gently she used her fingers to probe inside Jane's mouth, and press down on the soft palate at the back of her tongue. Jane arched her back, but didn't gag against the intrusion, or resist when Matilda's hand squeezed her neck.

'You see? You've started your journey, Jane. Your lips and mouth and throat will bring any man to ecstasy. And you will discover so much more that will bring you pleasure,' Matilda whispered, her mouth replacing her fingers in a long, deep kiss.

As the night wore on the empty beds filled. The redhead, women Jane recognised from the auction, two of her competitors on the racetrack. As dawn broke Sei crept into the darkened room. She fell into Jane's arms, smothering her with kisses, and crawled into the narrow bed between Matilda and Jane.

After tomorrow we will be free. Those were the words that sang through their dreams, during their last night in the care of the Ruskin Club.

Most of the next day was spent preparing the women for the evening. Ms Brentwood arrived early, and they were all waxed clean of any body hair, measured and inspected for any blemishes. When it came to Matilda's turn she examined the marks the birch had caused, with disapproval, but passed her fit for inclusion in the entertainment.

Jane looked for Anna when they were lined up by the lift shaft, but there was no sign of her. They were all dressed in matching white shifts over their corsets, and on their heads they wore crowns woven from bramble branches, the delicate flowers blooming and ready to disport their fruit. Ms Brentwood guarded the lift and sent them down in pairs. Jane manoeuvred in the queue so she would be coupled with Sei. Matilda was just ahead of them.

Jane clutched Sei's hand as the lift descended. Through the latticed grill they saw the wide hall, lit by the luminous paintings that crowded its walls. Still they descended until the lift shuddered to a halt in the darkness of the cellar. A hooded figure awaited them.

'Paul?' Jane whispered hopefully, but there was no response.

They followed the flickering candle, past the racks of dusty bottles, along a labyrinth of passageways to where the cellar opened up into a cavernous, brick-lined chamber. In the centre a small stage had been created, and Jane squeezed Sei's hand tighter when they took in the tableau upon it.

Anna lay on a raised, moss-covered platform, her locks of dark curls spread around her. Her eyes were closed and her palms upturned, as if she were floating in an imaginary stream. She wore a crown of hawthorns and a single rose lay by her side. She was entirely naked. Her small breasts rose and fell gently as she breathed, the only sign of life in her perfect body.

Around the dais gathered a crowd of indiscernible figures, dressed in long gothic capes. They moved their hooded heads in unison as the pairs of women were arranged in a circle around Anna's supine form.

'Tonight we honour John Ruskin, May Day being a favourite festival of the great man.' Jane recognised Sir John's muffled voice from behind one of the hoods, as he addressed the company. 'Our May Queen is depicted in the role of Ophelia, from the painting by one of the founders of the pre-Raphaelite Brotherhood, Sir John Everett Millais.' The audience murmured deferentially. 'However, before she is crowned we must remember the excellence demanded by our mentor.'

His cloak flapped as he clapped his hands, and allocated figures stepped from the crowd and anonymous hands seized the scantily clad women. They led them to the shallow alcoves at the perimeter of the brick cellar.

'Each student will finally fulfil her agreement by being tested in the way she has found hardest to master. We have two virgin orifices for our delectation, which we shall save for last.'

Haunting music drifted from speakers strategically placed high on the walls. Jane's struggles were futile and she was brought to her knees, facing the chamber. They ripped the flimsy material from her and chained her arms high behind her. In an alcove opposite Matilda was now lashing out at her captors, but still her legs were hoisted up and spread, so that her sex, for so long so valiantly protected, was exposed and vulnerable.

Sei was to Jane's left being shackled, facing the wall with her buttocks held high. Jane counted twelve women in all, and the guests outnumbered them by about three to one.

When the last of the women was tied in position, Sir John held out a set of cards, and each guest took one. The lucky ones held them up jubilantly, while others sighed in disappointment.

Jane shuddered with trepidation. Which of the shadowy figures would she finally be obliged to please with her mouth? She tried to concentrate on the memory of Matilda's fingers preparing her, showing her how to yield and accept male needs.

The entertainment began with Bessie's stout frame doubled over, her wrists fastened to her ankles. The man who had drawn her card did no more than open his cloak and slap some grease onto her broad buttocks, before he entered her, thrusting avidly between her fleshy cheeks. His orgasm came fast and his lusty groans clashed with the lyrical strains of the music, then before he moved away he slapped her quivering buttocks. She yelped and a ripple of approval filled the chamber as they moved on to the next unfortunate.

To Jane's consternation Ruby, the spiteful redhead, was tied in the same position as herself. Again the man designated to penetrate her revealed no more of himself than he needed to. Ruby's eyes opened wide as he prised open her mouth and held her head, tilting it a little to slide his straining erection between her lips. She gagged and spluttered but he persisted, until she succumbed and allowed him deeper.

Jane couldn't bear to watch, although a part of her revelled in her tormentor's downfall, and she frantically searched the remaining men for clues to their identity. She hoped that whoever had drawn her card would be gentle.

The group worked their way around the cellar. When each woman had been finished with she was rewarded with a chastisement to remind her of her humility. Sometimes with the palm of a hand, sometimes a short cane, or for women whose position made their breasts the only option, a horsehair switch. The extent of punishment was increased for those least able to disguise their pleasure.

As each alcove was visited the tension and excitement of the shadowy audience grew. All the time the haunting music played and Anna lay motionless on the dais, her naked flesh shimmering in the dim light.

By the time they reached Sei, Jane was close to fainting. She just had time to whisper a few words of comfort to her friend before she saw the man open his cloak. His cock was short but stout, like the man himself. It was already rigid, the head shining in the candlelight as he gripped it in his fist. He stroked until it swelled and Jane recoiled as it grew to fearsome proportions.

The man applied oil liberally and nudged at Sei's tight, puckered entrance. At first it didn't yield but he persevered, grabbing her slim hips and pulling her onto him, and Sei let out a short sharp cry as the man broke through the tiny ring of muscle. It only took a few more thrusts before he sighed hoarsely, signalling that he'd found his target. Tears smarted in Jane's eyes as she experienced Sei's discomfort as if they were her own.

The man rolled his hips, sturdy on his feet, lifting Sei's slight body with his motion. Jane shouldn't have been surprised when Sei's breathing changed and her body no longer resisted the penetration, or when a dull ache formed and throbbed in her own bottom, when she thought of how it felt to be filled there. Sei called out with passion, her orgasm coinciding perfectly with the hooded stranger inside her, and earned herself six cuts with the cane for her abandon.

The audience counted each swipe as it sliced through the air and striped her buttocks. Sei thanked her punisher, in a quavering but gracious voice.

'As I mentioned, before we move to our main event of the evening,' Sir John addressed his guests, 'we have two students who have withheld favours during their training.' He moved over to Jane.

'Of course, there is always a choice.' He loomed over her as he spoke. 'Lord Waterhouse has recently visited the Isle of Man and is, as you know, anxious to try out his new purchase.' Jane shrank back into the alcove. Any inhibitions that remained were quashed by the threat of the birch. After her actions the previous night to avoid it, she nodded without hesitation when Sir John asked for her decision.

Her heart was pounding and her mouth was dry when the man took up position in front of her. He was tall and his hands were tanned and smooth. The audience clustered around the alcove. She should have been used to it by now, but still she struggled to overcome the scrutiny of strangers. She closed her eyes to obliterate the glowering, hooded figures and tried to remember the advice Matilda had given her.

The room fell silent, and the macabre music was her only distraction. His fingers prised open her mouth, and when he opened his cloak his penis stood out stiffly and his salty odour filled her nostrils. Jane regarded its smooth length with awe and unease. He placed one hand around her neck and used the other to keep her mouth open. She took a deep breath and felt him press between her lips, and swell inside her as she prepared to surrender her remaining purity.

She felt the head nudge on the soft palate at the back of her throat, and rest there, just as Matilda's fingers had done the previous night. But he squeezed her neck, more firmly than Matilda had done, and inched his hips just a few inches forward. Before she knew it he'd slipped deeper and filled the entrance to her throat. She couldn't breathe and her head spun, but he kept up the pressure on her neck, massaging it until the urges began to rage more intensely than she had ever felt before. It was a stranger taking her, but he seemed to know her boundaries better than she knew herself.

He withdrew once, to let her fill her lungs, stroking her breasts as they rose above the corset. Her arms ached from the chains but she allowed him to re-enter her, trustingly, and to reach deeper than she thought possible. She felt her throat distend as he pulsed inside her, and she used her muscles instinctively to arouse him more. Her mind raced irrationally and her body heaved with unknown pleasure, and then he drew back enough to let her taste the first hot spurts and she swallowed them, like nectar.

He filled her mouth with his juices, and at the moment he withdrew, and she gulped in air, he plunged his fingers between her parted thighs; all she needed to bring the heady orgasm flooding from her.

'Quite a display for an ingénue!' Sir John's voice cut harshly through her reverie. 'Twelve strikes across her breasts for flaunting her wantonness.' The audience applauded his judgment enthusiastically.

Jane had screwed up her eyes to await her punishment when the moody melody stopped, the sudden silence disturbing the occupants of the cellar.

'Not just yet!' A figure stepped from the back of the gathering and grabbed the horsehair switch, brandishing it in the air. 'I think we have some business to attend to, don't you, Minister?'

Jane opened her eyes as the mystery guest threw back his hood. He spat the words in his host's direction, and it took her a moment to believe what she saw.

It was Ben Handford.

He turned and smiled sheepishly in her direction. 'Untie them,' he said, taking charge of the stunned audience.

'How did you get in here?' Sir John spluttered with indignation.

'I wasn't the only one on to you and your *brotherhood*.' Ben turned theatrically on Jane's unidentified seducer. 'We made a good team, didn't we Paul, once we'd pooled our resources.'

Tears of joy and relief trickled down Jane's cheeks, as the man in front of her lowered his hood. Paul gazed back at her, his soft brown eyes glistening with affection and appreciation.

'I made sure I drew your card tonight,' Paul whispered, as he kissed her and then tore himself away reluctantly to free Sei and the other women.

Ben Handford enjoyed every moment of his revenge. One by one he worked through the list. He began with the committee, matching their pseudonyms, derived from the followers of the pre-Raphaelite Brotherhood, to their real personas. He moved on to the heads of industry, architects, and city bankers. He reserved his former television boss until last, watching him shrink to the back of the chamber, hoping he had escaped exposure.

And when Ben had outlined the dubiousness of their sexual practices, he moved on to the cartels they operated between themselves. Gradually they lowered their hoods, their faces ashen with shock, as he produced detailed evidence of illegal art dealing, currency trading, awarding of contracts, fast-tracking of applications - the list was endless and ran back twenty years.

Only one character remained hooded and unidentified, so Ben took a chance. 'Gina?'

Gina Bent lowered her hood, her handsome face contorted with incandescent rage. Jane smiled and pulled the cloak Paul had given her further around herself. Ben was certainly thorough. With Paul's assistance from the inside they had compiled a decisive record of dishonesty and corruption - even if they had taken their time! She shouldn't have doubted either of them.

Jane started as Sir John revealed his face for the first time, instantly familiar as

Anthony Hazleton, the distinguished figure she'd seen on television, smiling benignly as he left Downing Street or speaking eloquently in Parliamentary debates.

His strong jaw jutted defiantly, even in the face of impending disgrace. 'So, Handford, what do you intend to do with your evidence? One exclusive in a Sunday paper and a book deal, then you'll be back where you started. A lonely old hack being feted by your fellow vultures, until they get bored of you.' He paused and ran his fingers through his shock of silver hair. 'That's if we let you out of here, of course.'

Several of the men stepped forward, emboldened by their leader's belligerent stance.

Jane noticed the Adam's apple bobbing in Ben's throat, just as she had done in the Camden office when he growled down the table at his team of blasé young programme makers.

'Don't worry, minister, your secrets are safe with me.' His lip curled into a combative sneer. 'Well, me and the PM's private office, that is. I took the precaution of lodging a dossier with them this morning. I'm sure they'll find it an interesting read.'

The Epilogue

The director gave Jane the thumbs-up from the gallery, as she came off air from her afternoon chat show. She acknowledged his praise with good humour and hurried out of the studio; she didn't want to be late.

Ben Handford joined her in her dressing room. He was clearly elated.

'Great news, Jane, the networks want the show for primetime. You're going to be the new chat show queen!' He leant forward to kiss her and the make-up girl stepped back respectfully. 'And the channel's got the highest ratings since we opened. We've made it, Jane!' He looked years younger since they'd arrived in Seattle. His face was tanned and the worry lines, which ravaged his features in London, had filled and softened.

Just then Sadie burst through the door and dropped her bulging bags of designer shopping on the floor. She was a long way from Soho but had lost none of her East End cheer. She blew a kiss to Jane before she threw her arms around Ben's neck and hugged him effusively.

'Hello *Mrs* Handford,' Ben beamed happily.

'Hello, *Mr* Handford,' she replied coquettishly. They had only been married a few months and still found the joke amusing. 'Have you heard, Hazleton's resigned?' she went on excitedly. 'Three weeks before the election... but not before you got what you wanted out of him!'

'No more than we deserved, Sadie,' Jane chuckled. 'Now we'd better hurry. Anna's concert starts at eight and I have to get home and change.' Anna was due to make her first solo appearance at the city's May Day concert, in front of thousands of people. Jane was so proud of her friend.

The doormen escorted Ben and Sadie to their chauffeured limousine. Jane waved them off and climbed into her new Italian sports car, and as she drove through the evening traffic towards her apartment she thought how perfect her life was. She lived in one of the most exciting cities in the world and her media career was flourishing. All her wildest dreams had been exceeded in just one year. In a few weeks she would celebrate her twentieth birthday on an exclusive, tropical island. Her closest friends would join her: Anna would take time out before she began a west coast concert tour; Sei would be flying in from Paris, where her husband had been appointed Ambassador; and Matilda would make the trip from Africa, where her foundation was building a modern hospital.

Hazleton and his powerful friends had certainly paid a high price to avoid public disgrace. Jane allowed herself the briefest stab of sympathy for her former tormentor now his political ambitions lay in ruins, and wondered what would become of Sir John and the Ruskin Club.

She let herself into the sunny apartment, in a hurry, as always, to see him. The pages of his novel were stacking up on his desk and he stood up to greet her, but before she crossed the room she lifted her cotton dress over her head. Beneath it she was naked and prepared for him.

'Display.' Paul pretended sternness, but a smile creased his features.

She raised her arms and crossed the cool tiled floor, giving him time to admire her breasts, and the sloping curves of her waist and hips. Jane sank to her knees in front of him and loosened the belt of his towelling robe.